# DASH

Editing by Jenny Sims of Editing4Indies
Cover design by Sommer Stein at Perfect Pear Creative

For more information about the author and her books, visit her website- www.shanteltessierauthor.com. You can sign up for her newsletter on her website. The newsletter is the only place to get exclusive teasers, first to know about current projects and release dates. And also have chances to win some amazing giveaways.

# DEDICATION

I wanna dedicate this book to my readers. I want to thank each and every one of you out there. You make the long hours and all-nighters worth it. Thank you

# CHAPTER ONE

*Dash*

I squint my eyes to get a better look at the car that stands out in the oncoming traffic on this California freeway. It looks like any black Charger, but something about it seems off...

Blacked out windows.

Blacked out rims.

Blacked out lights.

Solid black.

I watch it through the dark tinted visor of my helmet as it passes me. I glance over quickly, in time to see brake lights come on before it pulls to a quick stop and turns into the center median. Then I see the colorful lights come on that are hidden in just the right spots.

"Fuck," I cuss into my helmet.

Just as I suspected. It's a cop!

I look down at the speedometer on my bike and see that I'm doing ninety-two in a sixty-five. Fuck!

I reach back and tap the thigh of the girl who is sitting on the back of my bike—signaling to hold on. I feel her knees tighten on my legs as her arms wrap tightly around my waist. Her big ass fake tits, a high school graduation present from her parents, are against my back just as I rev the throttle more. I can pretty much bet my left nut that she's yelling at me through her helmet right now to slow the fuck down. But it's too late. I've already decided to run and now I'm committed to it.

I look down quickly to see I'm going well over a hundred when I look in my side mirror and notice the

Charger gaining on us. Usually, if you run on a motorcycle, the freeway is your only option to get away, but I see brake lights up ahead. Traffic is coming to a standstill. I need to get off the highway and try to lose him in a neighborhood on some backstreets. I see an exit up ahead and decide at the last minute to take it.

I look both ways and run a red light when I see both directions are clear. I swerve through traffic quickly as my adrenaline pumps. I know this road. I'm about a mile away from my best friend Blake's house.

I take my next right and see a cop car pulling out in front of me. His lights come on as well.

Shit! Of course, the cop on the highway has called for backup.

I let off the throttle and pull on the brake. I turn into a gas station, and without stopping, I exit out of the opposite side, getting back on the road.

I see another cop coming from the opposite direction. Fuck! I should have just stayed on the highway, but I didn't want the possibility of being stuck in traffic.

But what other option do I have? Fuck it! I need back on the highway.

I go to take the on-ramp, but there are already cops there as well. I'm fucked. I look over at the ditch. I could take it. It's not that deep. The bike could get me through it and back onto the highway in no time. They would never be able to catch me. But Valerie tightens her body around me, reminding me that she's also on the bike, and I won't risk her life.

I bring the bike to a quick stop. The front of Valerie's helmet hits the back of mine from the force due to my last-minute decision to surrender.

She starts to climb off the bike before I can even get my feet on the ground, almost knocking us over. I watch as she frantically pulls her helmet off and throws it to the ground. I cringe as it hits the concrete. Couldn't she have thrown it behind her in the grass? Stupid bitch.

I climb off quickly as well. I've been in this situation enough to know that the police will fucking tackle your ass while you're still sitting on your bike. And all that does is knock your bike over, and that pisses me off. Cops are dicks anyways, but they are ten times worse when you try to run from them and they catch you.

I take my helmet off as well and set it on the ground. They are also known to cut your helmet off. This one is my favorite — no way will I let that happen.

"Hands up in the air!" a police officer yells with his gun raised and aimed right at me. By now other cop cars are coming to a stop to join the show — lights flashing and tires squealing.

I raise them with a heavy sigh. Can't they see I'm not packing? Where in the hell would I keep it? I'm wearing shorts and a t-shirt.

"Is there a problem, officer?" I ask with a cocky smile.

Valerie lets out a cry, and I turn around to look at her. Tears run down her face leaving a trail of black mascara and eyeliner. I've always felt like she wears too much makeup. "What's wrong?" I ask her.

"Seriously?" she screeches. "You're a jackass, Dash!" she cries. "You shouldn't have run. Now we're getting arrested." She drops her head but keeps her arms raised. "My parents are going to kill me," she adds, and I roll my eyes. She never has been much of a risk-taker. Or an adrenaline junkie, like myself. Why did I once date her? How is that saying? Opposites attract. Or maybe the sex was just that good...? Nah!

"We got him."

I spin my head back around to look at the officer who is walking to me as he speaks into his radio that's connected to his uniform.

"Yes, sir," he responds to the person on the other end of it.

He reaches for my raised arms and yanks me toward him before he shoves me forward. He then grabs the back of my neck roughly and throws the front of my body over the back of his cop car. "Fuck!" I mutter under my breath from his force.

He yanks my arms behind my back and proceeds to place me in handcuffs as he reads me my rights. He doesn't need to inform me of them, though. I've been in this situation before. Hell, I've totaled a car and two bikes in my twenty-two years. And I've had my license revoked a handful of times. I always get out of it though. Money talks. And that is one thing that I have plenty of.

# CHAPTER TWO

## Dash

I stand in a jail cell with my hands still cuffed behind my back as I look around. "Where is the girl who was with me?" I ask the officer who sits behind the only desk down here eating a Twinkie with his coffee. They placed us in separate cop cars when they hauled us in. I was immediately thrown into a cell alone, but I don't know where she was taken to.

He looks up at me for a few seconds with his brown eyes before he turns his attention back to his afternoon snack, ignoring me.

I huff as I sit down on the hard bench. I try rolling my shoulders but can't due to the cuffs. "Isn't this illegal?" I ask, referring to the cuffs.

"Let's talk about illegal..." a man's voice I don't recognize says.

I look up and just then a man comes around the corner of the cell into view. His silver hair is combed back and his dark brown eyes almost look black, but the smile on his face is friendly and my eyes widen.

I know exactly who this man is. He's Mr. Knight. He used to be one of the world's biggest Formula One race car drivers. He retired and started his own racing team.

"I'm sorry?" I question, confused as to what he's doing here and what he means by let's talk about illegal?

His eyes drop down to the papers sitting in his hands. "Erik Dashling." He says my name with a smirk as he skims over the information on it. "Seems you have a need to break the law, son. Wanna explain to me why you were clocked by an officer doing a hundred and thirty on the interstate today?"

One thirty? That's all? My 1,000 will do every bit of two hundred. Easily! But I also had a passenger who I needed to think about. "It was a nice day for a ride," I decide to say with a smile.

He lets out a chuckle at my sarcasm. "Yes, I guess it was." He places the papers behind his back and straightens his stance in front of my jail cell. "I've been watching you for a while," he announces, and my eyebrows shoot up. "And I have come to a decision."

"A decision?" I ask standing up from my bench.

He nods. He then lifts a hand and the officer behind his desk drops his Twinkie and jumps up. He walks over to the cell and opens it up. I stay grounded to my spot, wondering what in the hell is going on when the cop finally walks over to me. He spins me around and takes my cuffs off.

I rub my sore wrists as I turn back around to face them both.

"I'm giving you a spot on my team," Mr. Knight says with a friendly smile.

I look back and forth between the two of them in confusion. He wants to make me an errand boy... "Community service?" Wouldn't be the first time I have had to do some sort of community service for my endeavors. It will definitely be the first time it's something I will enjoy though.

He shakes his head. "No. I'm offering you a job," he clarifies before he straightens the jacket to his Armani three-piece suit. "Like I said. I've been watching you for a while. And you are exactly what I need. I'm starting a new race team. A motorcycle race team. And I want you."

This can't be happening. There's no way Johnny Knight is offering me a position on his race team. I'm the kind of guy who would be a liability. I'm dangerous and sometimes out of control. People have a hard time with my sarcasm and say I'm hard to work with due to my inability to follow rules. "I have a record," I say in all honesty.

He shakes his head. "Had. It's clean. As of now."

"How did you...?" There's no way! Even my father can't get shit off my record. And believe me, he's tried. Not because of me, but because of how it makes him look to his friends. Like I give a fuck how they see him.

He smiles. "Son, I have a lot of pull in this town." I watch the officer nod his head, and he looks over at me. "And I promise you. If you produce half of what I know you're capable of, I will take care of you. This isn't a handout. I will work you hard to produce the results I want."

I run my hand through my hair as I release a deep breath. "I don't understand. Why take the chance with me?" I ask in all seriousness. He has to know more about me than just my record.

"You think I got where I am today without taking risks?" he asks with a smile.

I shake my head as I look away and a thought comes to my mind. "Where's Valerie?" His brows crease. "The girl who was with me?" I need to know where she is at before this conversation goes any further.

"Oh, your girlfriend? I had a car take her home. She was not in trouble for your joyride today."

I don't correct him on Valerie being my ex. I just nod once again before speaking. "Thank you, sir."

"So. Do we have a deal?" he asks, already reaching out his right hand to shake.

A deal? This is a once-in-a-lifetime opportunity. I mean, I'm twenty-two with a rap sheet longer than my left arm and a very powerful and rich man is standing in front

Dash

of me offering me the chance at my dream job. "What's the catch?" I ask crossing my arms over my chest, refusing to shake just yet.

"Don't push your luck, boy," the officer growls.

Mr. Knight lifts his hand to silence the officer as he smirks. "I like a man who wants to know all of his options before he takes a deal," he says to the officer, but his dark brown eyes stay trained on mine. "The catch is that whenever you are on the streets — whether it be in your car or on your bike — you abide by the law. I don't want you arrested or to get even so much as a speeding ticket. No drugs and no alcohol. I don't want you showing up for a race or practice runs hungover or exhausted or fucked-up. You are no use to me in a hospital or jail."

"That's it?"

He nods. "That's it. Do we have a deal?" he asks once again.

The alcohol might be a problem. I like to party. But the drugs? Never done them. And don't plan on it. This'll be easy. I give him a big smile as I uncross my arms and reach my right hand out. "Deal."

He smiles as he firmly shakes my hand. He then reaches into the pocket of his suit jacket and pulls out a card. "I will send a car for you tomorrow afternoon. Be ready for it by two o'clock," he says before turning around.

"Be ready for what?" I ask, placing it in my back pocket of my shorts.

He turns back around and gives me a smirk. "To sign your life away," he says jokingly, but I have a feeling he's being serious.

I look up at the officer once Mr. Knight is out of the room. "He owns you, boy," is all he says before he goes back to his desk, opens up his drawer, and sets my wallet

8

and cell on top of it next to my helmet. "Here you go. And your bike is sitting out front for you."

I take my stuff and hightail it out of there. But before I get on my bike, I make a call to my best friend, Blake.

"Holy shit, man. I heard what happened. Valerie called me crying," is how he answers his phone.

I roll my eyes. I bet she called him. Anytime she can play the victim, she does. "No big deal," I respond. "Hey," I say before he can say anything else. "I'm having a party tonight," I say with a smile. I was just given the opportunity of a lifetime, and I'm not gonna fuck it up. But I haven't signed anything yet. So tonight I'm gonna live it up one last time.

"Your place?" he asks.

"Hell, no. I'm not throwing a party at my house." During the last party we had at my house, a fight broke out and the neighbors called the police. Guess I shouldn't have beat the shit out of the guy on the front lawn for everyone to see. But, in my defense, the drunk bastard started it.

"Okay. Your parents' house," he suggests, and I can hear the smile in his voice. "They're out of town. And I can call this girl I've been seeing. Jackie. She has this hot friend who I know you would love to hit."

Bingo! "Great idea." Even though nothing is written in stone with Mr. Knight, I want to celebrate. And I know just how to celebrate. Some alcohol and a woman underneath me who is anyone but Valerie.

*Dash*

# CHAPTER THREE

## *Tabatha*

"You have got to be fucking kidding me," I repeat for the fifth time as I sit at a stoplight on Rodeo Drive.

"That's what I was told," Jackie, my best friend, says softly next to me.

"Who was it?" I ask curiously.

She shrugs before she looks down at her cell in her hands. "I don't know. They didn't say a name. I guess it was someone he was talking to when you guys got together."

In all honesty, it doesn't surprise me that the bastard was cheating on me. I mean, he is the type to have more than one woman. He likes power and that made him feel like he had some. Fuck, he was probably with her at times while we spoke on the phone. She was probably right there smiling while she sucked his dick or something.

"You did the right thing," she says before she reaches over and pats my arm.

I look over at her with no expression, and she exhales. "I know you loved him, but…"

"Stop right there," I say slamming on the gas as the light turns green. "I didn't love him," I say in denial, and she sighs heavily, knowing I'm lying. "But," I add, "I don't regret leaving that sorry bastard."

"Good girl," she says happily, and I tighten my hands on the steering wheel. That's what Rodger always said to me. Always!

In and out of the bed. The worst part is that I did everything he said in order to hear him call me that. I wanted to be his 'good girl.' I wanted his praise. I shudder at how pathetic he made me.

I sit behind the steering wheel as I drive us to my house, and my anger starts to rise. This is the first time I've actually got to spend time with my best friend in months. We used to be inseparable. But things started to change once Rodger and I hit the three-month mark in our relationship. He started having me cancel plans with my family and friends, saying he didn't have time for this dinner or that party. And he didn't want me to go without him. Blah, blah, blah. Same ol' bullshit, just a different day. At first, I didn't think anything of it and let it slide. Before I knew it, he had changed my cell phone number. Then he was driving me to and from school, telling me it was easier to ride together — which at the time made sense.

We first met a little over a year ago at college. He just happened to be in one of my classes. I fell hard and fast for him. I loved him so much that I actually hated the person I became. Rodger thought people were below him. His father is a congressman, and his mother is some Botox loving, face peel obsessive, highfalutin bitch.

I was raised with money, wore the expensive clothes, and had the prettiest jewelry. Hell, I still do, but that doesn't mean I walk around with my nose stuck up in the air. Some people are lucky in life and some aren't. I'm a lucky one. I will never take that for granted ever again. Can I be a bitch who throws tantrums? Yep! Can I be a suck-up and bait Daddy when I want something? Absolutely! Do I tell it how it is? Of course. I wasn't raised to hide what I feel. How is someone going to know what you feel or think unless you tell them?

Well, with Rodger, I kept everything inside. I kept my mouth shut and sat up straight. To him and the men in his family, women were seen not heard. A woman's place was in the kitchen cooking or on her knees in the bedroom.

Dash

I couldn't take it anymore; I can't hide who I really am. I am a smart-mouthed bitch who has anger issues and a right hook to prove it. If that meant I rolled around in the dirt with the ones he considered scum, then call me the fucking queen of the scum world.

But for some crazy damn reason, I fell in love with him. There was just something about him. I wish I knew what it was because I would have ignored it. He didn't like to fight or to have me disagree with anything he said. What he had to say was final. Well, last week I overheard a conversation, and I couldn't keep my mouth shut. It was our biggest fight yet.

"You shouldn't have said that," he says tightly as he shuts his bedroom door. His dark hair is trimmed short, and his dark green eyes are hard.

"Why not?" I ask trying to keep my voice low, but it's hard. I want to scream at him.

"Because my dad didn't appreciate that. That's why," he snaps before running his hands down his white polo shirt. I just ironed it two hours ago, and it already has wrinkles. He hates wrinkles!

I try to hold my tongue, but enough is enough. "What? I can't have an opinion about our future?"

He fists his hands by his side as he takes a deep breath. "Your opinion was not asked. Therefore, it was not needed."

Simple as that.

He and his dad were talking about where he would transfer to next fall. I was in his parents' kitchen making him fucking chocolate chip cookies when I had overheard them. Of course, I had stormed off into the living room to find out what the hell they were talking about. When I said that I think he should stay here, it had started a big debate between his dad and me. Was it wrong not to want your boyfriend to pack up and leave you behind?

Well, good riddance, you sorry bastard!

I pull up to my house and open the door for Jackie to enter before I slam the door shut and lock it.

"Whoa. You okay?" she asks setting her purse down softly on my kitchen table.

"Yes. I just need to blow off some steam," I say, rolling my shoulders.

She smiles as she pulls her phone out of her purse. "How about we go to a party tonight? I just got a message from Blake that his friend is having one."

"Sounds perfect." That's exactly what I need—a party and some alcohol.

"That's my girl. Go ahead and start getting ready, and I'll make you a pre-party drink."

# CHAPTER FOUR

*Dash*

"I can't believe that you are going to be racing for Johnny Knight," Blake says excitedly.

I shrug, trying to not be as excited as he is. I still find it all too hard to believe. And I won't be jumping up and down until tomorrow when those papers are signed.

He pushes my shoulder, trying to knock me off balance. "You know you're going to kick ass," he says before he looks down at his phone and sighs.

"Calm down, man," I say. It's like the fifth time he's looked down at it in the last two minutes. The party has been going for two hours now. The house is full. People I have never even met are showing up. Guess that was bound to happen from people posting the shit on the internet. Some are already starting to walk sideways from the alcohol they've consumed. So far, I'm on my third beer. Not really wanting to get hammered just yet, 'cause I would hate for my parents' house to get destroyed. Not because I care about their shit, but because I don't wanna clean up the mess.

"She said they were coming." He sighs. "But that was over five hours ago."

"Then they'll be here," I say lifting my beer to my lips. "What's up with you and this Jackie girl anyway?" I ask once I pull my beer away. "You two serious?" He's been talking about this girl for over a month, yet he hasn't brought her around anyone. I was actually starting to think that she was imaginary.

He shakes his head. "Not that serious."

I smile. It totally is, but I'll let him be in denial. "So, what's her friend look like?"

He shrugs, and then looks at me with a smirk. "You haven't even met her, have you?" I ask with a frown. He did say she was hot.

"No. But I'm sure she's hot. Hot girls hang out with hot friends," he says matter-of-fact. I laugh. "If she's not what you want, then you could always call Valerie. That's a guaranteed ride," he mumbles.

I shake my head. "Fuck that." Valerie is the last girl I want, but I'm sure she'll show up at some point here tonight. She's an ex. I took her out for a ride today because she needed some time away from her house. Then after I was let out of jail, she blew up my phone with how much she hates me and what a jerk I am and how I could have killed us. I would prefer not to hear that shit tonight.

I turn around to throw my beer in the trash when I hear Blake speak. "There you are, baby. I thought you weren't gonna show up."

I turn back around to see him pull a pretty petite blonde into his arms as she speaks. "Yeah. It took me a while to get Tabatha ready." She giggles, referring to her friend.

"Where is she?" Blake asks looking around the kitchen.

She turns to look at the entrance of the kitchen, and then I hear a female's voice snap, "Get out of my way."

I watch as the sexiest woman I've ever seen enters my parents' kitchen. The first thing I notice is her tight-as-fuck jeans. The kind that look painted on. They gather tightly around her ankles, highlighting her black heels, which make her look about six inches taller than she is. She's wearing a black shirt that at first glance looks see-through.

It makes my mouth water.

Dash

Her dark hair is pulled up in a high ponytail, and her lips are the color of a cherry sucker. You can tell she has makeup on, but it's not overdone. Honestly, she looks like she just rolled out of bed and said fuck it! It's hot as hell and sexy as fuck!

She walks in like she fucking owns the place—head held high and shoulders back. Her hips sway as she walks in her 'bend me over the counter and fuck me' heels. She holds up a red cup in her right hand and shakes it. Her beautiful red lips frown when all you hear is the sound of ice clinking together. Her light brown eyes look around, and she smiles when she sees the alcohol displayed on the counter as if she's at a buffet. She goes to fix herself a new drink when my friend, Brandon, walks in and notices her.

"Hey, sexy," he says walking up behind her.

She turns and gives him a look from hell that only turns me on more. "Go away," she sneers.

I chuckle as he turns and walks off rejected. Feisty. I like that in a woman!

"What's wrong with her?" Blake asks turning back to Jackie.

She sighs. "She just broke up with her boyfriend."

I smile. Bitches who are recently single are the best. They're looking for payback—and I'm willing to be that for her tonight. Big sacrifice on my part, I know. But what can I say? I'm a gentleman.

I stand back and watch her fight with the gin bottle for a few seconds before I make my way over to her. "Need some help?"

She looks over at me. Being this close to her, I get a better look at her eyes. They have a golden hue to them. Her beautiful eyes hold mine for a few seconds before she looks me up and down with a straight face. She huffs as she hands me the bottle as if just that act of defeat was intolerable.

16

"Here you go, sweetheart," I say handing it back to her once I open it.

She stands up to her full height, but even with her heels, she still has to look up at me. "Listen. I'm not here to be someone's sweetheart. If that is your plan for the night, then keep looking." And with that, she spins around and walks back out of the kitchen.

"Sorry," Jackie says, coming over to me as she holds hands with Blake. "I had already made her a few drinks. The ex keeps blowing up her phone. I think she plans on getting wasted."

I rub my hands together. No need for her to apologize. I think I can handle a woman who has an attitude. "No problem. But I'm telling you right now; she's not leaving this house wasted." I understand how bad breakups can go, but I won't allow her to leave this house. The possibility of her getting in a wreck is too big; I've put myself in danger daily, but that's my life. Others, I care about.

She gives me a big smile as she lifts a set of car keys. "I have her car keys."

Blake reaches up and snatches them out of her hand. "Now, I have them. I'm not letting you drive either, baby," he coos before he leans down and captures her lips with his.

I chuckle as I turn around and leave the kitchen in search of Tabatha.

# CHAPTER FIVE

# *Tabatha*

I open my eyes and moan at the bright light that assaults my sensitive eyes. I close them and place a hand over my face. I have a pounding headache in need of some Advil. I slowly rub my temples as I take a deep breath.

I open my eyes slowly this time and glance around the room I'm in. I don't recognize anything—from the cream walls to the immaculate clean tan furniture and spotless wood floors. Seriously, I could eat off them. I'm sure as hell not in my bedroom. Did Jackie and I not go home last night?

Beside me, I hear a faint sound of snoring. My head snaps to the left, and I wince from the sudden movement. But my breath catches and my heart pounds in my chest when I see the back of a head covered in brown hair that's a little longer than what I'm used to on a man. I quickly lift the sheets and look down at myself. I'm naked.

"Shit," I say a little too loud making the dark-haired man stir beside me.

What the hell did I do last night?

Last thing I remember was Jackie coming into my bedroom and telling me to get ready. I had a few hours before we had to be at Blake's party. Then I started drinking while getting ready. Rodger wouldn't leave me alone. She finally dragged me out of the house as she complained how late we were.

Then nothing. Until now.

I have to get out of here!

I take a quick look around the room to locate my clothes.

I spot my skinny jeans wadded up over in the far corner. They aren't hard to pinpoint since they are the only thing lying on this bedroom floor.

I throw the covers off and run over to them. I pull them up not caring about my underwear. Those babies are too fucking small to even look for.

I place my hand over my breasts and look for my bra — where is that at?

I spin around and spot my shirt tossed behind the couch. Who has a couch in their bedroom? I snatch it up and start to put in on when I notice that it has been ripped.

That motherfucker.

I smile to myself. At the time, I probably liked his enthusiasm. Now, not so much. I spot a man's t-shirt on the floor underneath the desk. I see Dash written across the back with a number 88 placed underneath it.

That's the only shirt I see, so I grab it and put it on.

Grabbing my purse from the other side of the room along with my heels, I step out without waking him or leaving a note.

Seriously, what would it say?

Thanks for a night I can't remember and for losing my favorite pair of panties? Oh, and when you find my bra, can you please return it?

No, that's just tacky. It's bad enough I woke up in bed with a man. And let me set the record straight — this sort of thing has not happened in a long time.

I mean, yeah, I like sex as much as the next girl and have had a couple of one-night stands before Rodger. I at least knew those men, though. It just happened once, therefore, one-night stand.

But I don't make it a point to sleep with random men I don't know at parties. That's how girls end up with a disease or worse, dead or missing. So, I'm just gonna chalk it up to a lapse of judgment and alcohol-induced horniness.

It's totally a thing. Plus, I just went through a breakup. Doesn't that allow me one night of craziness?

Slowly and quietly, I make my way through this mansion as I try to do the walk of shame without being seen.

Long ass hallways with expensive artifacts hanging from the walls make me think this guy does not own this house. He looked way too young. His parents probably own this, and he lives with them.

I roll my eyes. I always find the ones who need their mommy and daddy to support their asses.

That's why his room is so clean. I bet his parents are out of town for business, and he had the maid come and clean so he could throw a party. That's what I would do. And by looking at the beer cans and empty liquor bottles covering the floor, I would say he needs her to come back to clean once more.

I turn down another hallway and walk past several shut doors. I can hear movement behind the last door I come up on.

"That feels so good," a woman's voice says softly. "Right there," she moans.

I come to a stop and stare at a soft yellow painted door. Please don't be Jackie. She has to be here somewhere, right? And that could easily be her horny ass.

"You like that, Val?" a man's deep voice says next, and I release a sigh of relief. Not Jackie. "What are you?" he demands, his voice rising.

"I'm your bitch," she hollers out in a high pitch voice.

I cover my hand over my mouth trying not to laugh.

"I'm your bitch, baby," she repeats.

Okay, so the bitch is totally into her role, but he's not buying it.

"You can do better. Now. Tell Daddy what you are." I hear a slapping noise followed by a moan. And I can only guess it's his hand hitting her ass.

"I'm your little fuck toy," she calls out. "Fuck me. Use me," she continues.

I roll my eyes and walk away from the door.

Yeah, I don't need to know all the ways he feels he needs to degrade her. That's what Rodger did to me. Made me feel degraded. Made me do things that I wouldn't have normally done before him. I have more self-respect for myself now.

"Right," I mumble to myself. This coming from a girl who had a one-night stand with a stranger. I shake my head at myself.

"Thank God," I whisper harshly when I finally make it to the front door. I let out a sigh of relief that instantly turns to fear when I walk outside and don't see my car.

I see a black Bentley, a red Ferrari, a yellow Porsche, and a couple of sports bikes. Yep, none of those are my white BMW.

Looking down and digging through my purse, I locate my cell phone. Pulling it out, I thank the Lord that it's not dead. I also cuss out loud when I notice that I have three missed calls from the ex himself. I ignore them and call Jackie. The one who left my ass here. In my car. The bitch!

I impatiently tap my foot as I squeeze my eyes shut waiting for her to answer. Damn headache!

"Hello?" she sleepily answers on the third ring.

"Wake your hungover ass up and come get me," I demand, looking around to make sure no one is gonna walk out of the house and see me.

"Where are you?" she asks sounding more awake.

"Wherever you left my ass at last night," I snap.

She groans. "I'm coming."

"Hurry your ass up," I say before hanging up the phone.

I make my way down the stone steps and white stucco pillars. I walk past the cars in the circle drive and continue to walk down the long driveway.

I'm going to kill her!

Why would she leave me? We never leave one another behind.

As I start to come to the end of the long paved driveway, I stop and try to look through my purse for my sunglasses.

"Shit," I cuss when I realize they are not in there. I remember having them while driving to the party last night. They must be in my car.

I huff, throw my purse back over my shoulder, and squint trying to block the hot sun that is just intensifying my annoying headache.

I come to the end of the driveway and see a tall, wrought-iron gated entrance.

Well, this can't be good.

I come up to it and look for a button that I can push, but the only button I see is on the opposite side sitting in front of the guard shack.

Hmm well, so much for the Lord being on my side this morning. I start to look around to make sure I didn't miss something to help open it from this side. I could go back and try to see if there is a gate opener in one of those cars.

I turn around but stop before I can take a step. I really don't want to go back there and set off a car alarm. I'm trying to get out of here unseen. And what are the odds of them being unlocked? Not likely!

I look around once again to see if I can find another way out. When I come up with nothing on this side to help me with, I decide the best thing I can do is climb and jump over the fence. It seems to run the full length of the property. It's not like I can just walk a few feet down and walk off their property.

I shake my head at myself. I am too hungover for this bullshit. I squeeze my eyes shut and rub my hand over my throbbing forehead. Why did I have to drink so much last night? Everyone knows that alcohol is only a temporary fix. All you are left with the morning after is a badass headache. You're still gonna remember the heartache and betrayal.

Taking a deep breath and trying to forget about Rodger, I open my eyes. I notice a tree that stands off to the right. To any other person, it would be too hard to climb. Good thing for me, I started climbing trees as soon as I could walk.

I go over to it and adjust my purse over my opposite shoulder so it hangs across my chest. That's all I need — to climb this bitch and have it fall off once I get to the top.

I spit on my hands and then rub them together. I know, classy. I feel like a pitcher spitting on the ball. Nothing can be nastier than that. I dated a baseball player once. Why do we find them so sexy when they spit on the one thing they all touch? Oh yeah, the tight fucking pants that showcase those beautiful round asses.

It only takes a few seconds for me to figure out how to get up it. I grab ahold of the lowest branch and lift myself up. At this moment, I'm thankful Jackie made me take all of those stupid yoga classes with her back in the day, which has left me limber. Climbing far enough up, I swing my body around and come level with the fence.

"This is going to hurt," I whisper looking at how far the fence is from the ground. There's not a tree for me to climb down on the other side. I'm just going to have to jump. And I'm guessing the distance to be over six feet.

"Let's go to the party," Jackie had said. "It will be great," she had said.

"Great my fucking ass," I mumble. I remove my heels and throw them over. I cringe when my three hundred and fifty dollar pair of shoes hits the grass. I treasure my heels. What woman doesn't?

Taking one last deep breath, I swing my legs over the fence and jump down. My feet instantly sting when they hit the ground. I don't even try to catch myself, which could injure my body worse. I just let go and crumple to the grass.

I roll over onto my back as I let out a growl of frustration. The fact that I had to sneak out of the house — from some guy whose name I don't even remember — couldn't have been the worst part of my morning. No, I also had to listen to some dude take care of his morning wood. Then climb a tree and jump a fence. Yeah, today is not my day.

I groan at my sore body as I get to my feet. I don't even bother to brush myself off before I grab my shoes and start to limp my way off down the street.

I am in the process of dreaming about a hot bath and curling up in my bed for an early afternoon nap when Jackie passes me and then does a U-turn, coming to a stop beside me. I pull open the passenger door and fall inside, thankful for the cool air-conditioning.

"Do you want to drive?" she asks, car idling in the street.

"No," I growl. "Just get me home."

"What the hell happened to you?" she asks, looking me up and down with a sour look on her face. "Did you sleep outside or something?"

"Just take me home." I can explain the situation to her after I sleep off this hangover.

She looks from me to the clock on the dash. "Don't you have a test today?"

Shit! "How do you know that?"

"You told me that like thirty times last night before I left."

I look over at her. "Speaking of leaving…" I huff. "Why did you leave me?"

She frowns. "You said I could." But then she gets a dreamy smile on her face.

"Thanks." She sighs, and I can't help but scowl. Glad she remembers how good her night was.

"Just drive me to the college. Please," I say, pulling my sun visor down to look at myself in the mirror. I look like a horror movie gone wrong. My dark hair still looks freshly fucked, only with a few added leaves in it. What makeup is still on has smeared across my face. And my light brown eyes are bloodshot.

She frowns. "You're going to go to school like that?" Her dark blue eyes look me over and her frown deepens before she scrunches her nose.

"I don't have a choice, Jackie." I sigh. "If I miss this test, I'll be in deep shit with my dad. Just take me there. I don't think the test has a hygiene requirement."

She nods her head and starts to drive off. I run my fingers through my hair and try to take off what's left of my makeup, before I lean my head back against the headrest and close my eyes — trying to remember what the hell happened last night. I remember showing up at the party with Jackie. I remember making myself a drink in the kitchen. I remember Rodger calling me, and I remember pressing ignore before I ended up just turning my phone off. But this morning, it was on. When did I turn it back on? I don't remember.

Then we made our way to the back of the house to the game room where I proceeded to smoke a guy who asked me to play a game of pool. The same guy who had helped me make my drink in the kitchen...

I smile as I start to remember the color of his eyes. They were the sexiest gray eyes I had ever seen. I had eye-fucked him with no shame. His smile had caused me to miss a few shots, but I still beat him every time.

His strong jaw and dark hair.

My eyes snap open at that. Well, that answers that question.

I ended up sleeping with him?

I don't remember going to his room, though. Hell, I don't even remember kissing him. So, how did we end up there?

Jackie gets my attention as she rolls down the windows and cranks up the A/C.

"What are you doing?" I ask.

"You smell like booze, cigarettes, and sex," she says matter-of-fact. "It's making me nauseous," she adds. "And what happened to you?"

I laugh. "Well, it seems I got some action last night, but I don't remember it."

"Oh, you got some action all right," she agrees. "I thought you two were going to do it on the pool table. Or in the hallway," she adds with a laugh. "Did you end up doing it in the garden or something?"

I scowl. "Why didn't you stop me?"

She quickly looks over at me with a smile. "He was hot and why would I stop you? You were pissed off at Rodger for calling you and started drinking like a fish.

Plus, you were totally digging one another." She wiggles her blond eyebrows.

Digging? Who says that?

I shake my head. Even if she had tried to stop me, I wouldn't have listened. "Did you get some?" She better have left for me a good reason.

"Yep," she says with a smile on her face.

"Well, then, our life is complete," I say dryly.

I stretch out my legs and smile. At least the sex I got was good. I can tell it by the feel in my muscles. Whoever he was, he used every inch of my body, and I guarantee I loved every second of it.

"Do you want me to wait for you?" she asks as she pulls up to the college.

I shake my head. "Just come back and get me in an hour," I say digging through my glove box.

"What are you looking for?" she asks.

"Advil." I always keep some in my car.

I look over at her when she sighs. "I already took it," she admits with a small smile.

"What?" I snap. "You took the only two I had left?"

She holds up three fingers, and I let out a growl. She calls out, "Sorry," as I swing the door open and get out.

# CHAPTER SIX

# Tabatha

After Jackie had picked me up from the school, I dropped her off at her house. Then I stopped off at Starbucks for the biggest coffee they had, which I now know is called a Venti. And I hate coffee. But it just sounded so good. Well, it doesn't taste as good as it sounded. Plus, my tongue is numb from where I burned the hell out of it.

I make my way into our house. My parents have many houses all over the world, but I grew up in this one. The one I still call home even though I now have a place of my own. I actually just bought my first home last year. Against my parents' advice. I didn't want to live on campus or with my parents. I wanted my very own place, but it's on the other side of town. And my parents' house just happens to be five miles from the college. After the morning I've had, it was an easy decision.

I take off down the main hallway to head to the back of the house where my old room is located, when I hear my dad talking in his office. I go to walk past it and see his door is open. He looks up and spots me. Busted.

"Hey, sweet pea. How was your test this morning?"

"Fine," is all I say. I'm not a hundred percent sure that I passed. Guess I'll find out soon enough.

He lifts his hand and motions for me to enter. "Come here. I have someone I want you to meet."

I shake my head. "It will have to wait. I need a shower."

"Nonsense," he argues. "You look great. It will be quick."

I sigh but go ahead and walk into his office. I see his nose scrunch when I come up to his desk. I can't help but smile at the thought of smelling how Jackie had described. I can't smell much of it; I think my nose is used to it now.

I hear the leather creak from someone shifting on the couch behind me, but I don't turn around. I wait for my father to excuse me since he finally sees how awful I look.

"What did you do last night?" he asks with a frown on his face.

"Gardening…?" I offer, remembering what Jackie had said and the person sitting on my father's couch behind me coughs to cover up a laugh.

"Gardening?" My father's brows pull together. "Is that some new slang for something?"

"It's…"

He places his hand up to interrupt me. "I probably don't want to know."

I nod my head trying to hide my smile. He may end up reading it in the tabloids. See, my father is famous. He owns the biggest racing team in California. Formula One cars have always been his dream. He used to race them. That's where he started making his fortune. Then retired and started his own team. Come to find out, he loves being on that end just as much as he did being a driver.

"Anyways, as you know, your mother and I have been talking about branching out," he says with a smile referring to their company.

I nod my head. I have overheard this conversation. They want to dip their toes into other forms of racing.

"Well, it's official. We have started a new racing team that involves motorcycles. And you are already a fan." He gestures to my shirt, and I look down at the words DASH and frown before tilting my head in confusion. Then I hear the leather crinkle once again behind me. "See," my father says with a smile, looking past me to whoever is sitting

29

behind me. "I knew you would like her." He claps his hands together as if he's proud of himself, and I frown as the person moves behind me once again. What in the hell's wrong with them back there?

"Motorcycles?" That's not what I was expecting him to say.

He nods. His silver hair not even moving due to all the product my mother puts in it for him. I swear he is still a child and needs her to dress him. Feed him. And probably even bathe him. I shudder at that thought. Ugh.

"Yes. I want to introduce you to the newest member of our team." He gestures to the person sitting behind me. "Darling, say hello to Erik Dashling."

I quickly turn around wanting to get his over with so I can get the hell out of here. My heart starts to pound as hard as my head. I come eye to eye with those light gray eyes, chiseled jaw, and dark hair.

Memories of last night start to return. Like us making out on the pool table. Me stumbling into his room before he ripped my shirt off. Then me down on my knees before him. I couldn't get his belt and jeans off fast enough. Those memories are making my thighs tighten.

I blink rapidly to try to clear the memories that are coming back full force.

"Hello, ma'am," he says trying to sound formal. He stretches his hand out to me with a cocky smile on his sexy face.

"Hello," I say narrowing my eyes at him and crossing my arms over my chest. It's a little late for formalities.

He takes the hand stretched out in front of him and lifts it up to my hair. He pulls back and has a leaf between his fingers.

He chuckles. "Gardening? Looks like you've been rolling around in the grass."

Motherfucker.

He knows. Shit! I didn't think to look for any video cameras around his gate. I'm sure he has them.

His smirks grows as if he knows what I'm thinking.

"Nice to meet you, Mr. Dashling." I nod my head.

He gets a cocky look on his face and his eyes sparkle. "Please. Call me, Dash."

Oh, now the shirt I'm wearing makes sense.

I nod my head once and spin around to face my father. "I need to go shower and then get home. I have homework to do," I lie. "Excuse me," I mumble and walk out of the office and start down the hall when I hear Erik speak to my father.

"Will you excuse me, sir?"

As I'm nearing the stairs, I feel a hand on my upper arm. "What the..."

He pulls me into the hallway and presses me up against the wall. Before I can speak, his hands are on my face, and his lips are on mine.

I try to fight it, try to push him away, but his body pressed up against mine has my legs going weak. I wrap my arms around his neck to hold myself up. My body is still sore as hell from last night. And my pussy has been wet all morning. Although I can't remember what all he did, my body sure as hell can. His kiss is slow and sweet. He takes his time as his tongue makes long strokes.

He pulls away and a moan slips past my lips. "You taste as good as I remember," he mumbles. "Like candy."

I don't say anything as I stare into his eyes. He gives me a warm smile. "You left this morning without saying good-bye."

"If I remember correctly, we never really said hello," I whisper.

He chuckles. "You're correct." He leans back into me. "Hello," he whispers, sending chills down my body.

"Hello," I answer breathlessly.

"I have something you might like," he says with a smirk on his face.

"I'm pretty sure I liked it," I respond still feeling the aftereffects from last night.

"Pretty sure?" He frowns. "Well, I will have to remind you of how much you liked it later." He runs his fingers down the side of my cheek. "You screamed my name so loud my ears are still ringing." I inhale sharply. He lowers his face to mine and runs the tip of his nose down the side of my face. "You fucking loved every bit of it, darling," he growls as his hands tighten on my hips.

My body trembles. He nuzzles my hair and inhales deeply. "You still smell like sex." He pushes his erection into my lower belly. "Like me. And that shirt looks absolutely amazing on you."

His hands slip under the hem of his shirt I'm wearing. They softly make their way up my sides, and he cups my breasts. Thank God, I lost my bra in his bedroom. "We can't," I choke on the words as his aggressive hands massage them roughly.

He lets out another chuckle. "I know." He pulls back from me and my tits instantly go cold when he pulls his hands away and reaches into his pocket. Pulling out something black that is inside his fist, he holds it out in front of me. "This is what I thought you would want."

I look at his hand and he opens it to reveal my black panties. I gasp before I snatch them out of his hand. "How did you know?" I narrow my eyes at him.

Did he know who I was last night? Is that why he slept with me?

It wouldn't be the first time a guy wanted to sleep with me because of my father's fame.

He looks at me with a confused face. He goes to speak, but I hold up my hand. "I'm glad you had fun last night, but my father has already signed you, so that won't be happening again." I place my hands on his chest and shove him away from me.

"Wait. What?" he asks sounding confused. I go to walk away from him, but he grabs my upper arm.

"Erik, you ready to finish up this meeting?" I hear my dad ask.

He sighs as he holds onto my arm. "Yeah. Sure, Mr. Knight." He looks down at me and whispers, "This conversation isn't over," as he releases me.

I take the stairs two at a time and head straight for my shower. I turn the water on scalding hot and jump in, scrubbing every inch of my body until it's raw. He was right, I still smell like him, and I want it gone. The bastard used me. I mean, in a way, I used him as well—self-satisfaction. But he used me to help further his career.

# CHAPTER SEVEN

Dash

Just my fucking luck! The girl I slept with at my party is the one and only Tabatha Knight. Mr. Knight's daughter. My new boss!

"Dude. I had no idea," Blake says as he sits next to me on my couch while he holds my laptop. "I told you that I had never met her."

"Go to images," I say pointing to her name on my screen.

He does and pictures of her start to pop up—her in the winner's circle with racers; her dad by her side; her out at parties with a dark-haired man by her side. "Is that her ex?" I ask.

"One sec," he says before he clicks on the link to his name. "Rodger Heath the third. Son of Rodger Heath the second and Shawna Heath…"

"Wait. Rodger Heath? As in the congressman?" I ask, standing up from the couch and looking down at him in shock.

"Yes," he says just as shocked. He looks back down and starts to read the headline. "The two are still going strong after a year together. Are wedding bells in their near future?" He clicks on a few other links. A picture comes up of her and him walking out of a restaurant in New York City. She's wearing a black coat that she's tied tightly around her, keeping out the cold. Her long brown hair falls down—covering her face. She has her head down, and he has a hold of her arm tightly as if he's dragging her behind him. His face is hard as he stares straight at the camera. You can tell by his hard stare and his hold on her that he is not happy about something. Whether it was her or the cameras, I don't know. Blake then looks at a few more links. Not one mentions their breakup. How long ago did they split? Could it be possible that the press doesn't know about it yet?

"What are you going to do?" he asks getting my attention. He has a hard look on his face as he stares up at me from my laptop.

"What I always do. I always get what I want," I say simply. You think I give a rat's ass that her ex is Rodger Heath? Fuck, no!

"Dash, man, you just got the offer of a lifetime. You've already signed with him. You gonna jeopardize it for her?" he asks softly. "I mean, I get it, she's hot. But you just met her. And Jackie said they just broke up. The odds of them staying broke up…"

"I want her," I state, interrupting her.

"You've already had her." He says with a smirk now on his face.

I shake my head. "I want her again." She was different. She was wild, just like I knew she would be. Valerie was so boring, and I always had to be in control. Tabatha was crazy and full of passion. I could feel it in the way she touched me. Her body screamed for a release.

"You know her dad will kick you off the team if he catches the two of you together?" He closes the laptop and looks up at me. "I mean, look who she was with." He brings up Rodger again.

I roll my eyes, but inside, I am wondering the same thing. I mean, look at their fathers. Talk about a power couple. "Probably," I say in all honesty. But Mr. Knight told me that he isn't where he is today without taking risks. And she is a risk I'm willing to take.

# CHAPTER EIGHT

## *Tabatha*

"You're joking?" Jackie asks rubbing suntan lotion on her white as snow skin.

"I wish I were," I say, lying on a lawn chair by my parents' pool. Two days have passed since I came home to find Dash sitting in my father's office. And I'm still as pissed as I was the second I realized he knew who I was.

It was my fault. I was stupid enough to sleep with him without even bothering to find out who he was. I just wanted someone to get over Rodger, and of course, like a slut, I jumped in bed with the first guy who I found attractive.

"How could he have known who you were, though?"

"The internet." I roll my eyes behind my Dolce shades. "There are pictures of me on there with my father's racing team." She knows this. Then all the pictures of Rodger and me, of course.

"But, in the past, the guys dated you for a little bit while they tried to get close to your dad. Erik had already been signed."

I shake my head. "Technically, he was signing that very next morning," I remind her.

"It doesn't make sense. I can't see him doing that."

I arch a dark eyebrow. "Oh? Are you two best friends now?"

She shakes her head. "I just saw the way he looked at you at his party. Trust me when I say this. He was thinking about how to get you up to his bed—not how you could further his racing career." She then tilts her head to the side and frowns. "That sounded worse," she says, confused by her statement.

"Just forget it. It's not gonna happen again," I say, and I ignore her snort. She doesn't believe me. Hell, even I don't believe me. He just made me feel so free. So sexy. Have you ever been with a man who made you feel confident? Beautiful? That was how he made me feel. The way he spoke to me. The way his hands roughly held me. Just thinking about it makes me wet. I had cried out with every thrust. He took his time with me, yet fucked me. His cock was so big my pussy still remembers what if felt like…

I sit up quickly. "Fuck me!" I hiss.

"What?" Jackie asks sitting up quickly as well.

I look over at her, panicked as my heart pounds. "We didn't use a condom." I throw my hands over my face. "Oh, my God," I hiss. "How stupid could I be?"

"It's okay," she offers.

"It's okay?" I demand. "What is okay about that?" I throw my hand over my pounding chest. "I could be pregnant."

"You're on birth control."

"A disease?" How fucking stupid. I don't remember him having one. At all. "I'm totally fucked."

"You're worrying about it too much." I go to speak, but she raises her hand. "You had unprotected sex with Rodger."

"Yeah, but…"

"But nothing. It's not like he ever went and got checked."

I fall back onto my back and cover my face with my hands. I can't believe I let myself do that. What I allowed happen. I'm a total idiot.

"It's happened. Just try to forget about it. Relax," she says softly, and I take a few deep breaths.

I close my eyes as I turn over onto my stomach to let my back get some sun as I continue to remember that night. We lie basking in the sun in silence for a few minutes until I hear Jackie speak.

"I, uh, am going to go get something to eat. Want anything?" she asks sounding flustered.

"Sure. Bring me some ice cream." Aunt Flow is about to visit and my main craving is ice cream. Mint chocolate chip is to die for.

She doesn't respond, but I hear her get up and her feet slap against the hot concrete as she walks away.

I let out a long sigh as those gray eyes come to mind once again. I wish I could forget what happened that night at his party. It's all I see now. I liked it better when my memory was still hazy and hungover.


We crash through his bedroom door. He shoves my back against the door slamming it shut in the process. His lips are on mine as his tongue shoves its way into my mouth. I feel his hands on the hem of my shirt, and he goes to pull his mouth away to lift my shirt. But I grab a hold of him and pull him into me. His hands rise and rip my shirt off as I moan into his mouth. My bra disappears and his hand lands on my breast roughly. He takes my nipple between two fingers and pinches it so hard that I pull away and scream out.

I'm panting and pushing my hips into him, needing more. I drop to my knees and start to undo his belt. "Shit," he hisses placing his hands behind his head as I free his rather large dick. I lick my lips and take his hard dick into my mouth.

He then slams a fist against the door as the other hand finds its way into my hair. I pull him to the back of my throat and his nails dig into my scalp. I pull away as I lick up his long hard shaft. I come to the top and swirl my tongue around the head.

"God, Tabatha," he growls as his other hand finds its way into my hair as well. He grips it tightly and pushes his hips forward. I suck taking him to the back once again. "Fuck," he hisses. "I wanna fuck you so hard..." I moan around his cock in my mouth and relax my mouth giving him permission to do whatever in the hell he wants to me.

For once, in a long time, I want someone to fuck me so hard I can't stand afterwards.

"You're going to burn." A familiar man's voice cuts through my thoughts.

My eyes spring open, and I fumble to get off the lounge chair and up onto my feet. My feet get tangled in my chair, and I about fall into the pool when two strong arms grab me around the waist and I'm pulled into a hard body.

I let out a breath as my heart pounds against his chest. I watch the frown on his face from behind my sunglasses. I tighten my legs as the memory of what we did still lingers in my mind.

He reaches up and pushes my glasses to the top of my head. I blink a few times from the harsh sunlight. "You should be more careful," he warns.

"Of you?" Why do I sound so breathless?

He shakes his head. "I finally realized what you were so upset about. And I promise you that I had no idea who you were that night of my party."

"You're lying," I say, starting to get myself under control.

"I promise. I'm not."

"What are you doing here?" I ask, trying to pull out of his arms, but he doesn't let me go.

"I just wanted to talk to you. To make sure you understood that I didn't take you to bed with the wrong intentions."

I let out a rough laugh, hoping it hides my discomfort of wanting a repeat of that night. "Yeah. Because just getting your dick wet is a much better excuse."

He gives me a slow and sexy smile. "Darling, you wanted it just as badly." He then runs the back of his knuckles down the side of my cheek. "If I remember correctly, you instigated it."

"Me?" I gape up at him.

He nods. "The way your eyes raked over me. The way you bent over the pool table and pushed your ass out. I paid attention." I huff. "You knew what you were doing," he says, giving me a devious smile.

"I don't know what you're talking about." I play stupid. I just wanted one night to forget about Rodger. I just happened to have slept with a guy who my father signed. Why is karma coming after me?

"Now, who's the one lying?" He leans down so close his lips are almost touching mine. I lick mine. "And I just want another chance to show you just how much you enjoyed it. Preferably without as much alcohol involved this time."

I shake my head. "That can't happen."

"It can. And it will."

"No," I say firmly.

"What? Are you saying I don't have a chance?" He lifts an eyebrow and gives me a small smile.

I let out a breath before telling him the truth. "I had one intention that night and that was to forget my ex," I say, and his smile drops off his face. "So both of our intentions were not pure."

"You speak of my intentions as if you still don't believe me when I say I didn't know who you were," he says frowning once again.

I shrug carelessly. "Does it really matter? It happened. You're the one who won't let it go. And you also didn't use a condom," I add with bite.

He cracks a smile. "I had one, but you took it off." Of course, I did. He leans in and whispers into my ear, "You said you wanted to feel me as I fucked you." His breath hits my ear and makes me break out in goosebumps. "And it was the sexiest thing I had ever heard." He pulls away, and I look up at him through heavy eyes. "And you're right," he says softly. "I don't want to let it go." He runs his hand up my back. "I want you again and again. Why do you make it sound like such a bad thing?" He presses his lips against mine. I open up without hesitation letting him kiss me. It's just a kiss. What could it hurt?

My lips work with his as if they have done it a thousand times before. I feel his fingers brushing against my back and then his hand is covering my breast.

I gasp in his mouth when I realize he untied the top of my bathing suit.

He chuckles softly. "I want you right now."

"My dad..." If he saw this, he would shit a brick and both of our lives would be over.

"He's not here," he whispers.

"Jackie?" I ask. Why am I trying to get out of this? I want him.

"She has probably left already."

If I know Jackie, she is probably sitting in one of the windows, eating my ice cream while watching us. She's a freak like that.

"We can't do this," I finally say, pushing him away from me. My body shivers as his heat no longer touches me. My body wants him. Hell, my body has had him, and it knows how fucking good he feels.

I go to walk past him, holding my top over my breasts the best I can. Which is hard since it's just two triangles.

He grabs my arm and spins me around. He knocks my body into his, and I feel the air leave my lungs when he grabs my ass and lifts me up. He lays me down on top of the lounge chair.

"Dash…" I say breathlessly trying to get up.

He straddles me and pins my hands down by my head. I don't fight it. Instead, I lift my hips up to his, needing some kind of friction. I'm soaking wet and horny as hell. I want him to remind me how much I enjoyed it.

He slowly smiles then his eyes land on my exposed chest. Crap, I lost my bikini again. He sits there for a second as he watches my chest as I breathe heavily.

He bends down and places his lips on mine, slow and soft. His hands release my wrists and I wrap them around his neck. I just can't push him away. He makes me forget Rodger. He makes me feel alive again, instead of a pathetic little dog that obeyed every command. I wanna be wild and crazy for him.

He slides a hand between our bodies and inside my bikini bottoms. I spread my legs for him. "You're already wet for me, baby." He smiles against my lips when his fingers find my soaked pussy.

I moan as he slides one into me. "Tell me what you were thinking about when I startled you," he demands as he enters another one into me.

"You." I arch my back and let out a whimper.

He chuckles as he places soft kisses on my neck. "What about me?"

I pause for a second. Rodger never asked me how our sex felt, or what I liked. We always did what he liked. My opinion didn't matter. I like that Dash wants to know.

"The way you fucked my mouth," I say honestly and a deep rumble comes from his chest.

"I think about that all the time, too," he admits.

His fingers slide out and my body sinks into the lounge chair from the loss. "What are you doing?" I ask as he sits up. Please keep going.

"I believe it's my turn to fuck you with my mouth," he states with a smile as he unties both strings of my bikini bottoms and sinks down between my legs. I bend my knees and arch my back as he does just that. No tenderness. No holding back. He literally fucks me with his tongue, and it's amazing. He grabs my legs and throws them over his shoulders and his hands hold down my hips as they buck. My hands tangle in his dark hair and I scream out as he brings me to orgasm in minutes. Never slowing down. Giving me all he has. And it's amazing. Once done, he sits up but continues to hold me down as my body shakes from the aftermath. He leans down and gives me a soft kiss on my parted lips as I pant. I lick what's left of myself off his lips. And he moans into my mouth. It has me needing more. I lift my hips feeling his hard-on behind his pants. I need him inside of me. Fucking me. I reach for his pants but he grabs my wrists and pins them down by my head again and he deepens the kiss. Taking what little breath I had left away.

When he pulls away I'm gasping for air. "There's another memory for you to think about when I'm gone." Then with a smirk on his beautiful face, he gets up and leaves me there. I lie there completely spent as he gets up and walks back into the house to leave.

I throw my arm over my eyes and cuss myself. What in the hell did I just let him do? Did I really just let him go

*Dash*

down on me in the middle of the day on my parents' lawn furniture? Yes, yes I did! And it was fucking amazing!

"Girl…" Jackie screeches as she comes running outside.

I sit up and hold my bottoms between my legs. She's my best friend and has been since middle school. She's seen me naked more times than I could count, but I do not want her to see my pussy after what Dash just did to it.

"What?" I try to ask calmly. I pull my legs up and throw my arms over them trying to hide that fact that they are still shaking.

"What?" she repeats, placing her hand on her narrow hips. "You know what. I saw that."

"I knew you would watch, you sick freak," I say with a laugh.

She fans herself. "I didn't see much, but I do need to cool off after that. Oh, and he was hard as a rock as he walked out." She winks. "Big package, huh?" She then jumps into the pool, and I lie back down as I look up to the sky. I'm fucked! Getting involved with him is the last thing I need right now.

# CHAPTER NINE

## Tabatha

"Go away," I growl as I hear my doorbell ring again. I pull the covers up over my head and try to get back to my sex dream with Dash.

We're in my parents' pool and the sun has set. The full moon up above is the only light we have. He's shoved my back against the pool, and I've wrapped my legs around his hips. The water is somewhat cold, but his body warms my own.

"Dash," I say breathlessly as his lips run up and down my neck.

"God, you're so fucking beautiful," he says while his lips brush my ear. "So fucking perfect." His hands on my hips grip me tighter.

"Please," I beg and thrust my hips to him. I can feel his hardness resting against my lower belly. We've stripped naked, but he's making me wait for some reason. I'm going to explode before he even starts to fuck me.

"What have I told you about begging...?" I can feel his smile against my neck. He's enjoying this.

It won't work on him. I loosen up my legs a little and allow my hand to travel between our bodies. I grab a hold of his cock tightly, and he hisses in a breath. Slowly, but firmly, I run my hand up and down his thick cock.

I lower my face so that I can whisper into his ear. "I'm not begging. I'm telling you. Fuck me!" My body is tingling, and my pussy is throbbing. I need him to give me something and soon.

45

I feel his chest rumble as he lets out a growl from deep within his chest. His hand quickly grabs my wrist and pulls it away. He takes himself in his hand and pushes inside of me.

My head falls back, and I take in a deep breath as he stretches me to accommodate his size.

"I'll fuck you," he says through gritted teeth as his hands tangle in my hair. I whimper from the feel of the pinpricks, and my pussy tightens around him. "However you want it, baby," he says, pulling out and slamming back into me.

My back stings as its rubs against the pool wall, but it feels so good. He feels so good.

"Open up, Tabby." A fist hits the door a few more times, breaking my dream once again.

I growl as I bounce out of bed and storm to the door. "What the fuck are you doing here?" I demand, looking at Rodger. Not only did the bastard ruin my dream, but he also has to be standing on my front porch at the butt crack of dawn.

He gives me a look of disapproval with his green eyes due to my choice of wording. He always hated when I cussed.

"I came to talk to you." He looks behind me to my hall. "May I come in?"

"No," I say closing the door a bit so he has to look at me.

He fixes his tie and straightens his back. "Please?" he asks through gritted teeth. He doesn't believe in asking permission. To him, a man should receive whatever he wants, whenever he wants. Like every man on Earth is a God, and women are just little slaves. Just that thought has me wanting to slam his hand in the door.

46

"No," I say again more firmly. "It's over, Rodger. Go away." I slam the door in his face and head toward my bedroom. He ruined my dream for nothing. I look up at my clock and sigh. I have three hours before class.

I start to walk to my bathroom but come to a stop when a thought crosses my mind. I'm on Spring Break! I don't have to be anywhere today. I crawl back in bed, and as soon as I pull the covers up and over my head, my house phone rings.

"Ugh!" I say throwing the covers off my face. "What now?" I snap reaching over to grab the phone off my dresser.

"Good morning, sweet pea. Hope I didn't wake you."

"Hey, Dad," I say with a smile. I hate how much time I have missed with him and my mother over the last year. My parents really liked Rodger, so when I had to call and cancel a dinner date or birthday party for them with some lame ass excuse Rodger had made up, they believed me. Believed that I was just too busy with my 'grown-up life', as they would say.

"How about joining me for dinner tonight?" he asks happily.

"That sounds great," I say, lying back down on the bed with a comfortable sigh.

"You can bring Rodger," he offers, and my shoulders slump. "I haven't seen him in forever." I bite on my lip as I try to come up with an excuse as to why Rodger can't come, when he continues, "How about at the Gardens, say seven thirty?"

"See you there. I love you."

"Love you too, sweet pea."

I hang up the phone and close my eyes, getting back to my dirty dream with Dash.

I spent the day in bed daydreaming about Dash. Well, up until Jackie showed up to drag me out of bed to go to some stupid yoga class and then to the mall to do some shopping.

I pull up to the Gardens and leave my car with the valet. The waitress smiles as I walk in smoothing down my black dress. I chose something simple yet elegant. It's tight fitting on my chest and has a red belt that circles high on my waist. Then the pleated skirt flares out. It might be a tad short for dinner with my dad, but I bought it today and wanted to wear it out as soon as possible.

"Good evening, Ms. Knight." The hostess greets me.

"Good evening." I smile back.

"They are right this way." She turns and walks away from her station.

I follow behind her frowning. They? Who is my dad here with? Maybe my mother is coming as well. Not likely, though. That woman is busier than my father is most days.

The hostess walks us up to the table as my father stands. "Hello, sweet pea." He hugs me tightly then releases me. I turn to see Dash sitting there with a smug smile on his face.

"Can I get you anything?" the hostess asks as she places her hand on his shoulder. I have to hold back my eye roll as she eyes him like she would love to have him served on a silver platter.

"No. Thank you, though," he answers keeping his eyes on me.

I sit down, looking at him but speaking to my father. "I didn't know he was coming."

"Well, I knew you were coming." Dash smirks, and I can't help but remember what those lips did to me just a few days ago.

"Where is Rodger, sweet pea?" my father asks, and my eyes shoot to Dash. He rolls his shoulders.

I gulp down some of my water before I reply to him. "I don't know." I turn to him. "We broke up."

He frowns "Why? I thought that you two were in love?"

I sigh. "No. We were not in love, Dad." I was in love. I was an idiot who let my heart get the best of me!

"What happened?" he asks, still frowning. He wouldn't understand. To him, Rodger was a great guy who was ambitious and was going to one day rule the world. If I told him that our breakup started over me not wanting him to transfer to another college — he would side with Rodger. Not to be mean or unfair to me, but because he believes in doing whatever necessary to achieve your dreams. My father isn't selfish like Rodger, though. He actually cares for people.

"It just ran its course." That was a lame excuse, but it was the best I could come up with. Guess I should have prepared myself for this conversation.

"Why hadn't I heard about this?" he asks, clearly not going to let it go.

"It just happened," I say with a careless shrug, wanting him to know that I'm okay with it. That his little girl's heart is not torn open. It was but for different reasons.

"Well, I guess it's better off you guys break up before marriage." He nods to me.

I nod back not really knowing how to respond to that. At one point, I saw myself marrying him. Then at another point, I saw myself cutting him into little pieces and burying him in the backyard of our spring Villa where we would be living. Either way, I would have gone totally insane. The waiter chooses this time to come and take our order and then silence falls on the table as I look around the restaurant. It's a Saturday night, so it is fairly busy. Its lack of bright lights and whispers of others makes me comfortable.

"Tell me, Tabatha. What do you do?" Dash asks getting my attention.

Oh. So, he wants to play this game? The one where we act like we haven't rolled around naked. "I'm a student." I can play. I also work for my dad. But he doesn't need to know that.

He just nods. "What do you do besides race bikes?" I ask curiously. I had never heard of him before. I'm surprised my father chose him to join the team.

"That's about it," he says as he bites into a roll.

"College?" I question.

He shakes his head. "Racing."

I want to roll my eyes at him, but instead, I look over at my father. "Where did you find him?"

He looks offended that I asked. His eyes move to Dash before they come back to me. "He's the best there is." He gestures to him.

I expect Dash to give me a smug smile. Instead, he's watching me intently. He tilts his head to the side as his gray eyes continue to stare into mine. I want to look away, but that would show weakness. It would show him how much he affects me. So, what, we had sex once? I can handle that. I lick my lips as I remember the other things he did to me while lying by my parents' pool. The motion of my tongue has his eyes dropping to my lips, and I'm thankful to look away. I pick up my glass of water since my mouth is feeling dry all of a sudden.

"So, tell me more about this Rodger guy?" He finally speaks.

I stop my drink halfway to my mouth. "What about him?" I try to say nicely but fail. Why does he want to know about my ex?

"How long were you guys together?"

"A year."

"How did you meet him?"

"College."

"Why did you guys break up?"

I tilt my head to the side and narrow my eyes. "Why should any of this concern you?"

"Sweet pea," my father speaks, "he's just curious. And I am, as well."

I throw Dash a go to hell look before I turn and speak to my father. I already told them why. "It was just over." I shrug carelessly. I'm not going to admit that he had made me a different person or that I was suffocating.

"And he just walked away? Like that?" my father asks sitting back in his chair. Not buying it. "He seemed too much like a boy in love to just let you go so easily."

I hate how perceptive my father is. He sees everything! Even things I don't want him to see. "I broke up with him," I say. "He was thinking about moving away next fall for school, and he wasn't planning on me going. So where would that have left us? A long-distance relationship?" I shake my head. I wouldn't do that.

"He would move away from you?" my father says, giving his head a shake. "My sweet pea deserves better than that."

I actually smile. "I think he's changed his mind about moving. He wants another try," I state before thinking about what I just said. I look up at Dash; his jaw is tight, and his eyes look dangerously dark—I smile to myself.

He's jealous. He doesn't want anyone else playing with his toy.

We hear ringing, and my dad fishes his phone out of his pocket. "I have to take this."

As soon as my father walks away, Dash places his forearms on the table and speaks. "So, you still talk to him?" His voice is hard.

"Yes," I say, and he lets out a growl that I almost miss. "He showed up at my house this morning. It wasn't something I could have prevented. The bastard woke me up," I whisper.

He fists his hands on the table. "And?"

"And nothing." I don't want anything to do with Rodger anymore. But why do I want Dash to think I do? Because I like the way he looks when jealous? "I made him leave. I'm done with him. I'm done being that type of person." I whisper the last part as I drift off in a memory.

"Lock the door and come here," Rodger commands as he stands by the bed dressed in a pair of khakis and a polo shirt.

I do as he says and then walk over to him. "What are we doing up here?" I ask. We are at his parents' house for our usual Sunday dinner.

He doesn't answer right away. Once I'm a few steps from him, he reaches out and grabs my wrist. I yelp from how tight he's holding onto me. He pulls me to him before picking me up and throwing me onto the bed roughly.

"Rodger..." He places his hand over my mouth to quiet me.

"Shh," he says softly. "You don't want them to hear you, do you?"

I shake my head, and he removes his hand from my mouth. "Good girl." He places a soft kiss on my lips before his hands move up my thighs. He lifts the hem of my white cotton dress high enough to expose my panties. "This dress it too short." He sighs heavily — disappointed in my choice of outfit. "No woman who belongs to me should be showing off what's mine." His fingers dig into my hips, and I arch my back biting my lip to keep from making any noise. I don't wanna make him mad.

"I'm sorry," I breathe when he doesn't let up. The pain makes me cave.

He smiles. "Show me how sorry you are." He stands up off me and unzips his khakis. "Show me the good girl you can be instead of the slut that you look like."

"Tabatha?"

I snap out of my memory when Dash says my name. I blink a few times before I take a deep breath and let it out slowly, noticing our waiter brought our food out as well.

"What type of person?" he asks, and I frown.

"Excuse me?" I ask confused. What were we talking about?

"You said I'm done with being that type of person. What did that mean? What type of person were you with him?" His voice is soft and concerning.

I look down at the table and give a little smile to myself. Rodger had truly taken a strong-willed woman and turned her into a fragile piece of glass that he wanted to periodically break. See, to him, he was the only one able to glue me back together. That gave him power. I gave him the power. But now, now I'm stronger than I ever was before.

"Weak," I say as I look him in the eyes. "I'm no longer weak."

He frowns. "I can't see you being the weak type."

I let out a little laugh before I lean over the table and speak quietly. "Don't think you know me because I let you fuck me."

His dark eyebrows raise to his hairline, and I sit back with a sour look on my face. How dare him! He doesn't know me. He doesn't know how much I've hated myself. That one night at his party was supposed to be fun and bring back the old me. Instead, I had sex with someone who is currently not going anywhere.

Fuck! I can't catch a break!

"Sweet pea?"

I look up from my pasta that I haven't even touched and watch my dad as he walks back to the table. "Yes, Daddy?" I ask

"Are you okay?" He looks down at my food, and then back at me.

I nod with a smile on my face. "Yes."

"Well, I'm going to go make another phone call. I will be right back." He kisses me on the head and then walks off, leaving me there with Dash once again.

"I'm sorry; I didn't mean to upset you."

"You're fine," I say to my plate.

"I'm not going to pretend that I know you or what happened between you and him. But I want you to know that if you need someone to talk to, I'm here for you."

I sit and stare into his soft gray eyes wondering why he seems to care so much. For a man, he's beautiful. The button up shirt he wears shows off his broad shoulders and hard chest that I've run my hands up and down. He's rolled his sleeves back, exposing his tan forearms. His curly, dark hair is gelled, making it look as if it's still wet from his shower. His chiseled jawline and pouty lips make him look like he belongs on the cover of GQ. He's probably a player. A man who gets his kicks by making woman feel like they're special when in reality they are nothing to him but a piece of meat. A way to stroke his ego. Something I've done for him several times already in the past week. How many other girls have done the same thing just this week?

"Why?" I ask in all honesty.

He frowns. "Why? Because I want to get to know you. I want more from you than that first night. Or the few days after." He looks around the restaurant and then his eyes are back on mine. "There's something here, and you can't say you don't feel it."

I shake my head and drop my eyes. "I'm not looking for more than what we did," I state.

"I get it," he says. "I get that he hurt you. He messed with your head," he says, and I feel my anger start to rise. He doesn't know how much I changed. He doesn't know anything! "But I'm not trying to change you. I want to get to know the real you."

"You don't know anything about me except that I let you in my pants when I was drunk off my ass the first night we met," I say with bite. "So, to you, I'm probably some easy lay that you wanna keep around for whenever you feel like getting off."

He sighs heavily. "I'm not going to base who you are on what we did that first night. Hell, I wanted it just as much as you did, if not more. That doesn't make me like you any less."

I shake my head, trying to figure out his angle. I haven't even spoken to him. Hell, we haven't even exchanged phone numbers. Nothing!

"Let me take you to dinner? Just you and me."

Before I can tell him 'no thanks,' my father walks in.

"Sorry about that," my father says, joining us back at the table.

I stand and turn to him. "I have to leave, Dad." I don't give him an excuse. It wouldn't matter. Whatever I came up with, he would see right through as a lie.

He frowns. "I didn't get to spend much time with you." He looks down at his phone sitting on the table. My father is a hard worker, and I've never held that against him.

"It's okay," I say with a reassuring smile. "I will be free this weekend," I offer, and I instantly cringe at my admission. It makes me sound lame. Like I have nothing better to do. I was always so busy with Rodger that my father is going to think I have no life now without him.

He gives me a warm smile. "Why don't you come to the track this weekend then? Dash will be racing. We need to figure out what his bike will require. So we will be out there all weekend."

I really don't want to be around Dash. It's as if he can see right through me as well. No matter how bitchy I try to be, he can still see the weak person hiding behind the sarcastic, bitchy woman. But I nod. He'll be racing, right? He'll be occupied. I can hang with my dad. "Sounds good," I say before he stands and gives me a hug. I don't bother to face Dash or answer his question. I just turn around and walk out.

I make my way back to my house and just drop my purse on my bed. "Son of a bitch," I say a little too loud when I hear the familiar roar of a Lamborghini pull up outside.

I'm coming down the stairs when I see the front door swing open and in walks Rodger wearing a pair of plaid shorts and a polo shirt like he just walked off the golf course. "Leave." I point back at the door. I cuss myself for forgetting to lock the front door.

"Tabby," he whines. "Please, let's talk about this." He sounds sincere, but his jaw twitches. It shows me that he's irritated about how short my dress is as his eyes linger on my exposed legs.

"Don't call me that. You know I hate it." I point a finger at him. It makes my skin crawl when he calls me that.

"We can fix this. I love you," he says between clenched teeth.

I don't know if I should cry or hit him. He just told me that he loves me for the first time. Does he really love me? Or did he say it because he felt obligated?

I have wanted to hear those words from him for a year. A year. And he never said them. But neither had I. In all honesty, I know why he wants me back. It's a game to him. He hates losing, no matter how much his father disapproves of me. It's as if his dad wants me with Rodger because of respect. They want me to submit to their lifestyle.

I shake my head. "Well, I don't love you." I did — I had loved him — but in return, I hated myself. It was crazy and had me losing my mind. Thank God, I finally woke up and left his ass.

"Yes, you do." He takes a step toward me. "You can't deny it. I know how you feel about me." He gives me a smile that has my jaw twitching.

He's right; he always knew. And he took advantage of that. He knew how much I hated the way he changed me and how I had to bite my tongue and smile.

My anger comes back and I grab a small picture frame off the wall next to me and throw it at his face. He lifts his arm and blocks it. Damn! It hits the tiled floor and shatters. "What the fuck, Tabatha?" he shouts.

I smile and shrug. He takes another step toward me with his hard face. "You're going to come crawling back to me," he snaps.

The fuck I will! "Get the fuck out, Rodger!" I scream fisting my hands down by my sides.

When he continues to just stand there, I take a step toward him, closing the distance between us. My heart pounds in my chest and my hands are sweating. I'm actually terrified to stand up to him. But it's been a long time coming. The old me would fall to her knees and cry like a fucking child. Ask him to take me to bed and make me his 'good girl.'

Fuck that!

I take a deep breath and lift my hands. I shove him through the front door with all I have. He lands on his ass on the front porch, not expecting that.

"You fucking bitch," he growls, standing up and dusting himself off.

I smile. "Finally, you call me by a name I don't mind." God, it feels so good to stand up for myself. There's nothing else in the world like it.

"You're going to regret this," he sneers.

I ignore his threat. "Don't come back around, Rodger. We're done!"

I slam the door, lock it, and go back to my bedroom. I yank my dress up and over my head. I need a long, hot shower. I had just placed it on my bed and turn to walk into the bathroom when a noise stops me.

My doorbell rings... I fist my hands down by my sides. I swear the guy can't take a hint. Without bothering to put clothes back on, I make my way back down the stairs and swing the door open. "I said to leave!" I shout.

There, standing on my front porch, stands the only other guy I don't want to see—Dash! How does he know where I live?

His grayish eyes look me up and down before a smirk appears on his lips. He takes a step into my house, and I take a step back trying to keep my distance. He reaches up and closes the door once he's inside.

"You know," he says, taking another step toward me, "you shouldn't answer the door half naked and expect someone to leave." He licks his lips, and I wrap my arms around myself. He chuckles. "It's nothing I haven't already seen, sweetheart."

My blood continues to boil and nervousness sets in that he knows where I live. "Leave." I point at the door.

He shakes his head. "Not until I'm done with you," he says matter-of-fact.

"Well, you can't have me," I shoot back.

I go to take another step back, but I hit the wall. He's on me before I can even step around him. One hand tangles in my hair and the other is on my face. His lips attack mine, and he shoves his tongue down my throat.

I'm able to place my hands on his chest and shove him away enough for me to take a few deep breaths. "I'm so fucking tired of this bullshit game that you guys play," I shout, losing my patience.

He stands there looking at me with concern on his face as if I'm about to have a breakdown. "What bullshit? What game?" he asks cautiously.

"I mean the one where I act all submissive. The one where you guys demand that I be yours. And only yours. The one where I do things that make me hate myself to make you happy. And let's face it; that's not fucking possible!" I ramble as my arms wave around in the air.

He takes a step toward me, and I raise my hands to stop him. "Look, I don't know what you're talking about," he says softly. "But let's sit down and talk about it. Okay?"

I let out a sigh and shake my head. "Please. Just leave," I say, running out of air.

He turns around and looks down at the floor, and he stops once he sees the picture frame and broken glass on

59

the tiled floor that I had thrown at Rodger. "What happened before I got here?" he asks, spinning back around to face me.

"Nothing," I snap. It's none of his business. "I don't know why you act like you care, anyway. There's nothing going on between us."

As soon as the words are out of my mouth, his lips are on mine once again. I lift my hands to shove him back, but he captures my wrists and pins them behind my back. All it does is push me closer to his body and the feel of him so close to me has me surrendering. I want a distraction from Rodger.

I allow his tongue to stroke mine, and I even find myself wanting more when he finally pulls away.

"Can you tell me that was nothing?" he asks breathlessly against my lips.

I place my head down as I gather my thoughts. "What we're doing is wrong. I don't even know you." Why do I want you? Why do I feel so safe with you?

He releases my wrists and places his hand under my chin to urge me to look up at him. "Nothing we're doing is wrong, darling. And I'll tell you anything you want to know." He smiles at me, and I can't help but smile back. "Now. Please tell me what happened. Why are you so upset, and why is there a broken picture frame on the floor?"

I shake my head. "It's nothing you need to worry about."

He reaches up to push a strand of dark hair behind my ear. "Let me in, Tabatha. Was he here? Did he do something to you?" His eyes start to roam my exposed body.

I let out a sigh. "Yes, he came by. No, he didn't do anything."

His jaw tightens as he looks away from me and over to my stairs. "Is your bedroom upstairs?" he asks, and I nod slowly trying to figure out what he's thinking. Surely, it can't be sex at the moment.

He looks down at me and places his hands on both sides of my face. "Go upstairs, put some clothes on, and pack a couple of changes of clothes."

"Why?" I ask confused.

"Because I'm taking you to my house for a couple of days. I want you to be somewhere you are safe. And this place isn't it."

I want to tell him no. I want to tell him that Rodger isn't the type to hurt me. But he has before. Mentally and physically. He uses words as if they were his hands. Making each one bring physical pain. And when his words weren't enough, he would get rough with me. He never slapped me or hit me, but he would grab hold of me so tightly that he would leave bruises on my arms or my hips.

"Okay," I say before turning away from him and heading to my room.

## CHAPTER TEN

Dash

I needed her out of her house. She obviously wasn't safe there. And no matter how strong she thinks she is, no woman can fight off a man who is determined. Especially one fighting to get her back. She was right when she said I didn't know her. But I know less about this Rodger guy than her, and yet I feel like she wasn't being completely honest when she said he didn't hurt her. At the restaurant, she told me he had made her weak. As far as I can tell, she's not a weak person. So, in order for him to have made her that way, he had to have cut her down. Made her feel like she needed him to survive.

I pull into my driveway and get out of my car. I go to open the passenger car door for her, but she's already climbing out, so I make my way to the trunk to grab her bag.

"This is your place?" she asks with a smile.

"Yes. Why do you seem happy about that?" I watch as she walks up the steps with a smile on her face as she looks around. Her dark hair is pulled up in a loose bun and her fat white sunglasses cover up most of her beautiful face. Her light gray tank top hangs off one shoulder, showing off her simple black bra. She has a pair of white shorts on that makes my hands twitch. I just wanna run them all over her skin. Feel every inch of her. She's absolutely stunning and doesn't even realize it. She doesn't have to try to be seen or to stand out. She just does!

I don't know what it is that I feel exactly for her besides lust. But something else is there. I'm not saying I love her or that I want to run off and get married tomorrow. But I do want us to spend a couple of days in my bed and get to know each other better.

She lets out a laugh, which gets my attention. "Because I knew the place you had your party at was your parents' house," she says, sounding proud that she was right.

I nod my head. "You are correct, darling."

"Speaking of that party…?" she says shyly, and I know what she's thinking. She wants to know if I watched her climb the tree before she jumped over the fence. And the answer would be yes. I woke up and searched the entire house for her. When she was nowhere in sight, I checked the security system. Sure enough, she had snuck out. It was cute to watch how determined she was to get away though. And that's what made me want her again. She doesn't know me either, but she's about to find out just how determined of a man I can be.

I reach out and grab her hand. "Yes, I watched you escape," I say with a cocky smile.

"Escape? You make it sound like I was a prisoner," she says with a laugh. "And what about you having my panties in your pants the next day?" she asks arching an eyebrow.

I smile. "A gentleman doesn't tell."

"A gentleman doesn't carry around women's underwear in his pocket."

I had found them underneath my parents' bed. After spending time looking for her in the house, I ended up running late to my meeting with her dad. So, I had just thrown them in my pocket. You couldn't even imagine my surprise when I saw her walk into her dad's office wearing my shirt. I wanted to bend her over her father's desk and take her right then and there once again.

"Well, you shouldn't have left in such a hurry that morning. I was really looking forward to morning sex." I wink over at her before I unlock the front door and allow her to enter before me.

"I was still trying to remember where I was and who the hell you were," she says truthfully, and I chuckle.

"So, just how much do you remember from that night?" I ask dropping her bag to the floor in the entryway.

She gives me a sexy smile as she pushes her white glasses to the top of her head. "Some parts are still fuzzy." I have a feeling she's playing with me, but I'll play along.

I walk up to her and place my hands on her hips. "Then let me remind you, sweetheart." I lift her up, and she wraps her legs around me.

# CHAPTER ELEVEN

## *Tabatha*

He carries me to his room as I kiss him deeply. Placing my hands in his long hair, I yank hard, and he moans into my mouth. He doesn't bother shutting his door as we fall onto the bed. I get a glimpse of the huge bay windows to the right of me and smile when I see all the trees behind his house. It's as if there's a forest in his backyard.

He gets my attention as he pulls his shirt up over his head, revealing his hard chest. I sit up and run my hands over the smoothness of it. He reaches up and grabs my hair. I smile when he pulls my hair out of my bun.

"I wanna be able to pull on this," he growls, placing his hand in my hair.

I reach out and undo his pants as his fingers massage my head. "Whatever you want," I find myself saying as I release his hard cock from behind his pants and boxers. The hardness, yet softness, of his skin have my thighs clenching and my breaths coming quicker. I need to feel him on me, in me.

He pulls on my hair to get me to look up at him. "Don't say things you don't mean."

"I mean everything I say." My scalp prickles and my body breaks out in goosebumps as his fingers tighten in my hair. I inhale sharply, and my hand tightens around his cock.

Before I can take another breath, he bends down and places his lips on mine. I open up and let him have control. Even though Rodger was a control freak, it doesn't bother me to allow Dash that same power over me. I want him to take me, make me his. It's not degrading; it's exhilarating.

He pulls away quickly, and it leaves me panting for more. His hands fall out of my hair and they land on my chest. He roughly pushes me back onto the bed before he pulls my shorts down my legs and tosses them to the side.

He reaches down and grabs my legs as he continues to stand at the end of the bed. He doesn't even bother checking to see if I'm wet because he knows I am. I take a deep breath and arch my back as he slowly enters me, stretching me in the most delicious way. Not even bothering with a condom. I should tell him to stop and put one on, but I can't make my lips say the words. He just feels too good. And why bother when we've already done it without one? It just wouldn't be right to use one now.

He takes his time working in and out of me, filling me. "I'm gonna take my time with you tonight, baby."

I whimper as he thrust forward. "Please." I reach up and try to pull his body closer to mine. I want him to be as needy as I am right now, but he just smirks at my lame attempt.

His hands land on my thighs, and he slowly runs them to my hips. His grip tightens, and I arch my back, taking in a deep breath. "Begging won't get you anywhere with me," he says, moving his hips back and forth. "You're going to remember every little fucking thing this time."

How could I ever forget in the first place? I may not have remembered exactly what we had done, but my body had. "I need more," I whine as he slowly pulls out of me and then enters me again just as slowly.

He looks down at me and gives me a cocky smile. "I'm going to give you exactly what you need. In time."

I sigh as I reach up and massage my breasts. His hands leave my hips, and he bends over me. He takes my wrists in his hands, and he pushes them above my head, pinning them against the mattress. "I wanna be the only one to touch you tonight," he whispers as he places soft kisses on my neck. I arch my neck back, giving him easier access.

"Then touch me," I demand, lifting my hips to meet his, trying to get a little more forceful in his movement.

He releases my wrists, and his hands cup my breasts. I moan when he bends down and captures my hard nipple between his lips. "Yes," I say when he starts to suck on it.

His teeth lightly nibble, and I gasp as I lift my hands to tangle them in his dark hair. His hips pick up the pace, and I start to pant as he finally surrenders to what I need.

"How did you know where I lived?" I ask lying beside him, completely spent and naked. After we had our first round, he finally took the time to shed all of his clothes. But let's just say he wasn't as in control the second time. He let me take charge, and I like that.

"You told me that first night. You really don't remember, huh?" he asks chuckling.

I shake my head. "Thank God, you aren't a serial killer," I say seriously.

He laughs harder. "You had turned your phone on after our last game of pool and put my number in it, but you wouldn't give me yours." He smiles. "You were going to leave the party with Blake and Jackie but then decided to stay with me."

Hmm. Everything makes sense now. "So, what made me decide to stay?"

"I guess it was my charm," he says with a smile, and I laugh.

"Guess so," I agree before I close my eyes and enjoy the warmth of his body against mine.

"So, tell me something about yourself," I say after a few silent minutes.

"My name is Erik Dashling," he says, and I let out a little laugh. I at least know that much. "I go by Dash because I hate the name Erik and the name Dashling makes me sound like a fucking pussy."

"No, it doesn't." I playfully slap his hard muscular chest. "I like it."

He looks over at me with a serious look. "You would." He then looks back up at the ceiling. "I'm twenty-two. An only child." He frowns. "I have a tendency to do my own thing, which has gotten me in trouble more times than I can count."

"What kind of trouble?" I ask.

"The kind that gets you put behind bars," he says with no shame.

I sit up and look down at him with my eyebrows raised. "What kind of trouble do you get into?" I ask wondering if my father knows this. He takes his team and drivers very seriously. I mean, it's his life.

He smiles as if he's reading my mind. "Nothing too bad. I'm a little reckless, I guess you could say."

I let out a breath as I lie back down beside him. "That's nothing."

He turns onto his side and places a hand under his head to prop it up. "Really? You make it sound like you've been a little reckless as well."

"No. It just wasn't as bad as I was thinking," I say with a smile. He reaches up and pushes my hair off my face. "You make me feel reckless," I confess.

He pauses. "How so?"

I try to shrug it off, hating that it even slipped out. I go to roll over, but he gets up and straddles me, pinning me to the mattress. "Tell me," he whispers, leaning over me.

"I feel like we're breaking all the rules." My dad wouldn't allow this to happen, and he sure as hell would kick Dash off the team if he knew.

"We are," he says placing a kiss on my neck. I arch back giving him easier access. "That's what makes it so much fun."

I try to ignore the feeling that tells me this won't last much longer. "Well, at least when it's over you will still be able to race." But I will still see him.

He pulls away and looks down at me with a frown. "What are you worrying about? What did you mean by 'when it's over'?"

I shake my head, not wanting to tell him, but he is persistent. "Please. Don't be afraid to tell me anything."

I let out a sigh. "My dad…"

"I'm not worried about your dad. Will he threaten to kick me off the team? Probably. But will he? No. He was right when he said that I'm the best at what I do. And I will prove that to him. I'm valuable to him just as you are valuable to me," he states.

I smile at his words. "You wanna keep me around, huh?" I ask with a playful smile.

"More than you know," he says before he gets a big smile on his beautiful face. "Let me take you for a ride."

I laugh. "That's the corniest line I've ever heard," I say as I lift my hips, rubbing myself against him.

He chuckles. "No, I really wanna take you for a ride. On my bike."

I lift my head up enough to look at his clock sitting on his nightstand. "It's four-thirty in the morning," I say with a frown.

"And?" he asks arching a dark eyebrow.

"Where would we go?"

He leans down and places his lips on my neck. "You're right," he whispers against my skin. "We can go later." With that, I smile and allow him to take me on the kind of ride that I had in mind.

I yawn as I stand in his garage looking at his bikes. He has four. And three cars. And a truck. "Do you collect cars?" I ask scratching the back of my neck. I think we got maybe three hours of sleep this morning. He woke me up and told me to get dressed; he was taking me for a ride. I wasn't all that thrilled when I found out he meant on his bike.

"I like to keep my options open," he says as he reaches up and picks two helmets that hang on the wall in his garage.

"I bet you do," I mumble to myself.

"What was that?" he asks as he turns to face me.

"Nothing," I say waving it off. A man like Dash has plenty of options. They never settle down with one woman. I bet he prefers a different one every day like he prefers driving a different car every day.

He walks up to me and hands me a helmet. I look down at it. It's beautiful. It's white and black. It has skulls and wings all over it, and it makes it look kinda evil in a beautiful way. "Pretty," I say.

He smirks proudly as he looks down at it. "It's my favorite."

"Oh," I say holding it out to him for him to take.

"No, you're going to wear it," he states as he walks over to a toolbox. He picks up what looks like a seat. I watch nervously as he takes a little plastic section off the back of the bike.

"What are you doing?" I question as I watch him clip the black little seat onto the back of the bike.

"This," he raises the piece he just removed from the bike, "is a no-ho," he states.

"You're joking?" I ask, and he shakes his head with a smile.

"Nope." He pushes down on the seat, and I hear it click. He turns to face me as he taps it. "Come on."

I stay standing where I'm at. "I've never been on a bike before." And I'm totally rethinking it now.

"Here." He places his hand in his pocket and removes some earbuds. He then takes my phone from my hand and plugs them in. He pushes a few buttons and then smiles when he is satisfied. "There's only a few things that you need to know." He looks up at me. "Just follow my lead."

"How do I do that?"

"When we take a turn, lean into it with me." I nod as if I understand what he means. "You won't be able to hear me because of the helmet and the earbuds, but I will reach back and tap your thigh when I want you to hang on. Feel free to use your legs. You can tighten them against mine as tight as you want, it won't hurt me."

"Won't I be hanging on the entire time?" I ask as I start to panic. I look over to the bike. "What else am I supposed to hang on to?" I ask nervously.

He places his hand on my shoulders. "Calm down. It will only take you a few minutes to get used to it. And

Dash

once that starts to happen, you will loosen up and relax. You won't hang on as tight. But there will be times when you will have to hold on tighter than others. I'll let you know when those times are."

"Okay," I say as I swallow.

"No worries. I won't do any wheelies with you on the back."

"Wheelies?" I squeak. "You do wheelies? On that?" I ask wide-eyed.

He chuckles. "You're cute," he says before he leans in and gives me a soft kiss before he pulls way. He picks up a jacket off his bike and hands it to me. "This is a mesh jacket. It has holes for it to breathe, but it has pads in it in case we go down."

My legs start to shake. "You're not helping."

"It's just a safety precaution. I want you to be safe." He places it on me and then puts my phone in an inside pocket, before zipping it up. "Put these in your ear but don't turn the music on yet," he orders, and I do as he says.

I stand back and watch him as he places his jacket on and straddles the bike. He fixes his phone to the music he wants and then starts up the bike. It causes me to jump. "Come on."

I walk over to him, and he turns his body to look over his shoulder at me. He takes my helmet from me. "Place your left leg on the peg," he says pointing to it. I do as he says. "Now place your left hand on my shoulder and lift yourself up." I place my sweaty hand on his shoulder as he says and lift myself up. He holds the bike up as my right foot finds the other peg.

He leans over and hands me the helmet. "Don't be nervous. I would never put you in harm's way," he says softly before he grabs my left hand and brings it around to his face. He gives it a soft kiss, and then lets go of it.

72

I quickly put my helmet on and fasten it. I reach up from my earbuds and press play on the cord. Music blares so loud I cringe.

I sit there and wait for my ears to adjust to the screaming of some guy I've never heard before when I realize we haven't left the garage. Why haven't we left? Am I forgetting something? I have my jacket on. I have his helmet on. My music is playing. He said he would signal to me. Do I need to signal to him?

I lean over and place my right hand on the cool tank. And with my left hand I tap him on his shoulder, hoping that does the trick.

The engine revs up, and then he pulls out of the garage. The first five songs that play in my ear, I am a terrified mess. I hold my eyes tightly closed, and I squeeze him to the point he probably can't breathe. But he's right, every second that goes by, I get more comfortable. Every turn he takes, I lean more into him instead of trying to fight it. I just have to remind myself that he is the expert, and this is my first time. He knows what he's talking about.

I let my arms loosen, and I take in a deep breath. I smell him. The smell of him lingers in the helmet that I'm wearing, and it makes me smile. I close my eyes and feel the wind blowing on my skin through the jacket. It's an amazing feeling to know that there's nothing between you and the road. It feels as if I'm flying.

He doesn't take me far. Maybe ten miles on the highway and then he exits. But he gets right back on and heads back in the direction of his house. By the time he pulls up in his driveway, my legs are tingling from the roar of the bike underneath me. And my mind is full of nothing but him from smelling him in the helmet.

He pulls into his garage, and I slide off the back awkwardly but manage not to fall over. My back hurts from leaning over. My hands hurt from holding myself up while leaning over. And the inside of my legs hurt from straddling the back. But I know what can fix it. Him.

I rip his helmet off my head and unzip the jacket as he removes his helmet. I walk over to him and pull on his arm, spinning him to face me. I unzip his jacket quickly and then shove it off his shoulders as my lips land on his. He doesn't even try to stop me as his hands find their way to my hips. He pulls me into him roughly, needing me as much as I need him at the moment.

# CHAPTER TWELVE

*Dash*

I very slowly and quietly get out from underneath the covers without waking Tabatha. I make my way to the kitchen to grab a bottle of water for myself before making my way back to my bedroom and crawling in next to her. I take a drink and then place it on my nightstand. My eye catches the clock, and I see the time on it reads a little past six in the morning. The sun will start to rise soon, and I haven't had any sleep the last two nights. Tabatha and I haven't left my bedroom except for the one time we went to take the bike for a ride. And once to shower and use the bathroom. We actually stopped having sex long enough to order pizza, but we were even able to turn that into some sort of foreplay.

The woman turns me on like no other. Every time I look at her, my cock begs to be inside of her. My hands itch to explore every bit of her; no matter how many times they caress her, it's not enough. My mouth needs to taste her. My eyes need to devour her.

She lets out a little moan as she turns onto her side and throws her arm over my chest. I smile as I reach up and lightly run my fingertips up and down it.

I look back over at my nightstand when I hear my phone vibrate. I reach over and pick it up.

**Valerie:** *I'm sorry I blew up on you the other day. I got back into town last night and ran into Blake. He said that you got a spot racing for Johnny Knight. That's fantastic, baby.*

I roll my eyes as I exit out of the message, turn off my phone, and place my phone back on my nightstand. Of course, the bitch would only text me when she realizes the job offer I received. I haven't spoken to her since we got arrested. I was told that she had shown up to my party, but I never saw her, which surprises me. But I was too caught up in Tabatha at the time. I locked her and myself up in my parents' room the moment I got her away from the pool table and realized that she wanted to stay with me.

"Who was that?" Tabatha mumbles sleepily.

I lie down and turn onto my side. I wrap my arms around her and pull her body into mine—enjoying the heat her small body offers mine. "It was Blake," I lie. She doesn't need to know about my crazy ex. She's in the past. Within a couple of weeks, Valerie will move on and find some new guy who she can sink her money hungry claws into.

"This early?" she asks with a yawn. "What did he want?"

"He was letting me know that he'll be at the track later on today." Not a total lie. I spoke to Blake a few days ago, and he said that he was going to bring Jackie up to the track for my practice since he knew that Tabatha was going to be there.

"How much longer do we have?" she asks tightening her arms around me.

"An hour," I whisper as I lean into her and kiss her forehead.

She sighs heavily but doesn't say anything else.

I close my eyes and think how much I would enjoy her coming back to stay with me again tonight. And the next night. And then the next. Like I said—she's addicting.

76

I tear off my helmet and run my hand through my damp hair. It's fucking hot out here and all this leather gear that I wear for safety doesn't help.

"How was it? How does she feel?" Mr. Knight asks, crossing his arms over his chest as he looks down at the brand new race bike. We arrived at the raceway about an hour ago, but I just finished my first ride. She needs some work, but for being bone stock, she hauls ass.

"She handles really well," I say, letting my eyes run over the solid black bike.

"How's the suspension?" he questions.

"It's good." I reach up and point over at the track. "She felt a little soft coming out of the first turn, but other than that, she felt great."

"I saw that." He nods to himself in thought. "Of course, things will change once we meet with the crew chief and start adding everything that you will need." He looks up at me. "I just wanted to see how the suspension was for you."

"Perfect," I say with a smile. "I took it kind of easy on her since it was her first run. This time I'm gonna push her a little harder." She's fast and has a shit ton of torque, but it's nothing that I can't handle.

"Sure you wanna do that?" he questions, arching a silver eyebrow, but he has a smirk on his face.

I smile as my eyes slide over to Tabatha as she stands next to her dad. She's wearing a black shirt that hangs off one shoulder. Across the front in big silver glittery letters, it reads DASH. She made it this morning all by herself and informed me after the glitter dried that she was going to wear it. When I asked her if she was nervous about what her dad would think about my name across her chest, she reminded me that he already thought she supported me since she was wearing my shirt the first day we met. Her dad wouldn't know the difference. And I'm glad that she was right. He hasn't even mentioned it. "Some things are worth the risk," I say, referring to her.

She bites on her bottom lip to hide her smile, and I just wanna grab her and pull her into me and kiss her with all that I have.

"Well," her dad speaks, getting our attention. "I once told you that I didn't get to where I am today without taking risks." He nods. "So, I won't try to talk you out of it."

I throw her one last smile before I push my hair back out of my face and place my helmet back on to really push this bitch and see what she can do.

## CHAPTER THIRTEEN

# *Tabatha*

I stand next to my dad as I watch Dash work his way through the sharp turns of the raceway. It makes me nervous. What if he wrecks? What if the bike runs over him? I don't know much about racers on bikes, but I've seen crashes before on the internet—they are not pretty.

I smile like an idiot as I think back over our last two nights together. They were amazing. I just wish we didn't have to keep it a secret, but I don't want to jeopardize his future. He doesn't think my dad would kick him off the team, and maybe he wouldn't, but there would still be consequences and I'm trying hard to prevent that.

I look over my shoulder when I hear a car pulling up, thinking it's Jackie. She called me an hour ago and said she was coming up here with Blake. I frown though when I see a girl get out of the car who I don't recognize. She has a tiny skirt on that looks to be three sizes too small and a shirt that a six-year-old would be seen dressed in with no bra on.

"Valerie," my father says turning around to greet her.

"Hello, Mr. Knight," she says walking over to us. "How is he doing?" she asks as her eyes look over the track.

"He's doing great. Just like I knew he would," my father responds.

I stand stiff as a board as my eyes move back and forth between them wondering who in the hell this woman is and how she knows my dad.

Her eyes finally land on mine, and her smile drops off her face when she reads my shirt. "I didn't know you already had shirts made," she says looking back to my father.

"Hmm?" He looks over at me and smiles. "Oh, I just realized that," my father says with a chuckle but doesn't respond to her question.

"I'm Tabatha," I say reaching out my hand to her, trying to be polite, but I can already tell that I don't like this woman. Maybe she is Dash's sister? He did tell me that he was an only child, though.

Her smile returns, but it looks more evil than friendly. "I'm Valerie." She pauses. "Dash's girlfriend."

I stare at her waiting for her to laugh or to say she's kidding; there's no way she is Dash's girlfriend. He doesn't have one. Does he?

"Girlfriend?" I choke on the word. Have I been sleeping with a man who was unavailable in the first place? If so, where in the hell has she been?

"Yes, sweet pea," my father answers as he looks down at me with a look of concern for my hearing. "This is Valerie. She was with Dash the day I picked him up."

She laughs. "You mean the day you had us arrested."

"What?" I ask getting more and more confused. "When did you arrest him?" Her eyes narrow on mine as I have no concern that she was arrested, only Dash.

"It was no big deal. I called in a favor from the cops," my dad says, waving off my concern. "Dash was a hard man to get a hold of."

She looks over at my dad. "He was so excited. He ended up throwing a party that night at his parents'," she informs him, and I feel my heart stop.

Party? Parents? He had just been with her earlier that day and then with me that night? I think I'm gonna be sick.

"Does he know that you were coming up here today?" I can't help but ask. They look at me like I've lost my mind. Like I'm asking questions that I shouldn't be asking, but I need to get some answers because obviously Dash hasn't been telling me the truth.

"He does," she says slowly as she eyes me skeptically. "I've been out of town for Spring Break, and I text him early this morning."

I swallow nervously. Early this morning? His phone only went off once before he told me he turned it off — he had said that it was Blake. Another lie!

"Will you excuse me?" I mumble before I lower my head and start to walk to my car. I've been sleeping with her boyfriend. Hell, I spent two days in bed with him, naked.

I take a deep breath as I run my hand through my hair. This can't be happening! I feel my eyes start to fill with tears and my throat tighten. I'm not that type of girl. I would never get with someone who has a girlfriend.

I hear the sound of his bike nearing my father and Valerie as he finishes his last lap, and I angrily brush the tears off my face.

I walk around the concession stand and make my way to the parking lot when I'm grabbed from behind and shoved up against the brick wall.

My eyes narrow as I look up at Dash. Sweat covers his forehead and he's breathing heavy. He's still wearing his riding leathers, but he has them hanging off his hips. "I can explain."

"I don't need any more of your lies," I shout.

He looks over his shoulder to see if anyone is around to hear us before returning his eyes back to me. "It's not what you think. She's lying to you."

I fist my hands down by my side. "So, my father is also lying to me?"

81

Dash

He takes a step back from me giving me some breathing room as he runs his hand through his long dark and sweaty hair. "He thought she was my girlfriend when he arrested us. I didn't correct him," he says angrily.

"Why was she even with you?" I demand. "Did you sleep with her that day and then sleep with me that night?" I take a step toward him and place my hand on his chest shoving him out of my way, not even caring to hear his answer. I already know it.

I walk past him, and he grabs my upper arm before yanking me back. "No," he growls. "I didn't sleep with her that day and you're the only girl I've been fucking," he snaps.

My eyes widen at his words then they narrow. "You are nothing but a lying son of a bitch," I spit in his face.

"I'm not lying," he shouts as his dark gray eyes bore into mine.

Lie. "So that really was Blake who text you this morning?" I already know the answer. Why would she have lied to me? She doesn't have any reason to lie to me, but him…?

He releases me. He doesn't say anything as he breathes heavily and stares down at me with narrowed eyes and a tight jaw. His silence tells me more than his words can. He lied. It really was her. He really does have a girlfriend. And I really have fallen for him. 'Cause, otherwise, it wouldn't hurt this bad. The betrayal I feel wouldn't cut so deep.

I wouldn't be here fighting with him. I would have gotten into my car and left. I wouldn't have wanted him to tell me that she was lying. He would have had an explanation for everything I just asked.

I hang my head and take a deep breath trying to calm my nerves. My chest is tight, and my eyes sting.

I watch as his black riding boots take a step toward me, and then I feel his hands in my hair. I swallow the lump in my throat and close my eyes as he softly pulls my head up so I will have to look at him.

"She means nothing to me," he says softly.

And it makes my heart hurt even more. How can he treat her this way? She truly thinks that she is his girlfriend, and he has been stringing her along. How long will he do that to me?

"Please look at me," he begs, and I slowly open my eyes.

"I'm sorry," he whispers as he lets go of my hair and wipes away the tear that runs down my cheek. "I have lied to you." He closes his eyes and exhales as if to admit that hurt him. He opens them and looks back down at me. "And that ends right now. I'll tell you everything tonight. Please don't leave like this. Mad at me." He runs a hand through my hair. "I want to tell you everything. I just need one more chance."

"I shouldn't be giving you one more chance," I say truthfully. I mean, I've known the guy for what a week now, maybe two, and he's been lying to me.

He licks his lips nervously as he looks up and scans the back part of the parking lot. I know my dad is probably wondering where in the hell he is.

"I know." He sighs looking back at me. "But I'm begging you. Just give me one chance to explain everything to you, and then if you want, I'll leave you alone."

What could there possibly be to explain? If she's just an ex then why is she so important? Then a thought hits me and I freeze. "Do you guys have a child?" I love children. That wouldn't push me away if that were the case.

"No," he snaps and then lets out a long breath. "I have no children," he finishes through gritted teeth.

I nod my head, confused by his anger at my question. "I have to get back." His eyes soften as he speaks. "Please don't leave. Stay here. And I'll make everything right." He leans down and places his lips on mine. I stand totally still at first. But after a few seconds, I open up and allow him to kiss me. Once again, I fall into him and allow him to take what he wants from me. It's different with him than it was with Rodger because I want it from Dash just as much as he wants it from me. I wanna lose myself in him.

He slows the kiss down and pulls away. "I gotta go, baby." He lightly kisses my forehead and then looks down at me.

"Go," I whisper. "I'm not going anywhere," I say, and I give him a small smile.

# CHAPTER FOURTEEN

## *Tabatha*

*My heart pounds in my chest and my body trembles. I gasp, trying to catch my breath.*

*"You sure know how to stroke a man's ego," Dash's voice whispers into my ear as his hand slides between our bodies and his fingers find my clit. I gasp as he starts to massage it. He chuckles as he buries his face deeper into my neck.*

*I arch my back, allowing him better access, as I suck in another breath. "You're the one doing all the work," I pant as his body lies on top of mine.*

*I feel him smile against my neck. I let out a shriek as he rolls over and pulls me on top of him. He looks up at me with a smirk on his face. A few strands of dark hair stick to his slick forehead. "You can have all the control you want, darling." I'm momentarily paralyzed as his light gray eyes stare up into mine. The morning light coming in through the window makes them sparkle. The smirk grows across his face as he places his hands behind his head. Arrogant bastard. He knows what he does to me when he looks at me like that. Like I'm the only woman in the world. Like neither one of us has a past. Like we're not hiding from the present. I don't know what our future holds, but at this moment, it goes on forever.*

*I run my hands up his smooth and hard chest, the sweat from our bodies making it slippery. I want to taste him in every way. To the point that it may make me sound somewhat insane. Leaning down, I place my lips on his chest and give him a soft kiss. I continue giving him soft kisses as I slide my body down his.*

*He lifts his hips and he lets out a deep growl as I wrap my fingers around the base of his dick. I wet my lips and lower my mouth over him as his hands find their way into my hair. So* much for being in charge. I don't mind it, though. He can have all the control over me that he wants.

He moans as I pull him to the back of my throat. I let out a noise of my own when I taste myself on him. As I go to pull up, his hands in my hair grip me tighter and he lifts his hips, pushing deeper into my mouth. I try to fight the urge to pull back, to fight his control. He's not Rodger, I tell myself.

"Fuck...Oh..." I run my eyes up his body lying on the white sheets. His stomach muscles clench and his chest rises and falls quickly. His head is thrown back, his jaw tight, as he sucks in breaths through clenched teeth. It's a sight to see – how I allow him to take pleasure from me the way he wants. I relax, allowing him to have his way with my mouth as I just allowed him to have my body.

I take him as deep and as fast as he wants to go. And he wants it fast. He doesn't let up. My jaw is sore and my cheeks hurt, but it's worth it. Anything is worth hearing that man come with my name on his lips.

Once he's finished, he releases my hair and I pull away from him with a satisfied smile on my face. He grabs me by the shoulders and throws me down beside him. "You're amazing," he breathes as he pushes some hair off my face.

I take a deep breath. "Not so bad yourself," I tease.

His smile widens. "So much for stroking my ego," he mumbles.

I arch an eyebrow. "I think I've stroked enough," I respond, as his bedroom fills with his laughter.

I open my eyes and look at myself in the mirror. I have streaks running down my face from the tears I've cried in the last hour. It's crazy how that memory was from just this morning. We were lying in his bed laughing as we were getting ready for round two. Now I'm standing in the restroom at the hospital waiting to see if he's gonna be okay.

Dash crashed! It happened so fast that it didn't register at first. He was riding along on the track after our talk. I had almost left him. I was so pissed at the fact that he was keeping some serious secrets from me. Hell, I thought that Valerie was telling the truth and that she was indeed his girlfriend. My father even believed her and acted like he knew her. But after talking to him, I believed him. He wanted to explain and I needed to know the truth. So, he jumped back on his bike and went to finish his practice run.

*"Where were you?" my father asks as I walk back up to him and Valerie standing by the track. He's not being nosy just truly wondering where I had disappeared off to for the last few minutes.*

*"I was looking for something in my car," I lie not taking my eyes off the track.*

*"Did you find what you were looking for?"*

*I pull my eyes away from the track to look over at Valerie. Her voice was hard and somewhat sarcastic. "Yes, I did," I reply with a bitchy smile. Her jaw tightens, and she huffs out a puff of air. I would give anything to look her in the eyes right now, but we both have on sunglasses.*

*"We'll see about that," she mumbles.*

*"Excuse me?" I ask taking a step toward her. She goes to open her mouth, but that's when I hear it. A sound you can't miss. A sound of metal and plastic skidding across asphalt.*

*As I turn to look over the track, my father takes off running. My eyes catch sight of Dash picking himself up off the ground. He stumbles around as he takes off his helmet. Then my heart stops as he falls to his knees, then lies down on the track.*

The door opens to the bathroom, and I wipe the tears from my face. I don't wanna face my father like this. I need to look concerned for Dash but not over-the-top, bawling-my-eyes-out *girlfriend* status. That would send up red flags.

I take a deep breath and try to calm my shaking hands before I walk out of the bathroom. I straighten my DASH shirt and pull down my jean shorts. Have you ever noticed how freaking loud a hospital is? I mean, you have machines beeping, and you have nurses and doctors paged over the intercom. It's crazy busy. And cold as ice.

I wrap my arms around myself as I make my way back to the waiting room. I come to an abrupt stop when I see Dash's ex, Valerie, hugging an older woman while an equally older man shakes my father's hand.

"What happened?" the woman asks as she pulls away from Valerie. Although she asks about him, her voice is calm and holds no concern.

Valerie wipes the black from her eyes before she responds. "We don't know. He just wrecked," she cries before the lady takes her back in her arms once again.

"Now. Now," she coos as she rubs her back. "It's gonna be okay." She pulls away and looks down to give her a soft smile. "You know how many times Erik has had to go to the hospital?"

It sounds weird for someone to call him Erik. *He hates that name.*

"I told him this was going to be dangerous," the older man says as he shakes his head looking down at the floor. *Is this man his father?*

The woman turns to him and gently places her hand on his shoulder. "He's a big boy, honey."

*Big boy?* Boy does that contradict itself.

Valerie looks up and notices me. I swear she actually smiles as she remembers that I'm here. "Mom," she says getting the woman's attention, "this is Tabatha."

Great! Her mother is here. She turns around to face me. She looks like a million bucks. No wrinkles. No blemishes. She reminds me of Rodger's mother, and I immediately don't like her. You can have work done and still be beautiful, but I know this type of woman. They're fake on the inside as well—cold and heartless.

"Hello, Tabatha," she says with a kind smile. She reaches out to shake my hand, but the smile drops off her face once her eyes land on DASH written in silver glitter across my shirt. "Where did you get that?" she asks pointing to my chest.

I stand there confused as everyone stares at me like I'm on trial. "I made it," I say barely above a whisper.

Her eyes narrow on me and her pouty lips thin. "Tabatha is my daughter," my father announces with a proud smile. He is totally oblivious to what is going on here, but I'm not. Does her mother think that Dash and Valerie are still together as well? God, this is gonna kill me.

"I see…" she mumbles before she turns, giving me her back, and speaks to Valerie. "Erik will be fine," she assures.

I bite my bottom lip; this is so awkward. "I called his parents," she announces to my father.

"Great. Are they on their way?" he asks.

She shakes her head. "I told them no need."

"Mother," Valerie admonishes.

She looks down at her daughter. "They are on a business trip. I told them that I would keep them informed once I know something."

Wow. And they said okay? What kind of parents don't come when their child is in the hospital? I don't care how old he is. He could be dying, for all we know.

Valerie's mother turns around to look at me once again and gives me a chilling smile. "I told them that he can stay with us."

I try to keep my face blank. This woman has already clued in to my feelings for Dash, and I don't want another problem for us.

"And they were okay with that?" my father asks, sounding just as surprised as I feel.

"Yes," the man answers him. "He stays with us all the time. It will be no different now."

I'm gonna puke! How much has Dash lied about? Stays with them all the time? He also knew that Dash was racing for my father. The guy has to be joking, right? He has to be.

"Tabatha?" I spin around when I hear my name shouted. I open up my arms the moment that I see Jackie running toward me with Blake by her side.

She clutches me in a death grip. "Oh, Tabatha. Is he gonna be okay?" Jackie cries.

"I think so," I say trying to be positive. But I'm not as optimistic as the bitch standing behind me. She didn't see it. And at this point, none of us know anything.

"What happened?" Blake asks as he pulls Jackie away from me.

I take a deep breath before I rehash the event that I saw take place in front of my eyes.

## CHAPTER FIFTEEN

Dash

"I'm fine!" I say a little louder than I should have as I push the nurse away from me.

Her eyes narrow on me slightly. "Sir, we have to make sure that you don't have any serious injuries."

I shake my head, fighting the dizziness I feel. "I don't. Give me my clothes; I'm leaving."

"You were dressed in some sort of leathers," she says with a frown. "We had to cut them off you."

Fuck! "Well, find me some clothes so that I may leave." I'm sure this happens all the time. They have to have some extra scrubs lying around somewhere.

"Sir…"

"No," I snap. "You can't keep me here. I can discharge myself."

She nods her head with a long sigh before she turns and pulls the curtain back, walking out of my little cubby. I let out a puff of air as I rub my head. I have a pounding headache. It's like the worst hangover imaginable. Although I did not drink a drop, I crashed my bike. How? The brakes. I had none. My body hurts, but besides that, I feel okay. The helmet and the leathers probably saved my life.

A male nurse walks in as he reads over my chart. "I hear that you are refusing treatment and want to leave."

"I'm not refusing treatment. I don't need treatment." I've flipped cars before. Hell, I crawled out of one that was on fire before I was sixteen. I crawled out of it with my best friend, Blake, and then we ran home praying to avoid getting into trouble. We were stupid. Of course, my dad was going to see that his car was missing from the garage. I know what my body can handle. "I'm fine. I just want to go home."

He nods his head. "I understand, but it will take time. You have company out in the waiting room. Would you like to see them? That way they can see that you are okay."

"Send in Mr. Knight," I instruct, and he leaves with a nod. I need to speak to him.

Lying back, I let out a long breath as I rub my left arm. It's sore as fuck. It's what I landed on before I went rolling onto the grass. Thank God, it was the grass that stopped me.

"Are you feeling okay, son?"

I look up to see Mr. Knight walking into my little curtain room. I nod. "Yeah, just sore."

"The nurse said that you are refusing treatment."

I roll my eyes. "I'm fine. I just wanna go home."

His silver eyebrows that match his silver hair pull together. "Are you sure?" he questions. "I know that you are the only one who knows what your body is feeling, but I'd hate for there to be some serious damage and not know it."

"Thanks for your concern, sir. But that is not why I wanted to see you." I'm trying not to get pissed. It wasn't his fault that I wrecked, but I want out of here and my headache is getting worse.

"I'll make it happen," he says after a few quiet seconds. "But first, can you tell me what happened?"

"It was the brakes."

"The brakes?" he asks as his eyebrows draw together in confusion.

"They were out. I tried to slow down to go into the turn and there was nothing there."

"You didn't mention any problem with them after the first run." He sits down on the end of my bed.

I shake my head. "'Cause there were no problems. The bike was fine before then."

"Hmm." He looks up at me. "Our main concern is that you are okay." He stands. "Take a few days off. Recover. The bike has already been delivered to the shop. I will have it looked over and see if we can find the problem." He goes to walk out, but I stop him.

"How bad is it?" I didn't see much of the bike, and I couldn't hear much with my helmet on, either.

"Well, let's just say that I'm gonna have another one built for you."

"I'm sorry," I say as I hang my head. He gave me a once-in-a-lifetime opportunity, and I have already fucked it up. That's me.

"Don't be sorry," he says kindly. "This stuff happens. I'm just glad that you are okay. Take some time off…"

"I can be back at it tomorrow," I interrupt him. I'm not gonna back down or take time off.

He chuckles. "Recover, son. When the bike is ready, I will let you know and we can go from there."

"So, you're not kicking me off the team?" I ask, letting out a long breath.

"No," he says without pause. "This is part of the game, Erik. This is what guys like us live for. The adrenaline. The risk. I gave you this offer, and so far, you have kept up your side of the bargain. So, I will keep mine."

I nod my head in understanding, but I don't miss the threat. He said that I had kept up my side of the deal.

No drugs.

No alcohol.

No getting in trouble with the law.

What about falling in love with his daughter? Wonder what he would do if he knew that part about me? That I've been hiding a secret from him.

I lie back in the bed and let out a long breath as he walks out. I want to speak to Tabatha. But bringing her back here would be a bad idea. I just spoke to her father. He will inform her that I'm okay and that I'm going home. I will call her the second that I'm released and have her come over. Give me a little nurse action. I smile.

"Oh, my God," Valerie screeches as she comes barging into my room. "Are you okay?" she asks wide-eyed as she comes over to my bed.

"Fine." I push myself off my bed. "Who sent you back here?"

"Are you sure? You can barely walk." She ignores my question.

I glare at her. "I'm really fucking tired of being asked the same question, Val. I said that I'm fine."

She lowers her eyes to the floor and sighs heavily. She's so submissive that it's almost funny. She has always been that way. "I just worry about you," she whispers. Sure, she does.

I pull the hospital gown tighter around myself. "What were you doing up at the track?" I remember thinking 'oh shit' when I looked over to see her standing by Tabatha and Mr. Knight. That was when I brought the bike in. I saw Tabatha start to walk away, and I knew that Valerie had opened her mouth. I just didn't know what all she had said.

"I text you and told you that I was coming to the track."

"No, you didn't," I say remembering her text. "You text and said you were back in town from your Spring

Break vacation. You never said anything about the track. And I didn't tell you that I was there. How did you know that I was there?" I demand, getting pissed all over again.

Valerie and I go a little deeper than I've let on. We have been on and off since our senior year in high school. And at one point, we were gonna be together forever. Thank God, plans change.

She swallows nervously, and my jaw tightens. "I called my father. He said that he had spoken to your dad and you were gonna be there."

I turn away from her and fist my hands by my side. "Why do you continue to do this?" I ask between gritted teeth. Our parents are friends and that's what makes getting rid of her so hard. They all think that we are a match made in heaven. If they only knew what a little vindictive slut she is and how deep my hatred goes for her... "You know where I stand." She's known since the moment I broke off our engagement. Our parents just think I wasn't ready. They don't know that I caught her fucking a guy in his parked car outside of her parents' house. I learned a lot that day. She was the slut everyone said that she was, and I really didn't love her as much as I thought. I turned around and walked away without as much as a swing at the guy. She wasn't worth it.

I feel her hand on my back, and I spin back around to face her, afraid she may hit me where I'm already sore. That's one thing about Valerie. You don't turn your back on her; she will stab you then blame it on the person standing next to her. I learned that the hard way as well.

"How can you continue to say that?" she asks as tears start to fill her black eyes. "I love you."

I place my hands on her shoulders and give her a little shake. "I don't love you, Valerie. Not anymore."

Her bottom lip trembles, and she sucks in a deep breath. She pushes me off her and I sway. God, I'm gonna

_Dash_

fucking hurt for weeks. "Is it because you love her? Because we were just together a week ago," she cries. That has been my weakness with her in the past. Sex. She's willing to give it however I want, whenever I want.

"Dash...?" We both know exactly who she's referring to and I can't let her think that. Tabatha is great, and yes, I have feelings for her, but I wouldn't call it love just yet. If Valerie knows that I like her, then she will run with that information. I won't allow that to happen.

"No," I say softening my voice. "I don't love her. I don't even know her." I run the back of my knuckles down her cheek how I know she likes. Her skin feels ashy and her makeup is chunky from her tears and from her wiping her face with her hands.

She gives me a weak smile that makes my stomach flip in agony. You just gave her hope, you bastard. Take it back. "I just don't have time for this. For us. I need to work on getting a new bike built and getting back on the track. I can't race for Mr. Knight if I'm not a hundred percent in the game."

"I guess that makes sense."

Bingo. Stupid bitch! She was always easy to manipulate. And it helps that I always know the right things to say to her. Whether I want her to storm out of my house and leave me alone for days or spread her legs when no other bitch is around. That part of her is a plus.

"My parents want you to stay with us."

"What?" I can't do that. That would piss Tabatha off.

"They spoke to your parents. They can't come home for another few days, and they want you to stay with us. Make sure you are all right. My parents agreed to take care of you."

I sigh heavily. Everyone is working against Tabatha and me. Will she go to her dad and try to get me kicked off? Will she tell him what we did the night of my party

96

and what we have continued to do over the past week? What will Mr. Knight think of me? He will probably think the same thing that Tabatha thought in the beginning — that I used her to further my dream. I don't know her well enough to know what plan of action she will take. But Valerie — I know exactly what she will do; she will try to ruin my life. She will destroy what I have with Tabatha and my dream of racing for Knight. I know what I have to do, but for the time being, I will tell her what she wants to hear.

"Okay," I say, and she gives me a huge smile. "I'll stay with your parents, but only for a few days." Lie.

She throws her arms around me, knocking us into the wall. "Fuck," I curse loudly before shoving her off me. I bend over wrapping my arms around myself.

"I'm so sorry," she screeches.

"Goddammit, Val," I hiss trying to take in a breath. Pain shoots up my back and my side. My head pounds harder than it did before and my vision starts to fade in and out.

"I forgot," she cries.

I stay silent as I take a few deep breaths. Once I'm able to control my racing heart and the pain subsides, I straighten and narrow my eyes on hers. I refrain from cussing more as tears run down her face. "Just stay away. Don't touch me," I bark, and she nods her head quickly.

"I truly am sorry. I just…"

"I don't care."

# CHAPTER SIXTEEN

## *Tabatha*

I'm in total bitch mode and everyone knows it. Why am I so bitchy, you ask? Dash! I haven't seen or spoken to him in two days. Since the day that he wrecked at the track — when he promised to explain everything. He was going to calm my concerns and prove he wasn't a total lying douchebag.

Once the doctors informed us that he was refusing treatment and checking himself out of the hospital, he had requested to see my father. I was so relieved that he was awake, talking, and rather ready to leave, as the nurse put it, that I didn't realize he didn't ask to see me. After my father came out and told us that he seemed just fine and more determined than before to get on the track, Valerie made her way back to see him. When she came out, she announced very loud and proud that he had agreed to go stay with her parents.

What. The. Fuck. At that moment, my mood went from relieved to fucking pissy. I sat there like a fucking idiot for the next hour with Jackie and Blake giving me looks of pity. They knew that he wasn't gonna ask to see me, and I hoped to prove them wrong. They were right! But what did I expect? She had called him, and he had lied to me about it. You don't lie to someone unless you have something to hide. He obviously was still seeing her, and I was the side chick. I do believe that he wasn't sleeping with me to further his career with my father because being with me would just get him fired. But Valerie? I'm still confused to what that connection is.

After I waited an hour and heard nothing from Dash, we left. I stood and walked out without saying good-bye to anyone. Blake and Jackie followed me out. They ended up coming over to my house and hanging out, but they didn't stay long. They could tell my mood was getting worse by the second. The bastard didn't even text me to say sorry or even explain why he chose to go to their house. Hell, for all I know, Valerie went there and sucked his dick. Who knows what he sees in her. It's obviously not her personality, so the bitch has to have some mad bed skills.

I wanted to ask Blake about Dash and Valerie's history. I wanted to know what their current relationship was, but what good would that do? He wasn't offering any information, so I decided against it. Why throw salt into the wound?

Now I sit in my first class of the day. No makeup, hair up in a messy bun. I'm wearing yoga pants and a tank top. I didn't dress to impress anyone this morning. If my mother were to see me, she would tell me to cover up the dark circles under my eyes from the lack of sleep I've had over the last two days. To put on a dress and some six-inch heels. But thankfully, I no longer live at home, so I can look as distasteful as I want.

My face must say 'stay the fuck away from me' 'cause no one has spoken a word to me. But I can still hear them talking about who they did or where they went on their Spring Break. You would think that these guys have never been laid before. I mean, come on—mix alcohol, beach, and bikinis, and you're gonna get lucky no matter how much of a fucking douche you are.

I take a deep breath and close my eyes to try to calm my nerves. I don't have a class on Mondays. Yesterday, I did nothing but sat around my house listening to every song that resembled hating men. It helped a little. It mainly just fueled my fire to want to punch him even more.

I want so badly to lean over, grab my phone out of my purse, call the fucker up, and give him a piece of my mind. But what good would it do? Just make me look like a crazy bitch who felt more for him than he did me. I've been the fool before. Rodger made me that little puppy that followed him around and made him feel superior. I won't give Dash that satisfaction.

"Miss Knight. See me after class."

I open my eyes and look down as my professor tosses my test onto my desk. An F is scrawled across the top, and I slap my hand over it. Just fucking great!

I do nothing during class but stare at the wall ahead of me and contemplate what to do to put this anger to good use. By the time my professor dismisses class, I still have nothing.

I stomp my way down to his desk. "An F? How did I get an F?" I demand.

He leans back in his chair calmly and looks up at me. "Ms Knight, what you do outside of my class is none of my business. But I suggest that next time you come with your head on your shoulders and your mind working."

"Excuse me?"

He sighs and picks up my test. "You know this material. We both know you do, but that day you were not here."

Of course, I wasn't. I had a hangover from hell, and I was trying to recall who I had woken up next to. Naked. I climbed a tree to jump the fence. Who in the hell cared what I thought about this stupid class? I sigh. "I was having a rough day."

"Miss Knight, I don't consider a hangover being a rough day," he chastises. He takes a second to look me up and down, and he frowns. "Maybe you should concentrate a little more on school and less on partying."

Before I can respond, he hands me back my test. "I was once in college and understand how it feels to be young. I will give you one more chance. You will retake the test this Saturday." He returns to the papers before him, effectively dismissing me.

I shove the test into my backpack and then storm out of the classroom. I look down at my watch and realize that I have thirty minutes until my next class. I used to have that time to hang out with Rodger; now I want to spend it in the gym pounding on a punching bag to release my anger.

Looking around the big campus, I decide to head to the coffee shop. Don't ask me why—I hate coffee—but I need a pick-me-up. The moment that I walk in, I regret it. Rodger stands over by the wall talking to a pretty redhead who I know as Whitney. She's his best friend. I was never jealous of her 'cause, to be honest, he's not her type. She radiates class, the kind you can't buy. She's beautiful, but not the kind that has been added on. She stands tall and yet is down to earth. She's the only woman who I know could run for president and win by just the sound of her voice. When she speaks, people listen. She speaks clearly and is intelligent beyond this world, yet she has a way of making complicated sound so simple. She makes Rodger look stupid. But I never felt that way around her; she made me feel smart at times. She's not the typical girl who goes shopping and tanning on a Saturday. She spends her weekends in the library with her nose stuck in a book. She doesn't read romance. She prefers to read about the world we live in and the culture she wants her future children to grow up in.

I honestly only think Rodger is friends with her to learn from her. All he ever does is argue with her. She always wins, and it drives him nuts. She is the only woman in the world who would make him second-guess himself.

*Dash*

"Tabatha," she exclaims when she spots me.

Shit! "Hey, Whitney." I greet her with a fake smile as I walk over to them. I can't ignore her, but I can ignore Rodger.

"How are you doing?" she asks as she pulls me into a hug. Her red hair smells of citrus.

"Great," I lie.

She pulls away, and her baby blue eyes look into mine. "I was just asking Rodger about you. He said you had been sick." She frowns as she looks me over. "You should go home and get some rest. You do look awful."

I run my hand over my messy bun and remember that I look like hammered dog shit. I smile at her. Her words may seem harsh, but that is just how she speaks. She's not mean, just honest. Most women hate her for that—people hate to hear the truth.

I stiffen as Rodger throws his arm over my shoulder. "I called you just a few minutes ago, Tabby."

Tabby! He knows what the name does to me, how it pisses me off. "What are you doing?" I whisper when Whitney turns around to say hello to someone else.

He lowers his lips down to my ear. "You do look awful. You know? How could you leave the house looking like that? Didn't you know you would see me today?"

The words don't sound the same way coming from him. He makes it sound like I'm the scum on the bottom of his shoe that he needs to scrape against the sidewalk.

"Did you forget that I no longer have to look perfect for you?" I snap. 'No hair out of place' is what he once said to me before we went over to his father's for dinner.

"To the world, you're still mine, sweetheart." He speaks his words softly, but it is meant to be a threat. Our breakup is still not public knowledge, and I have a feeling his father has something to do with that. He probably paid someone a pretty penny. I know that we are not famous

102

actors or singers, but his dad likes to live in the limelight. So he will leak shit or pay to have stuff thrown out there for everyone. No matter how much he hated me, he thought my father's fame was good for him and his son.

I shove him away, and he stumbles over the table behind us. The commotion causes Whitney to turn back and face us. "Are you okay, Rodger?" she asks, her baby blue eyes wide as she reaches out to him. "What happened?" She looks over to me when he refuses her help to right himself.

"Sorry," I say as I fake cough. "You shouldn't get too close, babe. You may catch my cold."

His jaw tightens as I say babe. He hates that word. Actually, I do too, but I like to see that look of anger on his face. I actually give him a real smile.

"No worries," he says before he straightens his suit jacket. Who in the hell wears a suit to college? He does, every single day! It's annoying and unattractive!

"Are you taking your Vitamin C?" Whitney asks Rodger. He rolls his eyes at her. "Seriously, Rodger. You can prevent sickness with a daily consumption of Vitamin C," she finishes with a sweet smile. I can't help but laugh at her.

"Well, it's been fun chatting with you all. But I must go," I say needing to get the hell out of here.

"Okay," Whitney says and reaches out to hug me once again.

"I don't want you to get sick," I say taking a step back.

"No worries. Unlike your boyfriend, I take my precautions for this kind of event." She pulls me into a hug and then lets me go. I try not to cringe at her calling Rodger my boyfriend. We say our good-byes, and I don't even bother to say another word to Rodger.

I go about my day, sit in my classes, do my work, and try not to fall asleep. I yawn as I exit my car once I pull up to my house. Jackie has been blowing my phone up today checking on me and I haven't responded. I don't want to hear what a dick Dash is. That's what best friends do when a guy dumps your ass. They make them sound like dirt to put a smile on your face. But I also know that she and Blake are going out tonight—she told me that in one of her text messages. But right now, I need sleep more than I need alcohol.

Hmm. Never thought I would say that.

I put my key into the lock and hear the sound of a motorcycle engine. I turn around to see one of the bikes that was in Dash's garage the other day when he took me for a ride.

I stand frozen as I watch the guy get off it. "Tabatha," Dash says the moment he removes his helmet.

"No," I say shaking my head. "I don't wanna hear it, Dash," I announce before I spin back around and finish opening the front door. I rush through it and turn to slam it shut, but he shoves it open.

"I need to talk to you."

I laugh. A laugh that makes my blood boil. How dare this fucker show up here? I continue to walk toward the kitchen. He grabs my shoulder from behind and spins me around. "Don't walk away from me," he demands. For the first time since I've met him, I see him literally pissed. His gray eyes narrow. His nostrils flare, and jaw is tight. Too bad for him. I couldn't care less how mad he is.

"Don't you fucking dare!" I shout back.

"Please," he pleads, softening his voice, "let me explain."

I shake my head. "Your actions told me everything that I needed to know."

He finally releases me and sighs heavily. "You're wrong." He takes a step toward me, and I take a step back to match it. He reaches out once again and gently pulls my body into his. "I've been at your father's."

"No, you haven't," I reply immediately.

He gives me a small smirk. "I have, I promise you. You can even call him. That is who I went home with from the hospital."

I shake my head slowly not wanting to believe his words. "I heard her parents. They said that they had talked to yours and offered for you to stay with them. Valerie came out after seeing you and said that you were going to their house."

He places his hands on my face. "She asked me, yes. I told her that I would. I needed her to believe me."

"So, you lie often." I meant it as a question, but I said it as a statement.

"Yes," he sighs, "I lie to her often. She's is an annoying little bitch, and I can't stand her knowing what I'm up to or where I'm at."

"Geez," I breathe. "I'd hate to hear what you say about me when I'm not around," I huff sarcastically.

"All I do is talk about how great you are. How much I want you."

"Always about sex," I reply.

"No," he says but I can't miss the smirk growing across his face. "Sex is great with you, though."

"If this is how you plan on buttering me up, it's not gonna work." I pull back and cross my arms over my chest.

"I'm not here to butter you up. I'm here to tell you the truth."

"Why should I believe you? You haven't called me. It's been two days, Dash."

"I'm sorry. I went home with your father, and although I'm still somewhat sore, I've spent every waking moment with your father going over our plans. We needed a new one, and we are running out of time."

"I'm sorry that you're still hurting." I can only imagine what the crash did to his body. He's very lucky that nothing was broken.

His head starts to come down to mine. I reach out and softly place my hand on his chest and push him away from me. "Did you really think that you could show up here and expect me to just lie down and spread my legs for you?" I ask in all seriousness.

"What do you want from me?" he asks, taking a step back to give us even more space.

"The truth," I snap, finding my anger again. "I'm pretty sure that is what you promised me at the track."

He runs a hand through his hair with frustration. "What do you wanna know? That Valerie and I were engaged."

"Engaged?" I squeak. "How have you failed to mention that to me?"

"It was a long time ago." He shrugs as if it's no big deal.

"It couldn't have been that long ago," I snap. "You're only twenty-two years old," I remind him, in case he has forgotten.

"Okay. It was three years ago."

I release a long breath. Just fucking great! So this bitch is expecting to marry him. So much for him and I having any chance together.

## CHAPTER SEVENTEEN

# Dash

I didn't want to tell her about the engagement, knowing it would only lead to more fucking questions. But at what point do I stop hiding things from her?

"It seems like a lifetime ago," I say truthfully. "We had known each other for a long time. Our parents are best friends."

She gives a rough laugh. "Of course, they are."

I ignore her and continue. "Senior year, we got together. It didn't take long for us to get serious. I proposed, she said yes. And then, we split." I shrug carelessly.

"My gosh," she says wide-eyed. "Did it really not mean that much to you?" she asks as if she can't imagine a world where lovers fall in and out of love.

"Do you still love Rodger?" It's a simple question, yet her face hardens and her body stiffens.

"No." It comes out as a growl.

I take her hands in mine and squeeze them tightly. "See, it's possible to no longer want someone."

She nods her head in understanding. "But she won't give you up. Shit, my dad thinks you two are together."

"And Rodger is still trying to get you back," I say. "But we can fix the problem with your dad."

She eyes me skeptically. "What do you mean?"

"Let's tell your father." It's time to come clean. I can only keep so many secrets.

She starts shaking her head quickly as she pulls away. "Look, you wanted me to prove this to you, let me."

"You'll lose everything. We both know that he will drop you."

"I've been telling you from the start that I would risk everything for you, yet

I have risked nothing. We've kept it a secret."

"Because we have no other choice," she says frustrated.

"We have a choice. I have a choice." I place my hands in her hair, and she closes her eyes as I tighten my fingers in it. "I choose you, Tabatha. You're better than any dream I have ever had. Because you are real. You're right here in front of me." And with that, I lower my lips to her. She opens her mouth for me, allowing me in, and I take over. Pushing my tongue into her mouth and working our lips together.

When I pull away, I take her by her hand. "Grab your car keys."

"Why?"

"'Cause I'm still sore as fuck and I should not have ridden my bike over here."

We pull up to her father's house, and she reaches over to grab my hand. She squeezes it tightly, and I squeeze it back. "It's going to be okay," I reassure her once again.

"You don't know him the way that I do. And what are we gonna tell him?" Her eyes widen as if she just thought of this. "He's gonna ask how we met. When it happened? Why you didn't think of the team first."

She's starting to panic. I yank my hand out of hers and place them on her cheeks to make her face me. "It will be fine. Let me do all the talking. Okay?"

"But…?"

"No buts. I will take care of all of it." She's reluctant but nods her head.

I let go of her and get out of the car. I go around the car and open her door. I grab her hand and hold on tighter when she tries to pull away. We enter the house, and I close the door quietly behind us. "Dash, is that you?" I hear Mr. Knight call out from down the hall. It sounds like he is already in his office. I told him earlier that I had to run out and do a few things and then would be right back.

"Yes, sir," I call out as well.

Tabatha comes to a halt, and I yank on her hand to get her to walk again.

"Stop stopping," I say quietly. We come to the office door, and she pulls me up against the wall.

"I just don't think we should hold hands. It's not a smart thing. Let's see how he reacts first."

"Okay," I say running my hand through her soft hair. "Whatever makes you feel better."

I pull away and walk into his office. I would love to say that I'm as calm as I'm putting on, but I'm not. I'm just as nervous as Tabatha looks.

"Erik..." Johnny starts but cuts himself off the moment that his daughter walks in after me. "What are you doing here, Tabatha?" His voice has an edge to it as if she's interrupting whatever he wants to talk to me about.

"I...uh...wanted to talk to you about school," she stumbles as she looks him in the eye.

He waves her off. "Later. I have to speak to Erik alone. I'll speak to you about your schooling when I'm done." He then looks away from her. She wastes no time before she turns away and all but runs out of the office.

"What do you need, Mr. Knight?" I ask as I sit down and lean over, placing my elbows on my knees. I feel calmed getting a few extra minutes to collect my thoughts on how I'm gonna tell my boss that I'm with his daughter.

"We have a problem," he says, and his dark brown eyes stare into mine.

Does he already know about Tabatha and me? How could he, though?

"What's the problem?" I ask starting to break out in a sweat.

"You threw a party. The same exact night that I had you arrested." He speaks slowly letting it sink in.

I swallow nervously. The party that I slept with his daughter at. Hours after he told me no parties, alcohol, or drugs. "Yes, sir." I try to say it without sounding like I actually did something wrong.

He looks down to his table shaking his head. "I told you no parties. No alcohol. And no trouble with the cops."

I sit up straight. "Cops? Sir, I know you said no parties, but I had not signed yet. The party was tame and there were no cops…"

He slams his hand down on the table. "And you think that's okay?"

"I swear I had no idea who she was," I blurt out. "She…"

"She?" he interrupts me

"Yes. That night was my first night to meet her. I swear I had no idea who she was." God, I just broke like a little kid who stole a cookie out of his mother's cookie jar. But Mr. Knight is intimidating.

"I don't care who the hell you met that night or what you two did." Then he looks at me with narrowed eyes. "What does concern me is the parents who are threatening to sue you."

"What?" I ask as I jump from my seat. Ouch! A pain shoots up my back from my wreck. "Who in the hell is trying to sue me?" I demand. "And for what?"

He places his hand up and gestures for me to sit back down as if he is now the calm one. "An underage male attended your party and got drunk. He then drove and was involved in a car wreck."

"Shit. Is he okay?"

He nods. "The sorry idiot will be fine. But since he was over the legal limit, he was arrested. The parents are now threatening to sue you for all damages. The cost of the DUI, and the cost to repair the car and the property that his car destroyed."

"Can they do that?" I ask. "I haven't been notified of anything."

"I was just notified after you left here this morning. I told you that I had pull in this town, and I have very well paid attorneys who make sure everything involving my company or me lands on their desk. It has not gone public yet, but I have no doubt that they will try."

"So, what do I do?" How is this happening?

"Absolutely nothing! I'm gonna take care of it." Just as he says that, his fax machine alerts him of a new fax. "Just in time," he says reaching over to grab it. He speaks as he hands it over to me. "Do you remember this boy?"

It's his mug shot. He looks like he has been drinking for days. "I don't remember seeing him," I say looking over his messy hair and green, bloodshot eyes.

"So you're saying you didn't personally serve him alcohol?" he asks placing his forearms on his desk. "'Cause the parents said that you did."

"Not personally." I shrug before laying the picture back on his desk. "I didn't know every person who was there. And about three hours into it, I went to my parents' room…"

He lifts his hands. "With the girl you were speaking of earlier?" he asks and I give him a nod as I kick myself for saying that. I used to be great under pressure, but now, not so much. Guess when you have a lot at stake things are different.

"We should contact her. She may have seen him. Let me have her name and number. The attorney will also want to speak with her."

Fuck me! "Well…uh, she…"

My head shifts quickly and I flinch from the discomfort to look at the door when it swings open. "Dad. Let me explain." She was listening?

"Sweet pea." He stands from his desk. "I told you that we would discuss your schooling later. I am in an important meeting."

She takes a deep breath as she closes her eyes. When she opens them, she pushes her shoulders back and takes the three steps that have her standing right in front of his desk. She leans over and picks up the mug shot. She looks it over for a few seconds as her father and I stare at her silently. He has a look of pure confusion and annoyance on his aged face. My wide eyes go back and forth between them.

"I saw him," she announces before placing the paper down by her side.

"You know him?" her father asks as his brows draw together. "From school?"

She shakes her head. "I saw him, Daddy. At the party."

"You what? What party?" He looks over at me, and I shift in my seat under his black gaze. Here it goes! I can see the second that his face goes from confusion to livid that he has put two and two together. "Erik's party? You were at his party that night?"

"Yes, sir," she answers keeping her shoulders back and head high.

"What were you doing there?"

"I went with Jackie."

"I don't give a shit who you went with. I wanna know what you were doing there in the first place!" he demands.

"I had just broke up with Rodger and wanted to go have some fun. Jackie told me about it, so we went. I had no idea that you had hired Dash earlier that day." She rambles.

"Why would that matter to me?" he asks placing his hands on his hips.

"I...we..." She starts to fumble over her words again. And I realize what a pussy I've been.

I rub my sweaty hands on my pants and then stand. "Tabatha is the woman that I was with the night of my party," I announce, and she spins around to stare at me wide-eyed. What was I supposed to say? This is why we came here in the first place. I mean, I was going to leave out the part where I slept with his drunk daughter before I even knew who she was.

"What?" he barks, making her jump. "You were with him that night? With him how?" he shouts.

Okay. So maybe I should have worded it differently. I place my hands in front of me as if I'm about to beg for my life. "I swear it's not what it sounds like."

"Really?" he snaps, looking over at me. "Then what the hell is it? Sounds like you used my daughter to me."

"No, Daddy, it wasn't like that."

His head spins to face her. "And what in the hell were you thinking? You work for me. Do you know what this will look like when it gets out? 'Cause it will get out."

"What?" I question, looking at her. "You work for your father?"

"I didn't think it was that important," she mumbles.

He drops to his seat with a heavy sigh. For the first time since I met him, he runs his head through his silver hair messing up the perfect strands. "This is going to be big news when the media finds out."

"Why? I'm nobody," she says softly.

"Nobody?" he asks, shocked that she could have said that. "You're my daughter who is sleeping with an employee. Who has a girlfriend. They will eat it up."

"They're not together," she says as she starts to sniff.

"Oh?" He turns to face me once again. "Is that what you told her?"

"It's the truth," I say. "We haven't been together for some time."

He hangs his head as if this couldn't get any worse. And at that exact second, his phone rings. Reaching over, he picks it up. "Hello?" he asks and I turn to her.

"Hey," I coo, wiping the single tear off her cheek with my thumb. "It's okay. We will work through it," I assure her, but she shrugs as if she doesn't believe that is a possibility.

I take a step away from her and look back at Mr. Knight as he hangs up the phone. "Tabatha, leave," he orders, not even bothering to look over at her.

"But Daddy…"

"Leave!" he roars, and she spins around and runs out of the office, slamming the door

behind her.

"We have a new problem," he growls pointing at the couch for me to sit my ass down.

"What is it?" I ask reluctantly, not even really wanting to know what it is exactly. What could be worse than sleeping with his daughter?

"That was my main mechanic who is working on the bike you crashed. They just found the problem."

"Oh?"

"You were right. It was the brakes. They were cut."

"Cut? Cut how?" I ask in wonderment. "How was that possible? The first few rounds they were fine. If they would have cut them when I was off of it then we would have seen them."

He rubs his chin for a few seconds as he looks straight ahead thinking over what I said. "You came in. You got off your bike. Where did you go?"

Great. Everything from now on is going to lead back to his daughter. "I went to talk to Tabatha. Valerie had shown up. I knew that she was talking smack to her when I saw Tabatha walk away. I had to explain that she was lying." He nods his head as if he's starting to understand my reasoning. "But you were right there with the bike, right?"

"Yes, but…" he pauses, "I had a phone call. I walked away from the bike to answer it. It wasn't more than a three-minute phone call, but someone would have only needed a second to cut it."

"There was no one else there," I remind him.

"Yes, there was. Valerie."

She wouldn't. I start to shake my head in protest. "She knows nothing about bikes. How would she know what to do?" Would she go that far to kill me? Yep.

He shrugs. "You can learn anything on the internet these days. The question is why she would do it," he asks.

"'Cause she's a vindictive bitch who knows that I have feelings for your daughter," I say in all seriousness.

His eyebrows raise to his hairline. "Feelings?"

There it is. My opportunity to show him what it is that I want. "Yes, sir. Let me explain about that night of my party."

He shakes his head. "I spent months doing research on you, son." My eyes widen in surprise. "I know that you come from money. I know you're an adrenaline junky. And I know you live to race. But you're not who I picture when I see someone for my daughter."

"With all due respect, sir. The only thing you know about me is what your research has told you. You once told me that we are alike. And that we both take risks. I'm willing to risk racing for you, for her. That's what we were planning to tell you tonight. If you give me an ultimatum, I will pick her. 'Cause to me, she's worth more than some plastic and a track." I finish up and then stand from my chair.

He stands as well and sighs in acceptance. "We made a deal, and I'm not going back on it," he says with a smirk. "But I do have a request."

"Which is?"

"Keep it as quiet as possible. If you're going to see her, do it here. Don't go to her house. Don't go to your house together. Your crash at the track was all over the news. They know you were released and are staying with your boss. Myself! I can almost guarantee you that Valerie is not doing it on her own. She has help. Let's keep them blind to what is going on because, as good as you are for this team, I will kill you myself if my daughter is caught in the crossfire."

I nod in understanding. "I don't want that, either."

"Good." He sits back down. "Oh, and keep this a secret from Tabatha. As far as she is concerned, the wreck was a complete accident. Now go and calm her down. She's probably cussing me on Twitter or some other social network by now. I'm heading off to the shop to look at the bike myself."

Great! Another lie. As soon as I close the office door, I can hear her voice from the other side of the house. She's yelling at someone, and I figure it's her mother.

Making my way down the long hall, I round the end and find her standing with her back to me.

"Stop fucking calling," she yells as she holds her phone in front of her mouth. She hits end and then throws it down onto the table.

"Wow," I say coming up behind her. She spins around and looks behind me.

She wraps her arms gently around me, and I inhale her scent. God, it's been two days, and I've missed her like crazy.

"Are you in trouble?" she whispers.

"No. I'm okay." She sighs heavily. "But we made a few new deals."

"I won't walk away, Dash." My heart swells at her confession.

"You don't have to. We just have to be discreet." That will be hard with her. I always want her next to me, and when she is, I want my hands on her body while my lips are on hers. But it's to the point where her safety is involved and I won't risk that.

"Take me upstairs," she whispers once again before her lips brush against mine.

I let out a moan that shows my internal struggle. How am I gonna fuck her? I'm still sore as fuck.

"Don't worry," she says as if she's reading my mind, "I'll do all the work."

I smile down at her. "Show me the way."

She takes me back down the long hallway and then up the stairs. We walk down another long hallway. My eyes scan the pictures of her over the years that line the walls—from naked in the bathtub as a baby, to her senior pictures standing next to her dad's old racecar. I linger on that one a little longer and my feet slow. She tugs on me before I can see much more.

We walk into her room. Her walls are a soft yellow and the bedspread is a dark blue. It reminds me of the day out at the beach.

"Don't judge me," she says with a laugh.

"No judgment here," I say wrapping my arms around her and pulling her back into my front. I reach up and push her hair off her shoulder.

"Oh, no." She laughs pulling away from me.

"What?" I ask.

"In all of my madness for hating you, I have yet to shower today," she tells me.

"So?" I look longingly over to her bed. "Like I care."

"Well, I do." She starts to walk backward. She reaches down and grabs the hem of her tank top. She pulls it up over her head. "Join me?" she asks with a wink.

I chuckle. "Absolutely."

I follow her into the bathroom connected to her room. She flips a light switch on the wall and continues to walk to the end of the bathroom. She bends down, removing her shoes and her yoga pants before finishing with her bra and underwear.

"What are you waiting for?" she asks as she opens the door and enters the shower. I follow as quickly as my sore body will allow me. I'm not sure fucking in the shower will be best for me, but I'm gonna give it a try.

Walking in, I find her bending over to pick up her bodywash. I lean down and grab her arm. I pull her up and shove the front of her body into the wall.

"Thought I was gonna do all the work." She chuckles.

"Shut up," I say simply. I'll deal with the soreness tomorrow. As of right now, I can work it out on her.

She lays her head back onto my chest as I wrap my arms around her waist. My already hard cock pushes against her ass. My wandering hands make their way up her stomach and grab a hold of her breasts. She whimpers when I give them both a little pinch. "Hmm. You like that," I say with a chuckle myself. I pinch them a little harder and tug on them. She cries out as she rises up onto her tiptoes.

"Dash," she pants. Her chest rises and falls quickly making her breasts bounce.

"Fuck…" I growl as I hold them in my hands. I wanna fuck them. I want to fuck every part of her. I want to take my time and kiss every inch. Slowly make her fall apart underneath me. But that's just not going to happen right now. I need her.

I let go of them and she whimpers. "Bend over," I say placing my hand on her back. "Place your hands on the wall," I order and she does so without argument. I'm gonna have to fuck her this way 'cause I can't lift her to wrap her legs around me. I don't think my back could do that at this moment. But this way — her bent over and me behind her — I could do all night long.

I slide my hand up between her soft thighs and I smile when she spreads them further apart for me. I grind my teeth when I find her pussy just as soaking wet as the rest of our bodies. Taking my other hand, I grab my hard cock and position myself between her legs. At first, I nudge just the tip in. Slowly stretching, filling her as she moans and whimpers. I've dreamed of this for the last two days.

"How does that feel?" I ask as I push into her further. "Feels fucking great." I answer my own question.

I start to fuck her faster, and she cries out. Her head drops down and I reach up to grab a handful of her hair. I yank her head back and she hisses in a breath.

119

Dash

Her loud cries and the slapping of our bodies fill the bathroom and I'm thankful that we are here at her parents' house alone. Being the gentleman that I am, I hold out until she finishes before I allow myself to come. Once done, I pull her to stand. I can feel my body start to come down from the high and it aches. "I'm gonna get out. I'll meet you in bed," I say giving her a soft kiss on her cheek.

I must have passed out the second my head hit the pillow because the next thing I know, I feel her soft, naked skin sliding into her bed next to me.

"You okay?" she asks quietly.

I smile at her concern. "Never been better," I say wrapping my arm around her and pulling her into my side.

"What all did my father have to say to you?"

I lean over and kiss her hair. "Don't worry about it, baby. He knows about us and I'm still on the team. I told you. No worries." She sighs heavily. "What were you gonna talk to him about school?"

"I had a test the morning after I climbed your tree and jumped your fence. I found out today that I failed it. My dad's gonna kill me."

I chuckle. "Were you that wrapped up in me that you couldn't concentrate?" I ask trying not to laugh.

"Shut up," she snaps, and it makes me laugh harder.

"I'm sorry. I know it's not funny." I smile.

"No, I'm sorry," she sighs. "I'm just losing my mind." She pulls away from me and rolls over giving me her back. "So much has happened so quickly," she whispers.

I snuggle up against her back. "It's all gonna be okay." I kiss her bare shoulder. "What did your teacher say about your test?"

"The bastard is letting me take it again next Saturday."

"What a nice bastard," I observe, and she gives a little laugh. "I'll help you study for it. It'll be great."

# CHAPTER EIGHTEEN

## *Tabatha*

"I passed," I exclaim, running into my father's office with my test in my hand.

I don't get the congratulations party that I quite expected. My father sits behind his desk dressed in his dark blue suit that cost more than some people pay for their cars. Stacks of paperwork sit in front of him. Dash has his palms on the desk as he leans to look it over as well. I take a moment to admire the sliver of his lower back exposing some of the nail marks that I left on him from the quickie we had this morning before I went to school.

Dash and I haven't left my father's house this past week. Well, I go to school and his body is almost back to normal so he goes up to the track. He and my father are trying to get his new bike ready. Something is going on with what happened, but neither one is telling me shit. But at least Daddy is letting us stay here. Together. Every morning, we get up and walk down to the kitchen for Dash to have some coffee and for me to eat breakfast before school. My father just sits at the head of his table and stares at us. Like maybe he thinks it was a mistake to allow us both to stay here to be together. But he wants us to keep our relationship a secret from the world, therefore, we gotta keep it under wraps. And that wouldn't happen if we were at either of our own houses.

"Sweet pea?" my father says, getting my attention. Dash stands from the desk and turns to face me.

"Hey, baby," he says and then walks over to me. He wraps his arms around me and pulls me in for a long, slow kiss.

My father clears his throat, and I chuckle as I pull away.

"You can at least pretend to be discreet around me," my father says eyeing Dash.

"Sorry, sir," he responds with a head nod.

I hold up my test. "I passed," I say once again.

"That's great." Dash takes it from me. He reads it over and then looks at me wide-eyed. "You did more than passed, you aced it."

I give him a big smile. "That I did."

My father stands from his desk. "We should go out to celebrate." He smiles.

"Daddy. It was just one little test. That I had to take twice," I remind him.

"Nonsense." He waves me off. "We are going to dinner. I feel like you guys haven't been out of this house except for school and work all week." He sighs. "I remember when your mother and I were like that."

"Eeeeww, Dad," I say scrunching my face with disgust. I do not want to hear about my parents back when they were young. "Speaking of mother. Will she be joining us?"

"No. She has a meeting this evening."

I nod with a smile to hide my disappointment. She's always working. "Go ahead and get ready. We should be done in about thirty minutes," he states before he sits back down.

I look over at Dash, and he gives me a big smile. He leans into me. "So proud of you, baby," he whispers and then places a kiss on my cheek.

Geez, I've never been so proud to make an A.

*Dash*

You never realize how hard it is to keep your hands to yourself until you have to. Little did I know that my father had a hunch I would pass my test. He already had this dinner planned. I look out the dark black windows of my father's Escalade as his driver escorts us to dinner.

"So, how is the new bike coming?" I ask, looking over at Dash beside me. His hand rests in mine on his lap.

"Great."

"Is the new bike finished?" I ask my father who sits in the front seat.

"It should be very soon." He leans over and says something to the driver, who nods with a, "Yes, sir."

"If you ask me, I pay them too much to be this slow," he growls. "We are on a very tight schedule. Our first race is in three weeks."

"Three weeks?" I look over at Dash in surprise. "Will you be ready in three weeks?"

"Absolutely," he says with confidence and a smile.

We pull up to the restaurant and my father turns in his seat to look at our joined hands.

I roll my eyes as I pull mine out of Dash's. "I know the rules, Daddy."

"Just checking."

Just as I say that, Dash gets out and holds the door open for me. I thank him nicely and he gives me a flirtatious wink that makes me giggle.

I smooth down my red baby doll dress as we enter the restaurant. The hostess immediately seats us at my father's favorite table in the back.

It reminds me of the first time that we sat down to eat. It feels like that was a lifetime ago, yet it was just a few weeks. I give a little laugh.

"What's so funny?" Dash asks me.

"I was remembering when my father asked me to dinner and you just happened to be here."

Dash gives me a smirk. "That's why you asked to tag along?" my father asks, and Dash nods, still looking at me.

"Thought you would get lucky," I ask.

He shakes his head. "I already got lucky."

"Jesus," my father says shaking his head. "You two are going to be the death of me."

We both laugh at his unease. "But really, sweet pea, I'm glad you have time for me once again. I've enjoyed you being at the house. I've missed you." He looks over at Dash. "She never had time for her mother and me when she was with Rodger."

I duck my head in shame at his words. I hate how much Rodger took me away from them as well. I was just too weak to stand up for myself.

"Well, I would never do that," Dash replies in all seriousness.

I have a feeling that he feels that way 'cause of his own family. They don't seem to be very close. Hell, they wouldn't even come into town when Valerie's parents told them that he had crashed his bike and ended up in the hospital. And I haven't heard him talk to them on the phone since that incident, either.

I hear my father's phone ringing in the distance as I stare at Dash. He and my father are in conversation about his new bike as my father answers it.

"Mr. Knight," he says into his phone, and I take the opportunity to run my heel along Dash's leg under the table.

He leans over. "You better stop that. I'd hate to take you back to the bathroom."

I throw my head back laughing. As if I would actually do that with my father sitting out here at our table.

"We'll take care of it," my father snaps, getting our attention. "They have nothing to go on. He doesn't even remember the boy being there." Dash places his arms on the table as he leans over and watches my father intently. "That's what I pay you for. I may not be an attorney, but I know extortion when I hear it."

"Extortion?" I ask quietly looking over at Dash. He shakes his head at me but keeps his attention on my father. "Take care of it," he snaps once again.

"What's going on?" I ask.

My father slams his phone down onto the table, exhibiting his temper. My father has always been a laid-back type of guy, but if you mess with his family or business, you will see another side of him.

He looks over at Dash before he speaks. "The family says they have pictures of you serving him."

"What?" he barks. "That's a lie. I swear I don't remember seeing him there. I can't deny that he may have had drinks there. But I swear I never served him."

"He came in after me and Jackie got there," I admit, remembering the pimple-face kid walking in behind us. "I went straight to the kitchen for a drink, and he continued to walk down the hall."

"Are you sure?" Dash asks and I raise my eyebrows at his question.

"Of course, I am. Do you not believe me?"

"You were already drunk when you got there," he states.

"You were driving drunk?" my father growls. I ignore him.

I lean over the table and narrow my eyes on Dash. "Jackie drove me there. Yes, I had already had a few drinks, but I was just fine until you started shoving gin down my throat."

"Shoving gin down your throat?" he asks in disbelief. "You were the one trying to drown your sorrows in a bottle." I gasp. "What? Can't remember how much you were tore up over Rodger leaving you? And you had so much that wasn't the only thing you couldn't remember…"

"I left him." My voice rises. I slam my elbow on the table and point my finger at him. "And how dare…"

"Stop." My father's voice rings over ours. "Fighting about something so pointless isn't going to help us figure out the problem. It's just going to cause more."

I take a deep breath. As does Dash.

"And they no longer care about the alcohol."

"Then what are they saying now?"

My father looks over at me and then back to Dash. "They also have photos of you two together."

"What?" we both shout at the same time.

"They have photos of you two kissing out at the track."

"Jesus! Have they been following us? What in the hell do they want?" Dash asks.

"Money," my father responds simply. "They want money. At first, I'm sure they thought that they could get it from you. But now they feel that they have better leverage by bringing my daughter into it."

"Maybe they are lying?" I offer.

ash

"How would they know that?" Dash asks. "That is exactly what we did. I saw you leaving. I brought in the bike and ran to stop you."

"This is why you don't mix business with pleasure," my father mumbles.

Dash ignores him. "I begged you to stay. You did. We made out."

"How would he know that?" I ask. Dash having a day at the track was not big news. Then a thought hits me. "The wreck was on the news. It released his name and everyone who was there. Maybe they are just grasping for straws."

"There was only one other person there who knew that we walked off together," Dash says and I tilt my head in confusion.

"Valerie," my father answers.

"Does she know this kid?" I ask Dash.

"How in the hell would I know?" he snaps, growing angry again.

"How would you not know?" I snap. "You've known her forever. Have you ever heard her mention his name?" The bitch has called every day; she has even been to my parents' house. She had the nerve to show up two days ago, but my father told her that he was in a lot of pain and was sleeping it off.

"How many damn times do I have to tell you...? I don't know every little thing about the bitch." Dash snaps at me.

"Enough," my father roars as the waitress approaches our table. "Come back later," he orders her. She spins around and all but runs off.

"Call their bluff," I suggest.

"That's a stupid idea," Dash fires back.

"Did you just call me stupid?"

He leans back in his seat and chooses to ignore my question, but his narrowed gray eyes say it all. His hard face, tight jaw—Did I stutter look on his face.

"Call their bluff," I repeat, and he snorts.

"We've been hiding out for a week," he shoots back. "Why would we be willing to risk it?"

"Dash is right," my father agrees. "Why would we do that?"

"And why, exactly, are we hiding out?" I ask. This is what I meant by keeping secrets. "That day at the track you told me no more secrets. Why are you still keeping them from me?" I demand.

"Sweet pea…?"

"No, Father," I snap. "Dash is going to be honest with me or he's not gonna have to worry about the world knowing about us 'cause there will be no us." I know my voice sounds hard, but would I really walk away from him? I hope that I won't have to follow through with that threat.

He shakes his head as he looks down at the table with a hard laugh. "You just can't let shit go, can you?"

"Obviously not," I answer.

He looks up from the table and into my eyes. "The brakes were cut from my bike. Someone wanted that bike to go down. That's what I haven't told you."

"What?" I ask in shock. "Are you sure?"

"Of course, I'm sure," my father answers my question.

"But…why?" Who would want to hurt Dash?

"That's what we don't know."

"Do you think it was that kid?" I ask looking over at my dad. "He knew we were there. He says he has pictures…"

He shrugs. "Your guess is as good as ours."

*Dash*

I look down at the table as I realize why we are keeping a secret from the world. If they knew that we were an item, it would not only look bad for my father's company, but it would also make me a target as well. "What do we do?" I ask, feeling defeated.

"Exactly what we've been doing," Dash replies.

I lean back in my chair as my father finally signals for the waitress to return to take our orders. I don't know why, but the fact that Dash wants us to continue being a secret hurts. But I understand his reason behind it. Safety.

## CHAPTER NINETEEN

*Dash*

I sit in Mr. Knight's office once we get home for dinner. Tabatha went straight to her room. I can tell that she's upset about something. I'm just not sure which news I told her tonight has upset her more.

"I have an idea," Mr. Knight says as he sits down at his desk. "But you're not gonna like it."

Figured as much.

"How hard would it be to get close to Valerie?" he asks.

"Not very," I answer in all honesty.

"I figured, considering she showed up here the other day." I nod.

"Why would I want to get close to her again?" I ask, already knowing the answer.

"Because we need to know why she cut the brakes. That part doesn't make sense to me. She was the only other person who was physically there and could have done it. But why? She apparently loves you and wants to be with you. Why would she want to hurt you?"

I laugh. "Valerie is a bitch. She's vindictive and does whatever she can to get her way," I say. "But maybe it was a heat-of-the-moment type of thing." Let's give her the benefit of the doubt for one moment.

"I don't buy that. The brakes were cut so precisely, as if done with a pair of scissors. She knew what she had planned before she even got there."

"But how would she have known that she was gonna get a chance to be alone with the bike?"

He shrugs. "That's what we need to know."

"So, what...? You want me to invite her over here?" I'm skeptical of what exactly he has planned.

He shakes his head. "You're having a party."

I scratch the back of my neck. "That's not a good idea."

"It's our only idea. Get her drunk and question her."

"What if she doesn't fall for it? I mean, she's a fucking bitch, but she's not stupid. I've been ignoring her for weeks. What makes you think that she will tell me anything?"

His chair squeaks as he leans forward, placing his forearms on his desk. He links his hands together and looks at me. "Son, I love my daughter to death. The last thing I want is to see her get hurt." I swallow nervously, wondering where he's headed with this. "But I'm here to tell you that you need to do whatever you can to get this information."

Sex. He wants me to get her drunk and seduce her. "There's no way I..."

"You will."

"I understand that I work for you but..."

"You do!" he interrupts me. "You are the only racer who I have for my motorcycle team as of right now. You could have died. Hell, it cost us thousands of dollars when the bike went down. And it cost you practice time. She is working for someone. And we're gonna do everything we can to find out who."

I let out a long breath. "I get that. But you want me to risk what I have with Tabatha for something that we aren't even a hundred percent sure about?"

"We all take risks," he says simply. I risked my job to be with Tabatha. And now, I'm risking Tabatha for my job. How did this get so fucked-up?

I stand. "This is a risk that could cost me everything."

He leans back in his chair as he stares up at me. "You're right." He nods his head. "It could cost you your life."

# CHAPTER TWENTY

## *Tabatha*

I had to have heard him wrong. "Do what?" I ask Dash as I sit on the end of my bed.

His jaw tightens. "I'm sorry, but your dad has a point. I have to find out what's going on, and Valerie is my best bet."

When he came upstairs, he informed me of the party that my father wants him to have. And how he's supposed to invite Valerie. "So, you want to throw a party and what?" I snap. I stand from the bed and narrow my eyes on him. "You wanna get her drunk?"

"It will help get the information that I need."

My mouth falls open. "I can't believe you're doing this!" I whisper, starting to feel the tightness in my throat. "Just call her up and ask her," I offer in a rush. Please don't go see her.

"That won't work. It's just one night." He places his hand on my shoulder, and I jerk away from him.

"Just one night? A lot can happen in one night, Dash." I cross my arms over my chest. "What if she wants to have sex?" Even asking that question has me wanting to vomit. "Gonna go as far as she wants in order to get what you want?"

He runs his hand through his hair and sighs heavily.

"Oh, my God," I whisper as my heart stops. "You would."

He shakes his head. "You know that I wouldn't do that to us."

"Do I?"

"Yes," he says placing his hands on my face. "I wouldn't do that to us." I want to believe him, but they have a history. A part of him loved her. A part of him was once attracted to her. I'm not an idiot. He'll be drinking, too. He'll have to be. He can't just shove drinks down her throat and ask her a hundred questions without her getting suspicious. No bitch is that stupid.

"Dash…" I whisper, closing my eyes as I feel them start to sting.

"Shh." He interrupts me, and I'm actually thankful. I hate looking so weak. I don't want him to see how much I have fallen for him so quickly. I was so strong just two weeks ago. The girl who climbed his tree and jumped his fence wouldn't stand for this. But that girl was only fueled by hatred; she didn't feel love. How do I get back to that person?

I can't help but sigh in relief when I feel his lips brush mine. I open mine, allowing him to kiss me deeply and passionately. I moan into his mouth as I wrap my arms around his neck.

He pushes me backward and my knees hit the edge of my bed. I feel his hands on the hem of my dress before he pulls away and orders me to lift my arms. My dress falls to the floor, and I kick off my heels. He bends down further to kiss me again now that my heels are gone.

He softly pushes me, and I get the hint. I pull away and slowly make my way on my hands to lie in the middle of the bed. I look up at him just as he slowly removes his shirt.

The intense gaze in his gray eyes causes me to look away from them. Instead, I focus on the way he undresses for me. My heart beats so hard in my chest that I barely hear the sound of the zipper on his pants. Too quickly, he's naked and crawling onto the bed as well. The movement of the muscles in his chest and arms mesmerizes me as he settles on top of me.

*Dash*

"Tabatha?" he questions as he places a hand on my face.

I pull my eyes away from his body and look up at him. "It's gonna be okay," he assures me with a small smile. "I promise. We are going to be okay. I would never do anything to hurt you."

I swallow hard, knowing that promises are made to be broken. In the end, 'promise' is just a word spoken to prevent the inevitable that no one wants to see coming. I promise I love you. I promise you're my everything. I promise not to hurt you. Do you see a pattern? Promise makes you think that you have a chance. A candy-coated word to sweeten the pot.

"You are absolutely beautiful," he whispers before his lips are once again on mine.

*Dash,*

*I understand what you have to do. I hope you understand what I have to do.*

*Tabatha*

I lay the pen down on my desk and turn around. Dash sleeps quietly on my bed. His dark hair is messy and his lips are slightly parted. His naked body is sprawled on his back, and I can't help but feel my heart break. Growing up, my father always told me that we have choices in life that will make you weak or make you stronger. Last night while we made love, I thought he made me weak. The way he touched me, and the way he kissed me. The way he physically loved me was so overwhelming that I could see why Valerie wouldn't let him go.

But afterward, I lay there and realized that he made me stronger. Strong enough to walk away from him. Strong enough to step aside for him to do what needs to be done for him to continue with his dream.

I walk over to my bed and lean down, giving his parted lips one last kiss before I grab my purse...once again leaving him alone and asleep in a bed.

## CHAPTER TWENTY-ONE

I knock another shot of tequila back before I slam it onto my kitchen counter. I wipe the remaining dribble off my chin roughly with the sleeve of my shirt.

"Maybe she didn't mean it?"

I look over at Blake standing beside me. I yank the note out of his hand, wad it up, and turn to toss it in the trash. "She meant it."

"It was kinda vague," he offers. "I mean, that could have meant anything."

"Anything?" I turn to face him. Once again, I had woken up by myself after a night with her. At least this time she left me a fucking note. A note stating she left me. "I think it was pretty clear."

He sighs. "I just think that she needs some time. Things were moving pretty fast with you guys."

"How was that fast?" I mean, we might have feelings for one another, but we haven't even voiced them out loud.

"I'm just trying to help you."

"Then shut the fuck up," I bark.

He reaches for the tequila bottle and pours me another shot. I down it before he can even put the bottle back on the counter. I spin around and walk toward my bedroom as I pull my phone out of my back pocket. Dialing her number, I slam my door shut.

"Tabatha. Call me back as soon as you get this." I pull the phone away from my ear and press end after leaving a message. Of course, it went straight to voicemail. Tabatha

138

has turned off her phone. I'm not surprised. I should have never gone along with this damn party. Even Blake hasn't heard from Jackie. The girls are probably hiding out somewhere, or for all I know, they are out getting drunk themselves. I wonder if she's as drunk as I am. I'm feeling pretty damn bulletproof.

"What?" I snap when I hear a knock on my door. I don't want to listen to any more of Blake's bullshit excuses.

It opens slowly, and I give a satisfied smirk when Valerie peeks her head in. The party has been in full swing for two hours now, but I never doubted for a second that she would show. I knew that she would make an appearance, making sure to show off her only assets.

And she didn't let me down, either. She's wearing a white shirt that is so small it should be on a child. It has a deep V cut that shows off her big fake tits. Her skinny jeans look like they took some work getting into and her red heels top it off with some color. Black eyeliner lines her eyes a little thicker than usual. She looks like a cheap hooker that wouldn't cost me more than fifty dollars. It's sickening, and yet, I still find her somewhat attractive. Or at least my cock does.

"Blake said that you were in here," she declares, still standing outside of my room.

"Come in," I say nicely, and she frowns. I lick my lips, and I barely feel it. The tequila is doing its job. I didn't start drinking for courage to ask Valerie about the bike. I started drinking because of what Tabatha chose to do to us. And I hate to admit how fucking pissed I am at her for that. After everything I've said to her, she still doubted me. That stings.

She closes the door behind her, and I make my way over to her. "Having a party and didn't invite me?" she asks with a lifted dark brow.

I'm not in the mood for games. I place my hand on her chin and slam her backward into the door. She sucks in a deep breath. My next thought is that she's probably getting wet. She always liked rough sex. That's why it was so fun to fuck her. She would let me use her however I wanted. And usually that was like trash. If she only knew that I wasn't role-playing.

"Let's get one thing straight," I say leaning my head down to hers. "You fucked with my bike."

Her eyes widen, and she goes to push me away. I tighten my hand on her chin and her knees buckle. She closes her eyes tightly, and she sucks in a breath.

"I already know that you did it," I growl. "But why? Why would you do it?"

She tries to shake her head, but my grasp on her chin prevents it. "Why?" I scream in her face. The tequila coursing through my veins and the hatred that I feel for her makes me want to hurt her. While it also makes me want to rip that tiny little shirt off and fuck her.

I release her face and take a step back from her. I will do neither of those things. But God, it would feel so good.

"I'm so sorry," she cries. She allows her buckled knees to take her to the floor. She holds her head in her hands and she cries louder.

"Why would you do that?" I demand once again.

She cries loudly for a few seconds, and I roll my shoulders. Calm down, Dash. I need answers. I know how dramatic she can get. I'll get nowhere if we continue this way.

I take a deep breath and run a hand over my face. God, I could use another shot. Her soft sobs get my attention. Leaning down in front of her, I place my hands in her hair and gently lift her head to look up at me. "Tell me, baby," I coo. "Were you just jealous?" I ask smoothing the hair from her tear-streaked face.

She nods and my jaw tightens. I relax it just as quickly, not wanting to show her the madness that I feel. I have to play her. "What were you jealous of?" I ask trying to sound like I truly fucking care.

"Her," she whispers. "Mr. Knight's daughter. I know you like her."

"I don't like her." I love her!

She swallows thickly and licks her plump red lips. Even they look bigger than they used to. "I'm so sorry, Dash. I just wanted to get your attention. I never thought you would get hurt." She hangs her head.

"Thankfully, I didn't," I growl. But I've lost Tabatha because of her stunt. That's right, Dash. She dumped you. You're free to fuck whomever you want. My cock thickens.

"I love you," she whispers. "I know you say that you don't love me anymore, but we were still spending time together and you would call and text me." She pauses. "But after your party, you stopped. I know you were with her that night. I know the calls have stopped because of her."

"How do you know that?" She wasn't there. Was she?

"It doesn't matter," she answers through her tears.

I sigh heavily. What the fuck do I do now? Valerie has proven to be a threatening psychopath if she doesn't get what she wants. And Tabatha has left me.

I sit down on the floor and run a hand through my hair. I close my eyes and my body sways. Thank God, I'm sitting down. My state of drunkenness is getting worse by the second.

Valerie's crying has quieted and I hear the commotion in front of me. "Dash?"

I open my eyes and look up to see Valerie now standing in front of me. She's no longer crying. It's like a faucet she can just turn off. I sit speechless on the floor as she lifts her shirt up over her head. I swallow nervously when she reaches behind her back and unclips the tan bra that was trying to hold in her big tits. The alcohol and my cock remind me how much fun those big bastards were to fuck. To suck on. To come all over.

I shake my head. "I can't." Even my voice sounds pathetic.

She doesn't care what I have to say. That's the thing about an ex. They know exactly what to say, what to do, in order to get what they want. Hell, I was just doing it with her. And now she's doing the same thing to me.

Her hands lower to her skinny jeans and she undoes the button. The sound of the zipper is almost deafening even with the sound of the party in the background. My heart is pounding and the alcohol burns my insides.

She steps out of her jeans, slowly allowing my eyes to enjoy the show. I was always attracted to her body. The soft curve of her hips. The way she would sigh or scream when I fucked her. Everything about her but her actual face could turn me on.

Without thought, I stand and place my hands on her naked hips. My fingers dig into them on their own accord. I push her in the door once again and her breath hitches.

"I want you, Dash. It's been too long." Her hands find their way into my hair.

She pulls my lips down to hers, but at the last second, I let go of her hips. Grabbing both of her hands, I pin them above her head. Her tits press against my chest as she arches her back and whimpers.

I can't do this. I want Tabatha back. How would I prove to her that I'm worthy of her if she hears about this? And she will hear about it. That's only why Valerie is doing it. She already confessed that she thinks I like her.

What would she do if she knew the truth? But Tabatha left me! She doesn't want me.

"Fuck me," she says breathlessly. "Please. Fuck me," she begs, and my cock jerks. I've been drinking; that's what makes me want to fuck her. If I were sober, I could walk away from her—it wouldn't matter if she were naked or fully clothed. It's just the alcohol talking.

"Valerie…"

She leans in and her lips land on mine. My hands tighten around her wrists in anger as I hold them above her head. She gasps into my mouth from the pain. Without thought, my lips close around hers. I don't kiss her; I fucking dominate her—my body roughly pinning her against the door and my hands holding her wrists. My mouth takes hers over. Her hips press into my aching cock. Her body trembles as she moans into my mouth. She's not fighting. She wants me to have my way with her. And the best part is that she isn't bitching. She fully submits her body to me, and that's what I always fucking craved with her.

I could never be this way with Tabatha. She's strong. Even when we have sex, I hold back what I fully want to do with her. I give Tabatha the control. This is where Valerie allows me to be a man. Take what I want, as dirty as I want, and she doesn't judge me. What would Tabatha think of me if I asked to fuck her like a cheap whore? If I wanted to make her weak in order to feel powerful?

Walk away? She's walked away from me twice now. Why not take what's right in front of me?

Making up my mind, I let go of Valerie's wrists and pull away from her. Breathing heavy, I grab her arms and yank her down to her knees. She falls hard and whimpers from the force.

"Show me."

# CHAPTER TWENTY-TWO

# Tabatha

The glow from the neon lights and the alcohol is making me feel pretty fucking good at the moment. But I know that I'll feel like shit tomorrow. I'm only trying to drown out the memory of Dash. I remember the first morning I woke up in bed with him and how I wished I could just remember. Now, I'm just hoping to forget.

I left him! But that was the only option I had left. We had a secret relationship that was bound to fail.

"Another," Jackie yells over the music as she hands me a shot.

I smile over at her before I down it as she ordered. I couldn't ask for a better friend than her. She hasn't even spoke to Blake, or so she says. All I know is that she offered to go to Dash's party and keep an eye on him. I told her that it didn't matter anymore. I needed her here with me more than anything else. Thankfully, she understood that.

I turn around and let my eyes adjust to the flashing lights that cover the dance floor. My body vibrates from the music that shakes the floor underneath my heels.

I hate how unfair life is. I hate that the saying 'money can't buy you happiness' is true. Because I would pay every dime I have to put Dash and me in a bubble where we could live happily ever after. Where no one else can touch what we have.

"Wanna dance?" Jackie asks, placing her hand on my shoulder.

I turn back around to face her. "Not really," I shout over the music.

She throws her bottom lip out in an attempt to pout. "Come on. Let's have some fun. You called me for fun."

"I know." Jackie doesn't agree with what I did. But she's still trying to support my decision.

"Hey, remember that one time when we were eighteen and we bought fake IDs? We snuck into a club. They ended up being over occupancy and the fire department showed up?" She laughs as she recalls our first time at the club. "We accidently gave them our real IDs and they called our parents?"

I laugh along with her. We were grounded from seeing each other for two weeks. But we both got dates out of it. "Those firefighters were hot," I add.

She fans herself. "You're telling me. I lost my virginity to the hunk."

I laugh softly and then the smile drops off my face. "I'm just trying to tell you that we thought that was the end of the world. I don't think we have ever spent that much time texting and talking on the phone. Those two weeks were horrible. But we got through them."

I nod my head in understanding at what she is trying to say. "He loves you," she says leaning over to talk softer into my ear. "He wouldn't do anything to mess that up."

Even though I told him good-bye, I can't help but pray that she's right. Because no matter what has happened, I still love him. And if it came down to it, I would do anything for him.

"So..." she continues, ordering another drink, "tonight we are gonna have one hell of a girls' night and live it up."

# CHAPTER TWENTY-THREE

Dash

I jump off my bike and run up the darkened walkway. Once I get to the door, I bang my fist on it. "Tabatha!" I scream. Nothing. "She has to be here," I say between clenched teeth. "Tabatha!" I scream again.

This can't be happening. She has to be here. I couldn't do it with Valerie. I couldn't fucking do it! She kneeled down before me, ready and willing to suck my cock, and I couldn't even undo my pants for her. Yes, my dick was hard, but she wasn't the one I wanted. She wasn't the one who meant something to me. She had already confessed to the bike. I didn't need to fuck up what I had with Tabatha because I had one night with that bitch. I love her. I want to prove that to her. I want her to see that walking away was a mistake.

I spin around when I hear a car door open. Tabatha stumbles out of the passenger seat. She giggles as she leans over talking to whoever is in it. I swallow thickly. She's drunk. Standing upright, she slams the door shut and watches the car drive off. The moment she turns around, she stops, and the playful smile drops off her face.

"I'm so sorry," I say, making my way back down the steps to her.

She lifts her hand and stumbles, taking a step back from me. "Why are you here?"

"I've been trying to call you. You haven't answered. I need to talk to you."

She shakes her head. "Why? What could you possibly have to say?" Her voice rises. "Finished having fun with

146

Valerie so now you come over to have some fun with me?" she screams.

I grab her by the shoulders to help steady her as I lower my face to hers. "I didn't do anything with Valerie," I growl.

She snorts. "You smell like tequila. You're drunk."

"So are you, princess."

She pulls away from me and shoves me out of her way as she walks up to her front door.

I run a hand through my hair. "Please let me explain."

She stops at her door and spins around. "You didn't sleep with her?"

"No."

"Did she try?" she asks placing her hands on her hips.

"Yes."

Her lips thin and she looks away from me. "Did you kiss her?"

"Yes," I whisper. I can't lie to her. Not this time. I've lied to her before and it almost cost me everything.

"Dash…" she whispers as she drops her head. She shakes her head as she stares down at the ground.

"I'm sorry," I say, walking up to her once again. I place my hands on her face and lift it so she has to look at me. "What I did was a mistake. And I'm here to make it right. I love you." The words fly out of my mouth without thought.

Her eyes narrow at my confession, and she places her hands flat on my chest and shoves me backward. "Don't you dare say that to me!" she screams. "You think you can confess to kissing her and then just tell me that you love me?" she asks in disbelief.

Hurt. Pain. Rejection. Is what makes me respond the way I do. "You're the one who broke up with me. You're the one who left me. I was doing what I was told to do," I yell back. "You were the one who ran when shit got difficult. Don't make me sound like the bad guy."

"The bad guy? You are the bad guy. You kissed your ex. The same ex who is still in love with you."

I stand tall as I look down at her, furious at what she is saying. "She was the one naked and trying to fuck me. And I thought about it. I had every opportunity to fucking do it." Her eyes start to water, and she swallows. "I did kiss her. I could have lied to you about that. I could have not come over here at all. Hell, you look pretty drunk yourself. Dressed like a slut. How do I know that you didn't fuck some random stranger tonight?" She gasps. "What?" I snap. "It's not that hard to believe. You've done it before," I shout, fisting my hands down by my side.

She opens her mouth to speak but closes it quickly. Her body slightly shakes and tears roll down her face. She wraps her arms around herself.

I spin around, giving her my back—not wanting to see the pain that I just caused her. But it's not fair to make me out to be the bad guy. Kissing Valerie was wrong, I admit that, but she had dumped me. I stopped Valerie when my body wanted her. Don't I deserve something for that?

"Dash?" Her voice shakes.

"Don't worry about it," I sigh, not turning back around to look at her. "You were right to walk away." And with that, I walk down the darkened walkway and jump on my bike. I don't even bother to look up at her. Her rejection hurt too much. I told her that I loved her, and she did nothing. She said nothing. She doesn't love me. Not the way I love her. And in all honesty, I should have never come over here.

148

# CHAPTER TWENTY-FOUR

## *Tabatha*

I slam my front door and lean back against it as I hear his bike speeding out of the neighborhood. I place my head in my hands and slide down the door until I sit on the floor. My head pounds. My body is sluggish. What hurts the most is that he was right. After I had a few shots, I loosened up. Jackie and I danced with random men. And it felt good. I allowed them to place their hands on my ass and spin me around the dance floor. I hated the fact that Dash was with Valerie doing God knows what, and I was feeling sorry for myself. I had made a decision, and I needed to grow up and move on. Then he shows up here. He loves me? I didn't even let the words sink in before I went off on him. How could he love me? How could he just have been with her if he truly loved me?

I cry harder. I love him, too, but couldn't say it. What would he have done if I had said that I loved him? He would walk all over me. I don't want that type of relationship. I deserve better. I don't care what he says about me; his racing career will always come first. By throwing that party, he proved that. My father will tell him to jump and he will always ask 'how high'?

But another part of me feels like I should have told him that I loved him. That I hated knowing that he was with her. I was scared and jealous. I'm only trying to protect myself.

I jump when a knock sounds on my door. Spinning around, I open the door, ready and willing to do the apologizing this time.

My heart pounds in my chest when I come face to face with Rodger. "What are you doing here?" My words slur from the alcohol and the anxiety I feel that he's at my front door. His lips lift at the corners in an attempt not to smile. He then walks right past me; he ignores my question and enters the house. My house.

I close the door and turn to face him. His eyes look over my reddened skin from all the drinking and the smeared makeup from crying over Dash. I see his eyes harden. Reaching out, he wraps his hand around my throat. I try to scream, but nothing is coming out as he slams my back into the door. "Stop being a little bitch," he says calmly as I frantically try to pull his hand away from my throat.

I silently plead with him to let go before I lose consciousness. My vision is starting to fade and my legs are getting weak.

He sighs heavily and releases me. My already buckled legs can't hold me up and I drop to the floor. Gasping for breath, I rub my sore neck.

He stands quietly and calmly in front of me as if he wasn't just trying to kill me.

"Are you done?" he asks keeping his voice calm. I look up at him with tears running down my face, and I realize just how pathetic I must look. This is how he prefers his women. Kneeling before him.

He places his hands in the front pocket of his pants, and he stares down at me, waiting for an answer.

I swallow and it causes me to flinch from the pain. "Why are you here?" I ask quietly. My voice is scratchy and unfamiliar.

He frowns. But doesn't offer me an answer. "Come on," he says bending down and taking my hand. "Let's get you cleaned up." He jerks me to stand, and I fumble to get my balance.

"I'm not going anywhere with you." I try to shout, but it sounds more like a squeal.

"You're coming home with me," he says with a smile. Have I lost my mind? Did I trip and fall, causing a head injury of some sort?

"I will not!" I pull my hand out of his.

"Yes, you are." He pauses for a second as he reaches out and gently touches my face. I flinch away, and he just smiles. "It would be a shame if something happened to him."

My heart stops and what little breath I have catches in my throat at the words. "What?" I choke.

"It would be awful for Dash to have another accident. Because you don't want that precious Dash to have another accident, do you?"

I grit my teeth to the point my jaw hurts. Son of a bitch. "What did you say?" I ask, taking a step toward him.

"What would you do for him? To keep him safe?" His words make a chill run up my spine.

"If you hurt him…" I growl.

"I already have," he states simply.

I rush him and land my fist on his jaw. I wanna cry out from the pain it causes to run up my hand, but I hide it. Damn, they make it look easier on TV.

"Fuck," he sneers as he grabs my sore hand and spins me around. He wraps his arms around my shaking body. I'm so mad that I see red. He pins my arms to my chest as he holds onto me tightly.

"That's going to cost you, Tabby." He gives a dark chuckle into my ear. "I look forward to your payment."

"You son of a bitch," I hiss, trying to break free from him, but he's too strong. My throat still burns and my chest heaves. "What did you do to him?" I scream frantically.

*Dash*

"His bike, his brakes," he quips and then pauses. "That was just a warning."

I stop trying to fight him in total shock. "What…? But…That was…"

"Me."

I shake my head quickly and the notion makes me lightheaded. That can't be. Dash told me that Valerie confessed.

"So…" He continues to hold on to me tightly as he whispers into my ear, "What would you give up for him?"

I swallow the lump in my throat. After the way I just treated Dash, he deserves everything from me. I was a total bitch and regret not telling him that I loved him as well.

I close my eyes and a sob wracks my body. "I almost feel sorry for you," he whispers into my ear. "But I have a hard problem feeling sorry for others who put themselves in the situation at hand."

"Stop," I beg as I try to wrap my mind around what is happening. I shouldn't have drank so much. I shake my head as I try to clear it, but it causes my body to sway. I'm actually thankful that he's holding me up. Falling flat on my face would just make me look even more pathetic than he already thinks I am.

"One more time. What would you give up for him?"

I know exactly what he wants, and I hate that he's going to win. I won't allow Rodger to hurt Dash. It's not Dash's fault that Rodger and I have a past. And it's not Dash's fault that he wrecked his bike and could have been severely injured. It's all mine. If I hadn't broken up with Rodger, I would have never gone to Dash's party. It all starts with me.

I hang my head as Rodger continues to hold on to me, and I whisper as I feel my heart break, "Me." I give myself

152

to Rodger because that's what he wants. If I'm with him, he won't hurt Dash.

He continues to hold my back to his front, but he reaches one hand up and runs his knuckles down my face. I close my eyes tightly to try to stop the tears, but another sob wracks my body when he speaks.

"Good girl."

Good girl. I never knew how much two simple words could terrify me. "Please," I beg as my body shakes. I lick my lips and taste the salt from my tears. My body sways from the alcohol that I consumed tonight and my legs feel sluggish.

"Please what, darling?" he asks as he buries his head into my neck. His knuckles run down the side of my face, wiping off the tears. Then I feel it slide down my right thigh. My entire body tenses.

"No. No. No," I say quickly when I feel him lift the hem of my dress.

His lips softly touch my neck. "I just wanna feel how wet you are for me," he declares, and I shake my head.

"I'm not," I say shaking my head quickly.

I try to take in a calming breath. I can't panic with Rodger. That's what he feeds off of. You know this, Tabatha. I need to be strong. I need to fight him. I jump when I feel his hand cup me between my legs. Thank God, I wore panties. "Stop," I demand, and he chuckles into my ear. The sound makes my anger grow over my fear. He only has one hand holding on to me, so I take my hands and lift that arm up to my face. I open up and bite down into this flesh.

"FUCK....!" he screams out, before he yanks his arm out of my hold. I spit out his blood when he places his hands on my back and shoves me forward, causing me to hit my front door face-first.

My body stumbles, and my already drunk self falls to the floor. I look up at him as he bends over holding his arm as he hisses in a breath. I take the second to find my way to my feet and run. I'm that stupid girl. The one who runs upstairs. The one who thinks that a second floor window is my only way of escape. But the thing is that I have more objects to protect myself with up there. That's where my room is. That's where I spend most of my time. I grab the banister and yank myself as I shove off the last step, needing all the help I can get as I pant from exhaustion. My head is yanked back, and I scream as my arms go flying. Before I can fall backward, causing us both to fall down the stairs, he shoves me to the side, causing me to hit the wall. I fall down to my knees on the stairs and brace my face. I taste blood. My blood. And I can barely hold my head up because the room is swaying so much. He jerks my hands away from my face, and I look up at him through heavy lashes.

"You are so fucking pathetic," he growls. "You'll let random men touch all over you but won't give me what I deserve?" he demands.

"You don't deserve me." My voice is weak. Just as weak as my body.

"I don't deserve you? I made you!" he screams.

I throw my head back and laugh. A laugh that makes my entire body shake. It's the first true laugh he's ever given me. I'm sure it makes me look hysterical. "Made me what?" I ask once my laughter starts to die. He stands over me breathing heavy with narrowed eyes. One hand grips the banister, and the other pushes against the wall. "You made me hate you is what you did," I inform him. "I loved you." I start to speak the truth as the nausea sets in. All this throwing me around, and the liquor is about to come up. "I gave you all of me, and you took advantage of it."

He reaches out and slowly caresses my face. I don't pull away, but I flinch from the contact. "I only did what you were afraid to ask."

I gasp. "You think I wanted to be your play thing?" I ask in surprise. Does he truly think this way? "You think I wanted to be treated like crap? Not only did you use my body, but you also fucked with my brain."

"A whore is a whore in all aspects," he says simply, and my mouth drops.

"You sorry son of a bitch," I scream. "You are nothing. Nothing but a piece of shit who uses women."

"You make me sound like I'm the only one who has ever used you." He gives me a cruel smile. "You think he didn't use you?"

"Shut up." I place my hands over my ears. He can't talk about Dash. He doesn't know about what we had.

He leans over and rips my hands from my ears. "I heard the way he used you that first night. How easily you begged him to fuck you. It was disgusting." He spits in my face. "How easily you became a whore for him."

"What?" How would he know what we did? "What are you talking about?" Is he referring to Dash's party?

He rolls his eyes. "Don't act so surprised. Of course, I was there."

I shake my head. "You are one sick bastard," I mumble, yanking my wrists from his grip. "I did. I gave him everything that you wanted." I smile, and his eyes narrow on me. "And I'd do it all again. Maybe even let you watch…"

I feel the sting on the side of my face before my mind can comprehend what he even did. "You really think you can beat me?" he growls as he huffs. "After all I've done for you?" he shouts. "I was fucking nice to you. But now…now, I'm gonna show you what it's really like to be someone's bitch."

155

I turn over onto my stomach and start to climb the last two steps when I feel his hand wrap around my ankle. I try to stand to run, but he pulls on my ankle and it causes me to fall back onto the stairs. I hit my chest hard on the steps, and it momentarily knocks the wind out of me. He grabs my hair and yanks my head back. I still haven't caught my breath enough to even cry out. He shoves my head against the upper step, and I let out a moan of pain as I close my eyes. Maybe it's the alcohol, or maybe it's just the pain, but I can literally feel my skin tear open on my forehead and then the blood running down my face. "Rodger…" The word slips from my swollen lip, and I suck in a deep breath. I don't know what I plan on saying. Maybe beg for my life. But he would just get off on that.

He lays his body on top of mine, and it pushes me uncomfortably into the stairs. Fuck, I need to get us off these stairs. They're gonna kill me. "Say my name again." He breathes heavily into my ear from over my shoulder. "Beg me to forgive you."

"Fuck you, Rodger," I say before I spit blood onto the carpet.

I'm able to take a deep breath as he climbs off me.

He lets out a dark laugh as he grabs my ankle. He twists it to the point I scream out, and I have no choice but to turn on to my back. He yanks me down a few stairs, and I grit my teeth from crying out again as I feel the skin on my back scrape from the carpet on the stairs. I hate the fact that it pulls my dress up, exposing my legs and panties, but that's the least of my worries. He's going to kill me.

"I can play this game all day, sweetheart."

I can't. I already feel lightheaded and nauseous. If I don't stop this now, I'm gonna get sick. And the bastard is twisted enough to drown me in it.

He drops my ankle as he looks down at me with a cocky smile on his face. "You always were fun to play with."

"Go fuck yourself, Rodger," I growl with hatred.

"You always had a filthy mouth," he snarls. I look up at the ceiling and take a deep breath. I use my feet to shove him with all that I have, knowing that by pushing him backward down the stairs, he is gonna take me with him. I'm willing to take that chance.

## CHAPTER TWENTY-FIVE

*Dash*

I slam the door to my parents' house as I enter and look around at all the idiots who are still partying. I shouldn't have come back to the party. I should have gone for a long ride. It helps clear my head, but I've been drinking. And I am the one throwing the party. It would be rude for me to leave my guests.

I walk into my parents' kitchen, and the first thing I see is the back of Jackie's head. Blake's hand is in her blond hair as he kisses her deeply. "Take it to a room," I say loud enough over the music. "There are plenty to choose from," I mumble to myself, looking around the packed house and placing my helmet on the countertop. Some people have already passed out on the floor. A redhead catches my eye as a blond guy lifts her up and places her ass on the kitchen island. He reaches up and grabs her face as he kisses her deeply. It reminds me of the first night I met Tabatha. How hot she was for me. How her body demanded me.

"Back so soon?" Blake asks as he reaches over and pours a shot while Jackie licks her lips and smiles at me.

"What's wrong with you?" she asks, still smiling, and I wanna punch a fucking wall. I despise that look. The look where someone is in love and all giggles. It's annoying as fuck.

"I'm guessing it didn't go that well with Tabatha?" Blake asks.

"Tabatha?" Jackie asks as the smile drops off her face.

"No," I say, sighing heavily. "It did not go how I had planned," I confess, and Blake slides a shot across the countertop toward me.

"What didn't?" she demands.

I look at her and tilt my head to the side. "I poured my heart out to your friend, and she stomped on it. Let me tell you, it feels fucking great!"

Her eyes widen and then she pushes away from Blake. "I gotta go," she yells as she grabs her purse and storms out of the house. Leaving Blake and me staring at each other in confusion.

"Where's Valerie?" I ask when we hear the front door slam shut.

"She left."

"Thank you, God." I throw the shot back and then slide the shot glass across the countertop letting him know that he can make me another one.

"Why? Things went south with Tabatha and you want seconds with Valerie?"

"I didn't fuck her," I growl as I run my hand through my helmet hair. I turned her down for nothing. I could have at least gotten something out of tonight. Too late. I'm not gonna call her begging for it. Then I would look like a foolish idiot in front of two women. Pass on that.

"That's not her story." He tilts his head to the side. "As far as she's concerned, you were amazing," he says in a girly voice throwing his hand over his heart.

I roll my eyes. "Well, it didn't happen."

"I know," he says immediately. "Just letting you know what you have to look forward to."

"Lucky me…" I get interrupted as a male's voice rings out from down the hallway. I look up at Blake with big eyes, and he sighs heavily.

"Yes," he announces, lifting a shot of his own. "My brother has arrived in town. Now you know why Valerie left." Blake's brother is a total dick. Most women hate him; well, the ones who don't seem to fall for his witty comments and shallow gestures. But he has his reasons for being the way that he is. But, then again, don't we all? Love can be an ugly bitch.

A muscular arm lands over my shoulders, causing my already drunk legs to buckle a bit. "It's great to see you, Dash," he says excitedly before he removes his arm and walks over to his brother, Blake. He smiles brightly as he reaches up and rubs his knuckles over his head. Blake cries out like a little baby, and I laugh at him.

"Some things never change," he says, turning to me. "You two idiots throwing parties and I have to show up to tell you how to do it." He reaches for the tequila bottle and throws it back, not even bothering with a shot glass. Jake always showed us up when it came to drinking. We'd wake up hungover the following morning, and he would still be wide-awake throwing them back. "I hear you have woman troubles, Dash." He arches an eyebrow. "That's what happens when you mess with girls." He chuckles to himself. "Although, Valerie doesn't look like a girl anymore." He places his hands on his chest as if to inform me that Valerie now has fake tits.

"Trust me…" I reach over and grab the tequila bottle from his hand. "She's still a little bitch, though." I tilt back the tequila, and he laughs as I take a big shot from it and grimace.

"Dash has fallen in…"

"WHOA!" I interrupt him, pulling the bottle away from my mouth. They both stare at me wide-eyed. I don't care to talk about Tabatha tonight, and that's exactly what Blake was about to bring up. I slam the bottle down on the countertop and give him a fake smile. "How about an old-time drinking game?" I challenge, and without saying a

160

word, Jake walks over to the other side of the kitchen where the redhead and blond guy are still making out. I'm pretty sure he has his hand up her skirt.

Jake ignores them as he reaches up and grabs some shot glasses from the counter. He hands them off to Blake before he grabs more liquor bottles out of the freezer. "Who's ready to get fucked?" he asks knowing that he's gonna drink me and Blake under the table. And that's exactly what I'm in the mood for. As Blake starts to pour the shots, I look over at the entrance to the kitchen as if I expect Tabatha to walk in. I instantly look away and shake my head. Forget her, Dash. It's never gonna happen again.

# CHAPTER TWENTY-SIX

## Tabatha

I lay in a hospital bed as a nurse stands next to me stitching up my face. I have twenty stitches so far in my forehead. When my body finally hit the bottom of the stairs, I could barely move, let alone breathe. I had hit my head on the bottom of the banister, and the fact that he had already taken a few swings at my face didn't help. Rodger was out cold. I was trying to get up from the floor to call the police when my front door swung open. It was Jackie. After dropping me off, she had gone over to Dash's party where she had found out that Dash had come to see me. She came back to see if I was okay. Thank God, she did. She called 911, and I clung to her while we waited for them to arrive. I felt safe with her there as we both sat there and waited for Rodger to wake. Thankfully, he hadn't woken up by the time they arrived and placed him on a stretcher. I admit that I felt proud of myself at that very moment. Until it was ruined two seconds later when I threw up all over a paramedic.

My father was called and the police have shown up at the hospital to get my statement. I expect to be escorted to the county jail the moment I'm finished. I did almost kill my ex. And the fact that the cops are right outside of my room waiting to talk to me has not calmed my nerves.

"All done," the nurse says as she throws some stuff onto a tray and starts to leave. She walks out and the cops walk in. The one on the left has gray hair like my father and a beer belly that could be the results of too many donuts. The one on the right looks to be about my age. His dark brown hair is slicked back, and he has his hands on his hips. "Miss Knight. I am Officer Jones and this is

Officer Thomas. May we ask you some questions?" asks the one who looks to be my age.

I nod. "Yes, sir," I say softly, and he smiles gently at me.

They ask what Rodger was doing there and how long we have been together. I inform them of our breakup and my relationship with Dash. I tell them they can check my phone records and that I have had no contact with Rodger whatsoever. That he is the one who keeps contacting me. I tell them about Dash's wreck, and about how Rodger admitted to it.

"Has he filed a report?" he asks regarding Dash.

I shake my head. "Not that I'm aware of," I say truthfully.

"Go on," he says before he writes a few things in his notebook.

Their eyes get bigger and bigger with every sentence that I speak. I think they considered this a domestic dispute between two lovers, but that was not even close to what it was. I was trying to save my life. I was trying to protect Dash and myself. Even though he hates me. Shouldn't he? I couldn't even tell him what I was feeling. I couldn't even tell him how much I have fallen for him, and I blame Rodger for that. He taught me that people can use that against you, and I didn't want Dash to use me like that. I wanted what we had to be special. Now, it's just ruined.

"Thank you, Miss Knight," the heavyset officer, Thomas, says as he writes down in his little notepad. "After what you have told us, it's clear that it was self-defense."

"You're not going to arrest me?" I ask stupidly.

"No," he says crossing his arms over his chest. "But I do highly suggest that you come down to the station." I frown. "You need to file a restraining order."

*Dash*

"A restraining order? But we go to the same college. How would that work?"

"Ma'am," he says before he licks his lips, "you need to protect yourself. Next time, it could be worse."

"But a restraining order is just a piece of paper," I inform him, and he sighs.

"As true as that might be, it legally protects you. And if he violates that paper, he will see jail time."

## CHAPTER TWENTY-SEVEN

Dash

I wake up with a pounding headache and a sore body. I groan as I roll over, giving my back to the bright light assaulting my sensitive eyes. I lift my hands to my head and grip it tightly trying to quiet the pounding in my ears. "Shit," I hiss as a sharp object digs into my side. I shift and reach to grab it when I feel the coldness of a longneck bottle. Without even opening my eyes, which feel like they are about to pop out of my head, I lift the bottle, unscrew the lid, and take a swig out of it.

My dumb ass almost chokes on it, considering I'm still lying down, so most of it dribbles down the side of my face when I cough it up. "Son...of a...bitch," I try to say through another cough. I put the cap back on it and throw it to the end of the bed before I kick it completely off and onto the floor.

Then I pull my knees up to my chest and cuddle up to them as if I'm an infant. I got my ass handed to me last night just like I knew I would. At one point, I found myself running to the guest bathroom in the hallway. I fell to my knees and hugged the toilet for a good thirty minutes. When I finally got my legs to work, I walked out with squinted eyes. The room spun, and I couldn't seem to stand up straight. I'm pretty sure I saw Jake kissing the redhead in the hallway who was with the blond guy in the kitchen. And Blake was lying face down passed out on the countertop in the kitchen with a bottle of Fireball in one hand and a Corona, his chaser, in the other. It was then when I found myself reaching for his bottle that I knew I needed to give in to defeat. I had lost. I was considerably fucking drunk and alone. So I dragged myself to bed with my tail tucked between my legs like a good little lap dog and passed the fuck out.

That had to have been only a couple of hours ago. I yawn and close my eyes tightly, allowing my body to fall asleep because this is all I plan to do today. I plan to sleep off everything that I drank last night. I just get back to sleep when I hear my bedroom door open and then a loud banging sound as it hits the wall.

"What the fuck...?" I growl as I sit up in bed and open my heavy eyes. The room sways, and I close my eyes for a few seconds to get my bearings straight. I see Blake run into my room. "Get the fuck out, dude. It's too early." God, even my words sound slurred. I reach up and rub some drool from my chin.

He grabs the remote off my nightstand and then plops down on the end of my bed as he turns my TV on. He seems to be moving pretty damn well for a man who was passed out on my parents' countertop just hours ago. I sigh as I fall back down on my bed and place my pillow over my head. He was always that way. He could drink as much as he wanted and still make it to class or work the following morning. Me, not so much.

"What the fuck are you two doing in here?" I hear Jake's voice ask as he enters as well.

"I'm trying to sleep. Go away. Both of you," I mumble. I lick my lips just to see if they're still attached. They feel numb.

I hear Blake flip through the channels and then I hear a woman's voice... "The incident happened sometime last night...Mr. Knight of Knight Racing...Daughter...Tabatha...."

I sit up quickly and throw the pillow to the floor. "What the fuck is she saying?" I demand as I blink to try to get my hazy eyes to focus.

"Didn't you go see Tabatha last night?" Blake demands as he turns to face me.

"Yeah…" My dry throat makes my voice squeak, and I wish I hadn't thrown that bottle off my bed.

"See who?" Jake asks curious as he plops down beside me.

"She fucked him up. There was footage of him being taken out on a stretcher," Blake says in surprise.

"Who? What are you talking about?" I ask, confused as shit. Am I dreaming this? I always have crazy dreams when I drink. I motion for the bottle on the floor like a child who reaches out for a bottle of milk. Jake reaches down and hands it to me without question. I pop the top and take another swig.

"Rodger," he says, and my eyes widen. "He and Tabatha both went to the hospital…"

I frantically start to feel the covers around me as I look for my phone. I have to have one, right?

"What are you looking for?" Jake asks.

"Phone…" Before I can say another word, he throws it in front of me. My eyes are blurry, and it's hard to read what the tiny screen says. I somehow am able to get to the brightness, and I reduce it for my eyes to read it better. When my eyes focus, I see that I have twenty missed calls from Mr. Knight. "Fuck!" I jump out of bed and wobble on legs that feel like jelly as I grab my pants off the floor.

"Where are you going?" Jake asks. "I'm so confused," he admits calmly, and I ignore him.

My fingers frantically work to call Mr. Knight back. I'm in the process of placing my shirt on backward when he answers.

"Dash," he growls. "Meet me at the police station."

"Sir…?" I need water. My tongue feels like sandpaper. "I just…Sorry…"

"Get your ass together," he demands, and I straighten my back as if he can see me, although it doesn't help my limp legs.

"I..."

He doesn't allow me to explain. He can tell I'm fucked. "Rodger admitted to cutting your brakes. The cops need your statement of the incident." What the fuck is happening?

"Tabatha...?" I remember the news mentioning her.

"She's gonna be okay," he says, and I let out a deep breath. "Now get up here to the station." Click.

"Drive me to the station," I order Blake. I don't know what is happening, but she's gonna be okay. That's what is most important.

"Who the fuck is Tabatha?" Jake asks, getting concerned now. "And why are you going to the police station?"

"Why can't you drive?" Blake asks, ignoring his older brother, as he follows me out the bedroom door.

"Because I've already had two shots of whiskey this morning. And I was still drunk when I woke up; I really don't wanna get arrested today."

I walk into the police station not feeling any better. The coffee that Blake stopped and made me drink has not helped my drunkenness, although I do feel like I'm on speed. My hands are jittery, but at least my legs are working. I just wanna find out what in the hell is happening and then go to bed. I plan to stay under my covers for a few days. Of course, Jake had to come along with us. He's as nosy as a chick. I approach a police officer to ask where I need to go when I see the back of Mr. Knight's head. My palms start to sweat when I see that Tabatha is sitting next to him. I didn't think she would be here. Why is she here? He said she was fine. "Come on, man," Blake say giving me a reassuring pat on the back.

I walk toward them and Mr. Knight looks over his shoulder at me. "Dash," he says in welcoming, and I look over just in time to see her body tense from him saying my name.

"Hello, sir," I say and have to clear my throat. God, this is hard. Hard to see her. Hard to be so near her. I hate that I care so much for her. Did he hurt her? If so, how bad?

Mr. Knight stands and places his hands on my shoulders as his black eyes stare down at me. "You look like shit, kid," he whispers, and he starts to straighten my shirt. The same shirt that I partied in last night. The same shirt that I wore as I laid on the bathroom floor after puking up the red shit known as Fireball. I can still taste it in my mouth, and it makes me wanna vomit again. Don't puke on your boss!

Instead, I straighten my back and try to pull myself together. "I apologize. I didn't expect to be speaking to the police this morning," I say through gritted teeth.

He releases me. "Come on." He doesn't even allow me to speak before he starts to pull me back to the front door I just came through. He all but shoves me outside, and I stumble to stand up straight.

"Good God, Erik. Have you even been to bed yet?" he asks judgingly.

I pinch my nose between my fingers as I try to squash this headache. Why is the fucking sun up? "It was a long night," I admit. "And I have no idea what is going on." I release the bridge of my nose and look up at him. "Why is Tabatha here? Why am I here?" I ask squinting my eyes. I need sunglasses. "I saw the news this morning. What happened to her? To Rodger?" With each word I say, I seem to sober up a little. My mind seems to be understanding that this is real life. That some horrible shit went down last night and I'm not gonna like what happened.

"Rodger admitted to cutting your brakes."

His words make me think I'm not sobering at all.

"No. That can't be," I say holding my hand up to him. "Valerie admitted it to me last night at my party." I point a finger at him. "The party you told me to throw in order to get information. And I got exactly what you wanted." My voice starts to rise. "She admitted to fucking with my bike." And I almost fucked her.

"I'm sure she was the one who did it, but she was not the mastermind behind it."

"Why the fuck would Rodger care about my bike?" I ask confused.

"Tabatha." That one word has my anger rising.

"What are you saying?" My hands now tremble for a different reason. Fear. Fear for her. He tried to hurt me because of her. Would he hurt her because of me?

"I'll let her explain that to you," he answers.

I snort and his eyebrows pull together. "That won't happen," I say crossing my arms over my chest.

"Ah," he says after a few awkward seconds. "I see."

"You see what?" I demand.

"You two are fighting. That's why she wouldn't call you to come up here."

I want to yell at him. I want to tell him that because of that stupid party he made me throw that I lost the best thing that has ever happened to me. But he'll argue with that statement. He is my boss, after all. And as far as he knows, I'll risk anything to keep my job. Because that's exactly what I did. I threw a party and invited my ex-girlfriend because that's what my boss told me to do.

I realize what I've been doing wrong, and there's a simple answer. "I quit."

# CHAPTER TWENTY-EIGHT

## Tabatha

I sit in the same spot as when my father left. I didn't want Dash to come up here, but I had overheard my father call him. I knew he was on his way but even that twenty minutes didn't give me any time to prepare myself. Especially after the night that I have had. My ex-boyfriend wanted me to be his personal slave in order to save the man I loved from future harm. And the guy that I want to be my boyfriend told me that he loved me and I turned him down like watering down a flame. It's over. Whatever Dash and I could have had is now over. I can't just tell him I'm sorry and that I love him. Things have changed too much for that. Hell, for all I know, he went back to Valerie last night. Who could blame him for that? I'm sure she had been throwing herself at him. He had even admitted that she had been naked and he kissed her. I know he was hurt from my rejection. Who wouldn't go seek out some love? Even if that love was only physical.

"Tabatha?"

I look over my shoulder to see Blake standing there with a guy who I've never seen standing next to him. "Hey, Blake," I say softly not wanting to aggravate my pounding headache. The pain pills the doctor gave me are starting to wear off.

"Oh, my God," he says as his eyes widen. He walks up to me and kneels down beside my chair. "What in the hell happened to you?" He reaches up and tilts my face to the side to give him a better view of my bruised face. "Did Rodger do this to you?"

"I'm fine," I say, gently pulling away from him. I don't wanna be that girl. The girl who others pity. The girl

172

who others talk about behind her back. How could she allow him to do that to her? I finally stood up for myself, and it felt good.

"Where was Jackie?" he asks frowning. "I thought she was with you?" He starts to look around the busy police station.

I drop my head down and look at my hands in my lap. "I've been trying to call her..." he continues.

"She's here," I inform him. She hasn't left my side since the police left my hospital room. But eventually nature called. "She's in the restroom." Before the words even finish leaving my mouth, he takes off in a mad dash toward the bathroom.

I thank God for allowing me a second of silence. I need to think of what I'll say to Dash, if anything. Maybe he will make it easy on me and just ignore me. I would ignore me.

The seat that my father was occupying next to me is pulled back and I see a person fall into it from out of the corner of my eye. "I...." I pause when I see it's not my father. Soft blue eyes look deeply into mine. A sharp jaw twitches as his eyes stray from mine and seek out the stitches on my face and then the cut on my lip. "Excuse you?" I ask cautiously. The police officer had said that I needed to talk to a detective; maybe this is the guy.

"Hi. Tabatha, is it?" He reaches out his right hand. "Jake."

I sigh heavily. "Are you the detective?" I ask not bothering to shake his hand. I'm really not in the mood for courtesy. They keep asking me if I'm comfortable, and I wanna stab them with a pen and scream that no I'm not. But that would probably get me locked up in a padded room and then Rodger would win. And I continue to tell myself that won't happen. I didn't get my ass kicked last night to give up this morning.

"No," he says slowly.

"Unless you're a police officer, I don't wanna talk to you," I say looking away from him.

He chuckles to himself. "I knew I should have gone into the force."

I turn back to look at him. Is he flirting? "Who are you?" I ask letting curiosity get the best of me. He did know my name.

He's pretty. The type of guy who looks too pretty, yet he looks like he's a mess at the same time. His dark gray shirt fits tightly showing off his hard chest and muscular arms. His big hands sit on his thighs as his legs hang loosely open as if he has this fuck off nature about him. The type of person I used to be. I wish I could find that Tabatha again. The last time I allowed her to come out, I had a one-night stand with Dash. Look how well that turned out.

"Jake," he says again. "I'm Blake's big brother."

"Jake and Blake?" I mumble to myself, but he hears me.

He laughs once again. "Our parents weren't all that creative."

"I didn't know he had a big brother," I say truthfully. He goes to speak, but I beat him to it. "I'm seriously not in the best of moods. I really just need to be alone right now." Before he can respond, I get up and walk away from him. I make my way to the front doors, wanting some fresh air, but see my father and Dash standing on the other side of them. Dash's hands fly around in the air as he speaks quickly, and my father hangs his head as if he's trying to calm his anger.

I spin around and walk away quickly, not wanting them to see me. I don't want to explain things to Dash. The wounds he has caused me hurt more than the cuts on my face that required stitches.

I walk until I find a quiet hallway. A bench sits up against the far wall. I plop down on it and place my head in my hands. I take a deep breath and close my eyes. Do you ever think back and regret every decision you have ever made? Do you regret the person that you allowed yourself to fall in love with? I regret that I ever allowed myself to feel anything for Rodger. He wasn't the right kind of guy for me. I also regret that I ever got in bed with Dash. He is not the type of guy who settles down. Hell, he kissed Valerie, and then twenty minutes later, he told me that he loved me. Who does that? A man who doesn't know what he wants, that's who. A man who is keeping his options open.

"Tabatha."

My head shoots up, and I stand quickly when I hear my name called by the last man that I want to see. Rodger's father stands before me in his perfect black suit and red tie. Just looking at him, you can tell he's wealthy. From the smell of his expensive aftershave and the way his dark eyes stare at you. They always unnerved me. It's like they are looking into your soul. As if they are trying to suck the life out of you. It's sad, really; if you were to just see him passing on the streets, then you would think that he is good looking. His square jaw is mouthwatering and intimidating at the same time.

"What are you doing here?" My words come out in a rush, and he smiles at me, as if he can hear the concern in my voice. I straighten my shoulders and take in a deep breath and the smile drops off his face. He hates when women show any kind of power. Or any kind of happiness, for that matter.

He places his hands in the front pockets of his black dress pants, and it causes his chest to bow out even more. "I came to bond my son out of jail." If he's angry with Rodger, his voice doesn't show it. Rodger had woken in the hospital and only had minor injuries. He was taken in, but obviously, he won't be staying long.

"And what? You want to me apologize?" I say placing a hand on my hip.

"I…"

"You're wasting your breath with me." I interrupt him, and his eyes narrow on me. No woman interrupts him. "I won't give him shit." By the time I finish saying those five words, I'm breathing heavy. My heart is racing, and my hands are sweaty.

"Are you finished?" his deep voice demands. I just nod. I've already said too much. "I was going to tell you that you will not have to worry about Rodger anymore."

"I won't?" I ask with surprise.

"No. He has embarrassed me and our family enough over something that's not worth his time." He wrinkles his nose as he looks me up and down. I know I look like a mess. I have yet to shower. I probably still smell like the club along with the sweaty men I danced with and then my fighting with Rodger. I look absolutely awful and feel just as bad.

"Not worth his time?" I ask taking a step toward him. He makes no move but looks down at me as if I'm a bug he wants to smash under his shiny black shoes. "Maybe he's not worth my time. Maybe if he would have left me alone like I told him to do, then he wouldn't have been arrested," I shoot back, finding my anger. I lift my right hand and shove my finger into his chest. "You treat that man as if he can walk all over women. And I assure you that I'm not the one for him to fuck with."

Once I realize what I just did, my body wants to cower to him. To take a step back and crawl under the bench I was sitting on, but I don't. I stand tall. I'm tired of men making me want to be someone who I'm not. My father raised me to be a powerful woman and to know right from wrong. And what the men in his family do is wrong.

He stands tall with his hands still in his pants pocket. His eyes fall from mine and they look down my exposed legs that this short dress puts on show. Then his eyes lift up to my messy hair. I have the urgency to run. I hate the way he looks at women. As if he's waiting for them to serve him dinner and then lie flat on their backs waiting for him to service them.

"It's a shame, really," he says with a sigh. "My son had no idea what he had." He pulls his left hand out of his pocket and reaches up grabbing a lock of my hair. I hold my breath in true fear. He leans down and whispers into my ear, "I could break you. Easily. The confidence that you think you have is nothing but your fear. But I'm in no mood to do my son's dirty work." He pulls back, and I stare at him with big eyes. "My son is arrogant and immature. But he will learn. I was right when I told him to walk away from you. That you would destroy him. You were a good learning experience for him, and I appreciate that." He actually gives me a smile. "I give you my word. You will not have to worry about him ever again."

"Your word?" I breathe. "Why should I trust your word?"

His smile widens. "Because my word is the truth."

Arrogant son of a bitch. He then turns around and walks away. Just like that.

I fall on my bench once again and close my eyes as I fist my sweaty hands in my lap. Although that man scares me, I know that what he just said is true. I will never have to worry about Rodger again. That's one problem dealt with. But I still have Dash...

I hear a pair of shoes coming down the hall this time, and I open my eyes to see the devil himself as he comes to stand in front of me. He looks as bad as I do. And I hate how much it makes me feel for him. His long, shaggy hair is messy and standing every which way. His gray eyes are red and puffy. His beautiful lips are frowning. He actually looks sad. As if he regrets something. As if he made a mistake. Well, get in line, buddy. He might regret kissing Valerie, but I regret ever sleeping with him. I regret that he made me fall for him. I regret that I wasn't strong enough to walk away when I saw him in my father's house the morning after I slept with him. He was a stranger.

His face starts to harden, and his gray eyes narrow as they search my face. He looks at me as if he just realizes what my night has consisted of. A physical fight with Rodger. Whereas, I'm sure he got drunk and laid.

I actually throw my head back and laugh out loud. I laugh so hard my body shakes, and it feels good. I lift my head and look up at him as he stares at me with those beautiful gray eyes. They look hard as I watch his eyes follow the line of the stitches that are on my face once again.

I throw my hand up as I continue to laugh. He frowns when I snort, and it makes me laugh even harder. "Sorry…" I try to calm my laughter; it makes my aching body hurt, but it feels so good to laugh. "But this is just too comical."

"Your ex-boyfriend beating the shit out of you is funny?" he questions. "I don't see how that can be funny."

My laughter dies immediately. Instead of standing, I lean back against the bench and cross one leg over the other. His eyes quickly scan my bare legs, and I feel my body heat start to rise. No! Don't go there, Tabatha. You regret ever sleeping with him, remember? "No, the fact that you keep showing up is what I think is funny. The fact that you think I wanna talk to you is funny." Oh, good one. Make him buy it.

"You wanna talk about funny?" he asks raising his voice. "I have woken up to you running away. Not only once, but twice. What the hell is your problem?" I take a deep breath that makes my chest rise. Is he really gonna do this? "And why was Rodger there after I happen to leave?" Oh, he's going all the way. "Huh? Did you call him to tell him how bad I hurt you?" My mouth drops open. "Did you ask him to come over and kiss your wounds?" he shouts.

I stand and shove my hands into his chest pushing him backward. "Don't you dare accuse me of something you know nothing about," I shout back. "You were the one who had just been drunk and with your ex moments before. And you kissed her." I do air quotes around kissed. "Who knows what else you did with her."

"I was just doing what your father told me to do. Get information," he says matter-of-fact with a wave of his hand.

"Oh? And he told you to stick your tongue down her throat?" I demand.

"No. His exact words were to do whatever I had to do in order to get the information that we needed."

"Lies." I spin around giving him back for a second before I turn back to face him with my hands clenched down at my sides. "All you do is lie," I yell.

"And all you do is run away," he sneers in my face. "Not all of us are as heartless as you and can just turn our backs on others at any given moment."

I feel the tears start to sting my eyes, and I blink them away. He truly hates me now, but this is not the time to fall apart. After everything I've been through tonight, I can keep it together for just a little longer. I swallow the knot in my throat and lick my dry lips. "Well, you made it pretty damn easy," I lie. He hasn't made anything about us easy. It's so damn hard to stand here and be a bitch to him. My legs are tired, and I would give anything for him to pick me up and hold me in his arms. But that ship has sailed. "But I sure as hell can't stand the fact that you keep coming around." Stay strong, Tabatha. Don't apologize; you can't take those words back now no matter how big of a lie it was.

I expect him to yell in my face for what I said. For him to shoot the hurtful words right back. But instead, his hard eyes look me up and down, and he snorts as he shakes his head. That hurts worse than any words could. He looked at me as if I was nothing.

He runs his hand through his shaggy brown hair and speaks. "Well, I'll make something else easier for you. I quit."

I look down the hall and spot my father, and he hangs his head. I know immediately what he means. He quit the team. "Dash...?" I reach out for him, but he pushes me away and walks off.

He has to push his way through my father, Blake and his brother, and two police officers as they stand there staring at us. Who knew we had an audience?

"Dash? Man..." Blake calls out after him before he takes off to follow him.

I straighten my shoulders and push down my short dress as I avoid their eyes. As I try to walk away with some dignity left. Which, let's face it, I have none.

"Sweet pea..." my father starts in on me.

I raise my hand to stop him. "Please save the lecture for later, Daddy," I ask, still trying to hold in my tears. "I just wanna go home." I look over at the officer who looks surprised by my fight with Dash. "Am I done here?"

"Yes, ma'am," he says with a head nod, and I don't wait. I walk through the hallway to the front doors and shove them open. I take the front steps two at a time and almost fall flat on my face once I realize I'm still in heels. I stop in the parking lot remembering I didn't drive. "Shit," I curse out loud. I reach into my clutch to call Jackie, but

180

she comes running out the front door of the police station and rushes down the stairs. "Sorry," she says, as she passes me. "Come on. I'll take you home."

I shake my head quickly. "No." I sniff and quickly brush the tears from my face. "I don't wanna go there." I don't wanna be in that house alone.

"Wanna come stay with me?" she asks with a small smile.

"Thanks, but will you take me to my parents' house?" I question, wrapping my arms around myself. I can lock myself in my room and be left alone there, but not really be alone. If that makes sense.

She nods her head and continues to walk to her car.

I thank her as we pull up to my parents' house and I make my way into the house. I shut the door quietly and walk down the long hallway that passes my father's office. Then up the stairs before walking into my bedroom. I shut the door. I kick off my heels and leave them where they fall to the floor. I continue to walk through my bedroom and into my attached bathroom as I reach down and grab the hem of my dress. I rip it off and hiss in a breath as I get an ache in my side. I avoid the mirror as I turn on the bathtub and pour some bubbles into it. I remove my panties and bra and then place my hair up in a high clippie to get it out of my way. I get into the tub and very slowly lower my body into the hot water. I close my eyes and allow myself to relax, even though my back stings from the carpet burn I got. Today could have been very different if I had given in to Rodger. I don't know what he and I would be doing right now, but I do know that it wasn't all bad. He wasn't always bossing me around. There were times that he was very sweet. But there were just times where he would just give me this look, as if he was about to lay his hands on me. I had never been in that type of relationship before, and it was terrifying. Therefore, I did whatever he wanted me to do.

I sigh heavily as I lower more of my body into the scalding water and try to clear my head. I don't wanna think about Rodger. As scary as his father is, I believed him when he said I had seen the last of Rodger. Their family hates defeat and the fact that he got himself arrested is just unacceptable. Plus, it was all over the news. I had seen the headlines on the news when I was in the hospital. Public humiliation is another thing he can check off because of me.

I place my hands in the water, pushing away the bubbles to cup some water in my hands. I splash my face with it and then my hands drop to the water again. I really don't wanna think about Dash either, but what he said keeps going through my mind. I was just doing what I was told. I don't believe that. Why should I? He's lied several times to me now, and I hate to be taken advantage of. I refuse to be that woman who is with a man and is blind to everything he is doing wrong when the rest of the town knows. If he had been honest and upfront about what was going on, then maybe this could be something that we could work through. But even thinking that sounds crazy.

Then he told me he quit. He quit his dream because of me. God, that makes me feel fucking low. Has anyone ever given up a dream for you? It hurts to know that you took something from someone that they wanted before you were ever even in their life. Now I'll never see him again. A part of me was thankful that I would still see Dash at the races and around my parents' house every now and then. Now, he's gone for good.

I sigh heavily as I close my eyes tightly and wrap my arms around myself. My life is officially over. I filed a restraining order tonight up at the police station, which I think means that I can't go to school Tuesday. I doubt Rodger will be there, but I sure as hell don't even want to risk it. I feel like my life has officially taken a turn for the worse.

I jump back and water splashes over the side of the tub and onto the tile of the floor when my bathroom door comes flying open.

"Oh, my God," my mother says dramatically as she comes tearing into my bathroom. She falls to her knees by my tub as her hands reach out and grab the side of my head. She kneels in a puddle of water in her three thousand dollar suit.

"Mom," I say breathlessly, trying to calm my racing heartbeat. "You just scared the shit out of me," I say as my chest rises and falls quickly. "What are you doing here?" I ask trying to cover my chest.

Her brown brows pull together and her beautiful lips turn down into a pout. "Why wouldn't I be here?" she questions softly. "Your father called me when he was on the way to meet you at the hospital. I told him to send me the jet."

I drop my eyes to what's left of my bubbles in my water, which I lost half of when I shifted so quickly. "You shouldn't have come home, Mom. I'm okay."

"Bunny…" She calls me by my childhood nickname, which tells me just how upset she truly is. "How can you say that?" She removes her hand from the side of my head and gently runs her fingertip over the stitches placed above my eyebrow. I flinch even though it didn't hurt.

She leans back on her heels and lowers her hands to her lap. "I just don't understand," she says softly. "I thought you were happy with him? Was he…Had he been hurting you this entire time?" Her bottom lip starts to tremble, and I hate that my mom and I aren't closer. I love her to death, but I have always been a daddy's girl. Mainly because my mother was always the one to tell me that I couldn't do something. My father only knew the word yes.

183

"No," I lie, and she lets out a long breath as if she doesn't believe me. "It wasn't all bad," I try to reassure her. "I…we…" I shake my head. "I think he only hurt me because of Dash," I say, trying to explain it to her without telling her too much about my and Rodger's relationship. But Dash, I'll tell her everything about him.

"Your father filled me in on him as well. And I think we need to talk about him also," she says, straightening her back and hardening her beautiful features. She's giving me her business face. And I understand why. Dash rides for my father. Well, did. I just cost them their prized racer.

She stands, and I can't help but laugh at the water that drenches her pants from where she kneeled in it on my floor. She looks down and lets out a little laugh, too. "Finish up in here and then come down to talk to me." She leans over and gives me a soft kiss on my temple then turns and walks out, closing the door behind her.

I close my eyes and take a deep breath before I place my face under the water.

After finishing up, I got dressed in a pair of comfy shorts and a tank top. I make my way down the stairs and into the long hallway. I peek into my father's office to see if he's in there, but it's empty. I continue down the hallway and hear my mother in the kitchen. I walk in and sit down at the table when she turns around and sees me. She smiles as she walks over and sets down a cup. I look down into it, and it looks nothing like coffee. I frown.

"It's wine," she says, sitting down across from me with a cup of her own.

"In a coffee cup?" I ask.

She shrugs. "We don't have a wine glass big enough to accommodate the kind of day you have had," she says simply, and I agree with her. No amount of wine could fix what happened last night.

"Where's Dad?" I ask as I lift the cup and take a sip.

"The police station."

"Why?"

She sets her cup down and leans back in her chair getting comfortable. "He's still up there with Erik. Guess he had to give a statement and is pressing charges against Rodger. And your father informed me that he had some begging to do." I guess she means my father needing to get Dash back on the team.

It's so weird to hear my mom call him Erik. As if she's talking about someone I don't know. But how well do I really know Dash?

"Tabatha?"

I look back up at her and she gives me a soft smile. "You love him." It's not a question.

"I don't know him." I tell her how I feel.

"You don't need to know someone to love them," she says with a shrug. "I loved your father before I knew him."

"That sounds crazy when you say it like that." How can you love someone you don't know?

"I met your father at a young age," she starts. "He was so attractive," she says with a smile, and it causes me to smile. It's crazy how much they love one another after all this time. Yes, they are both very busy with their careers and everyday life, but they always make time for one another.

I wrap my hand around the cool coffee cup and speak. "What you speak of is lust. Not love, mother."

She tilts to her head in confusion "How so?"

185

"You don't just fall in love with someone by the way they look." I roll my eyes.

She chuckles. "I agree. He may have been attractive, but that wasn't why I fell in love with him."

"But you said…"

"I fell in love with him because of the way he made me feel. Not my feelings toward him, but my feelings toward myself. I lit up when he walked into a room. I had a smile on my face that wouldn't go away. My skin would tingle whenever he would look at me." Her eyes drop to the cut on my lip, and I lick it nervously. Her eyes meet mine once again, and she continues. "I loved myself first. I fell in love with the person who I was when he was around. And in loving myself, I fell in love with him."

"I wish it was that easy," I say, and she sits quietly, waiting for me to fill her in. "I fell for Rodger fast and look where that got me?" I chuckle to myself, but she stays quiet.

"You have a big heart."

"No, I'm just stupid."

"Don't be so hard on yourself."

"Mom…" I throw my hands out to my side. "Rodger was an awful person, and I didn't even see it until it was too late."

"I hate that he hurt you." She reaches up and wipes a single tear from her cheek. "But you fought to get away. You know what you deserve and you're not gonna settle for less. This Erik boy… maybe he is the one."

"How is Dash any better than Rodger?" I question. "He has lied to me, Mom. More than once. I can't trust him."

"Maybe he can't trust himself," she offers.

"What does that even mean?" I ask placing my elbow on the table and dropping my head into my hand. I'm starting to get a headache, and I'm exhausted.

I hear the legs of her chair scoot across the tile floor and her heels clink as she walks into the kitchen. I still have my head down and stare at the table when she returns to my side. She places the pill bottles in front of me and runs her hand over the back of my hair. "It means that maybe he doesn't trust the person you make him want to be. People experience love in different ways, baby. Rodger changed you," she declares, and I look up to her as she stands beside me, "in a way where you lost yourself. I can see it now. I didn't before." She frowns. "And that's my fault. I wasn't looking close enough. And I apologize." She never saw it because he kept me from them. And I allowed that. It's my fault, not hers. "Maybe Erik doesn't understand what you make him feel." She leans down and kisses my hair. "Give love a chance. It doesn't matter if your heart breaks a hundred times. You'll eventually open your heart to that one person who makes all that pain go away. It'll be that one love that's worth it." She takes the coffee cup that is filled with wine from me and pushes the pill bottle closer to me. "Take this antibiotic and this pain pill. They help more than wine."

## CHAPTER TWENTY-NINE

*Dash*

We pull up to my parents' house, and I growl. Cars are parked everywhere. I forgot that I had left the afternoon after my party to go to the police station. Of course, these drunk asses are still here passed out. "Fuck," I hiss as I get out of Jake's truck. He insisted on driving us, and I wasn't gonna argue with him 'cause I sure as hell couldn't drive. He might have drank the most out of the three of us, but he looked the most sober.

"What's wrong?" he asks, getting out of his driver's seat.

"I forgot all these people were here." I sigh. Some have already left but there are still cars here, informing me that some are still passed out from last night. "I'm in no mood to fuck with them at the moment."

"I'll take care of them," he says simply.

"Thanks," I say, walking up the stairs. I frown at the two people passed out on the front porch swing.

The moment we walk into the house, Jake starts yelling that the party is over and for everyone to get the fuck out. I ignore the grunts and moans from the drunks and make my way to the kitchen. I open the fridge and grab a bottle of water. I have almost half of it down when Blake and Jake walk into the kitchen. They both stand there staring at me.

"What?" I demand.

"You quit," Blake says, and I roll my eyes.

"It was my only option." And I really don't feel that bad about the decision I made, even if I didn't really think it through.

"You finally got your dream, and you quit because of a girl?" Jake questions.

I point a finger at him. "Shut the fuck up, Jake. I'm not in the mood to listen to your opinion. You have no idea what has been going on here."

He shrugs carelessly. "It's not hard to see. You fell in love with a girl. And then you fucked it up."

"I made a mistake," I yell, slamming my water down. "I allowed my dream to fuck up something bigger." I hang my head, and I take a few deep breaths. "I thought I could handle them both," I say truthfully. "I thought that I could race for Knight Racing and still be with Tabatha." I look back up at them. "And look where it got us. You think I care that I quit the team? The racing isn't what is important anymore. She is. I would have given it up at any time for her, and now I've lost her completely." I shake my head. "And that motherfucker, Rodger, hurt her." I squeeze the water bottle to the point where what's left comes pouring out of the top and onto the counter. "I was too busy being fucking pissed at her for not feeling the same when he attacked her. He's fucking never gonna leave her alone." I truly believe that. He has proven to me more than once that he's never going to go away. He wants her, and he's going to do everything he can to take care of her. He just strikes me as that guy who thinks if I can't have her, no one can. Sick twisted fuck!

The way her bruised and stitched face looked. She looked so broken—so not herself. And that's what made me so mad. That was why I yelled at her in front of everyone. I should have taken her in my arms and held her. I should have apologized and told her that I was there for her. Instead, I did more harm than good.

I grab my keys off the countertop and start to walk away. "Where you going now?" Blake asks.

"To take care of business," I throw over my shoulder.

The first time I ever found myself in jail, I was fourteen. Blake and I had decided we wanted to go for a joyride in my father's favorite car. Blake was over one day, and my parents were gone, like always. So we grabbed the keys and took it out. I knew how to drive, or so I thought. Try controlling a fast as shit car when you go around a corner. I ended up flipping the car; thankfully, we were both wearing seat belts. So when it finished rolling, we both crawled out with minor injuries. Then we ran as it started to burn to the ground. The cops came to our house and arrested us and called Blake's parents.

I laugh out loud as I remember that day. It seems like so long ago. So much for not wanting to get arrested today.

"Why are you laughing?" Jake asks as he sits on the bench next to me.

"I was just thinking how some things never change," I say with a smile as I fist my sore knuckles.

"And what times would those be?" Blake asks as he sits on the other bench across from us.

"The first time we got arrested," I say.

He chuckles to himself. "At least this one was worth it," he adds, and I have to agree.

When I walked out of the house a few hours ago, I knew exactly what I was going to do. I was going to beat the shit out of Rodger. Thanks to Google and social media, it wasn't hard to find his location. The guy checks into his own home. Little did I know that Blake and Jake were following behind me. Once I found his place and got off my bike, they pulled in behind me. I told them to stay out of it. I wasn't a coward. I was gonna fight him on my own. One on one. They stayed back as I asked, but that didn't stop the cops from arresting all three of us and now we are back at the police station. And although I am very much sobered up, I still have a pounding headache.

"What do you think this does to the charges you pressed against him?" Jake asks.

I shrug. "I don't care." He got what he deserved, and I'd do it again. The bastard deserves to die for laying his hands on Tabatha. How could anyone want to hurt her? I know he did; but I don't care how mad I get at her, I would never lay my hands on her.

"Hey?" Blake turns around to face the police officer sitting at his desk. "Where's our one phone call?" he demands, and the cop completely ignores him.

"Take it easy," I say stretching my sore neck from side to side. "We've only been in here for like an hour."

Jake sighs. "You two are a bad influence. I just wanted to drink."

We all laugh. We hear a phone ring, and we all look over at the cop who sits behind his desk. He picks it up and nods his head a few time. "Yes, sir," he says before he hangs up.

He stands quickly as he rattles his keys in his hands. He comes over to the bars and unlocks them. "You two are free to go," he says pointing to Jake and Blake.

They both turn to look at me as if I need them to stay and hold my hands. "Go ahead." I nod to the door.

They quietly stand and walk out and the cop goes back to his desk and sits down. I frown as to why he left the door to the cell open.

I look down to my bloodied hands resting on my jeans. I knocked him around pretty good. I even saw a tooth fly at one point. I wasn't a complete asshole. I allowed him to get in a couple of punches on me. I let him build up his ego when he thought he was gonna kick my ass, and then I let him down slowly when I knocked him to the ground.

"You think you can treat her like trash?" I yell as my right fist connects with his jaw. He stumbles back, and his arm knocks over a lamp. "Answer me," I demand, before I land a punch to his gut.

He falls to his knees as he wraps his hands around his waist. "You're no better than me," he says as he spits blood onto his white carpet. "And she knows it."

I kick him in the face and watch as his head snaps back. He rolls over onto his side as he cries, sobbing like a fucking child as he holds his face. "I'm nothing like you," I spit out.

He rolls over onto his back and looks up at me. Blood runs down the side of his face. "I know you used her for your own satisfaction. Don't make it sound I'm the only one who fucked her over."

I let out a laugh as I tighten my fist down to my side. "You fucked her. And I...I love her."

He laughs and it causes him to cough and then moan at the pain. "You wouldn't be saying that if you had seen her at the bar earlier that night."

He swallows. "All the men who were dancing up on her..."

"You followed her?" I demand.

"Of course, I did." He places his hands on his chest as he takes in a deep breath. "I'll never let her go."

Just what I thought. I take a step toward him. "That's why I'm here," I say with a smile right before I straddle him and let my hands go to work on his face.

I couldn't stop beating the shit out of him. He fought for a while and then he ended up just lying there unconscious as I pounded my fists into him over and over again. The guys finally had to pull me off him. And, of course, the police showed up. But I was expecting that since I had tripped his alarm system when I knocked down his front door. I was actually surprised at how badly he already looked from Tabatha. I smile, proud of her. Finally standing up for herself.

"So…" I stand from the bench when I hear a familiar man's voice. "It's like déjà vu," Mr. Knight says as he walks right into the cell.

"You don't seem surprised to find me in here," I say casually.

"I'm not." He unbuttons the top button of his suit jacket and sits down on the bench across from me. "I had a feeling you would do something stupid."

I arch an eyebrow. "Beating the shit out of your daughter's ex is stupid? The bastard deserved to die for what he did to her."

"I agree," he says without hesitation. "That was why I knew you would do what you did. But I hate to tell you; I just came from the hospital, and he isn't going to die."

"Shame. I knew I should have hit him some more," I mumble.

"Then you would be spending your life in prison, son. For murder."

I drop my head to look at the bloodstain on my hands. "You're saying you wouldn't kill for your wife?" I ask as I look up at him.

He takes a deep breath and rubs his hand over his chin. He bends over placing him elbows on his knees. "I would. But…"

"But nothing," I interrupt him. "Quit trying to make me think that what I did was wrong. I did what I did because I love Tabatha, and he deserved every bit of it. If he would have died…" I shrug. "Then I would be going to prison. That's a small price to pay for love. Don't you think?"

"You love her?" he questions as if he's surprised.

I fall back down on the bench and sigh. "More than anything."

He runs his hand down his shaved face as he looks at me with an expressionless face.

I sigh. "Why are you here? I quit."

"I remember that very well. Considering that was only hours ago." He sits up straight and runs his palms down his pants. "I got the call that you had been brought in. And here I am." He reaches his hands out to his side. "And now you're free to go." He stands.

"That's it?" I ask as I stand as well. "I almost beat a man to death, and I just get to go?" I ask, totally confused. I was prepared to do my time.

"I told you once, son. I have pull in this town." He places his arms over his chest. "But it's going to cost you."

I hang my head. "Why didn't I see this coming?" I mumble to myself.

"When I hired you to race for me, I knew you would be a pain in my ass, but I knew you would be worth it. What I didn't expect was for you to be a quitter."

I open my mouth to speak, but he holds him hand up to quiet me. "You're free to go. But I expect to see you showered and wearing freshly washed clothes next time I see you."

"And that is?" I question with a heavy sigh. The least I can do is show up for a man who is keeping me out of prison.

"In two days." He looks me up and down. "I'm going to give you a couple of days to rest and get your shit together. Then you will be ready to get back to work. Do you understand me?"

"But I…"

"Do you understand?" He asks again.

I nod. "Yes, sir."

He then spins around before walking out of my cell.

I'm not sure if it's the fact that I just beat the shit out of Rodger, or that I just got my racing job back, but I walk out the cell with my head held high and a fuck you smile on my face.

# CHAPTER THIRTY

# Tabatha

I sit in a lawn chair as I soak up a beautiful day on the beach. It's been three days since Dash, Blake, and Jake were arrested for going over to Rodger's house, and I still can't believe it.

"I don't know what you expected," Jackie says from beside me as she sits in her lawn chair while she watches the waves wash up on the beach.

"Well, I sure as hell didn't expect him to go and beat up Rodger." I have to say I was shocked at first, but then the shock wore off and I couldn't help but laugh at the situation. I never in a million years thought that he would go and stand up for me.

"Plus..." she adds. "Blake spoke to him this morning, and I guess he's back racing for your father now. You're going to be seeing him all the time." She gives me one of her evil smiles, and she even laughs.

I look straight ahead through my sunglasses as I watch the waves come in, crashing into the shore. I wish they would just carry me out to sea with them. "Maybe I should move," I offer, thinking out loud. New scenery could be nice.

Her head snaps over to look at me. "Move? Because of a man? You're kidding, right?" she asks. "Since when do you let a man get to you like this?"

I shrug. "Because of two men. I could transfer schools." I can't just up and quit school. But I also don't want the possibility of running into Rodger. I have a restraining order against him and shit could get ugly. Hell, his father told me not to worry about him, but that was before Dash broke into his house and got a hold of him.

"You can't run from your problems."

This time my head snaps up. "Why not? People do it every day."

She shakes her head. "You are not going to leave me behind."

Oh, is that what this is about? "You can come with me." I sigh when she ignores that. "I just need a fresh start," I say truthfully. I need to find myself; I feel so lost.

"Then start over fresh. But do it here. With your friends," she says softly.

"You're my only friend," I say with a soft laugh, but I hate how true it is. How much I have managed to fuck up my life in a matter of weeks.

"Not true."

I look over the back of my chair when a man speaks. I smile when I see Blake walking up to us. "I'm your friend," he says with a wink.

"You're the enemy's friend," I say, looking behind him to see if Dash is with him. I hate how disappointed I feel when he is nowhere to be seen.

"Ouch," he says placing a hand over his heart.

"And I could always use a new friend," his brother, Jake, says. "So what about it?" he asks as he plops down in the sand in front of my chair.

"I don't know. I'm pretty sure my friend list is full," I joke, and it feels good to smile.

His mouth drops open dramatically. "You only have two people on it. A second ago it was just one." He points over at Jackie. "And I heard she once left you at a party. That's not a very good friend." Jackie lifts her glasses and glares at him.

"One is all I need," I say truthfully, and it makes them all laugh as if I was joking. "And for leaving me at the party…" I pause as I remember that night with Dash.

197

_Dash_

His hands on my skin. His lips on mine. His body taking over mine. "Some things are worth it."

The four of us spend the day out on the beach. Jake actually turns out to be quite funny. And the guy has a ton of stories. He travels a lot. He said his dream is to travel the world growing old and fat as he samples food from foreign countries. I found myself enthralled in what he was saying. It sounded so tempting. What he was saying was the exact same things I was thinking. I had just told Jackie that I wanted to escape, and here, he was talking about leaving. I thought it would be hard to leave everything behind, but he made it sound so easy. It's not like I couldn't return whenever I wanted to.

I found myself nodding my head, agreeing with everything he said. Like some love-struck teenager, but the truth is, I'm the teenager trying to run away from the love that I have here. Seeing Dash the other night at the police station brought back all kinds of emotions. Love being the biggest one. And pain. A lot of pain. Pain that no amount of makeup could cover up. These bruises on my body will fade, and these stitches on my face will be removed, but my broken heart will remain broken forever.

I'm laying back in my lawn chair laughing at something Blake just said, pretending I'm not a shattered mess, when Jake's phone rings. I try to continue the conversation with Blake and Jackie so I don't look like I'm being nosy. But we all quiet as he starts to say good-bye.

"That was my friend, Joe," he informs us. "He is having some friends over tonight. Who wants to go?"

"I do," Jackie says raising her hand. She's always down to party.

"Sure," Blake says with a shrug.

They all turn to look at me. "What about you, Tabatha?" Jake asks with a smile. "It'll be fun,"

"Yeah," I say already regretting the word. A party? Is that really what I should be doing right now? I just said I wanted to leave town, not stay and party. It's been two days since my attack with Rodger, and I still have my bruises, but I'm sure I could cover them with makeup...?

"Awesome," Jake says excitedly, and I can't help but feel better about my decision. I really do wanna spend time with Jackie. The last two nights, I wanted to be alone, and I found out that it's not all what it's cracked up to be. Being alone sucks. All you have is your thoughts. I sat in my bedroom in silence, yet my mind screamed at me. And right now, I don't wanna think about anything. I don't wanna argue with myself about what I should and shouldn't feel. I just want to have fun and hang out with my friend.

Jackie jumps up from her lounge chair quickly and starts to pick up her bag. "What are you doing?" I ask, sitting up as well.

"We gotta go. We have to get ready for this party."

I look down at my hands sitting in my lap and twiddle my thumbs. I wonder if Dash will be there. Would they ask him to go when they know I'm going? And if they do, will he ask if I'll be there? See what I mean? Thoughts like these keep me up all night. "You okay?" she asks, placing a hand on my shoulder.

I look up and give her a smile. "Yes." I stand and start to dust the sand off my bag. "I'm ready."

I stand there awkwardly as I watch Blake give Jackie an intense kiss. I look away when his hand travels down and cups her ass over her white bathing suit bottom. "I'll pick you girls up," he says as he pulls away from her. "That way you ladies don't have to drive."

"I can drive us," I offer, and they turn to look at me as if I just spoke in a different language. "I don't plan on drinking," I add.

"Nonsense," Jake says as he throws an arm over my shoulder. "What's a party if you don't drink?" He chuckles to himself.

I sit on Jackie's bed fully dressed and ready to go. I decided on a pair of jeans tonight. After what happened last time I wore a dress, I think I'll avoid them for a while. I chose a pair of white jeans that have extra flare. You know the kind that are from back in the sixties. They're so long that they cover my entire heels. I chose a light blue razorback tank top. I did my makeup light and left my hair down to cover the part of my face that still has bruises.

I open my purse and pull out my little mirror to redo my lip-gloss while I wait for Jackie to finish. The more time that passes, the more nervous I become. She hasn't mentioned Dash at all, which I find odd. I mean, that's what girls do; they talk shit about your ex to make you feel better. She hasn't even asked me if I've spoken to him.

"Why are you acting so weird?"

I jump when she speaks as she exits her bathroom.

I sigh. "Why haven't you asked me about Dash?" I just come out with it. What are friends for if not to help you?

She frowns. "What do you want me to ask you?"

I rub my sweaty hands on my jeans. "Is he gonna be at the party?"

"No," she says without hesitation.

I release a long breath. "Why didn't you tell me that? I've been a nervous wreck thinking that I'm gonna see him." I can't see him. I can't allow him to corner me and tell me that he's sorry. Sorry will just suck me back in. Or worse, but if he's not sorry for the things he said? And if I see him, I may fall to my knees and tell him I'm sorry. Either way would not be good.

She sits down next to me and her soft blue eyes look at me nervously. "What is it?" I ask quickly. "Is something wrong with him?"

"I just didn't think you wanted me to talk about him. I spoke to Blake earlier and he said that Dash had been invited to the party, but he said he wasn't going. I guess he had gone out last night. So, he had plans to stay in tonight."

I don't know what hurts more. The fact that I thought I was gonna have to see him tonight or the fact that I won't see him tonight. I have avoided all social media pages the last few days ever since I saw what the news was saying about Rodger and me. I don't know how many times I've started to snoop on Dash's pages but made myself put my phone down. It's just not healthy. I'm going crazy!

"He and Blake went out last night?" She had called me at one point in time and said she was with Blake.

She shakes her head slowly. "Blake wasn't out with him."

I hate the pain in my chest. Sometimes, I think it would be better to be physically stabbed because that pain would eventually go away. But this pain I just can't seem to shake. The kind that takes your breath away. "He was with her, wasn't he?" He had to have been with Valerie. Why wouldn't he? She practically throws herself at him. And he once loved her.

"He didn't say," she says softly as she reaches over and grabs my hand. "But let's not worry about him. Okay?" she tries to give me a reassuring smile. "You've been through so much in the last few days. Let's just go to this party and relax."

"I'm not really in the mood to party," I say truthfully.

"I spoke to Blake a while ago, He said it's gonna be a small party, and it's gonna be real relaxed. Nothing crazy or anything. And I promise I won't let you get drunk and sleep with some random guy." She laughs, but her words sting. Because that night Dash was just some random guy, but that morning after he became something more important. That seems like forever ago.

"Promise you won't leave me?" I ask, laughing at myself. I sound like a child.

"Never again." She reaches up and pulls me in for a hug. She holds on to me tightly as her hand runs up and down my back. "I love you, Tabatha. And I promise to help you get through this." She pulls back and gives me a smile. The same smile that I see her give Blake all the time. It makes her eyes light up and her dimples show. It's hard not to smile back at her.

I nod. "Let's party."

# CHAPTER THIRTY-ONE

*Dash*

I told Blake I wasn't gonna go to the party, but I changed my mind. I spent most of my afternoon at the track with Mr. Knight. If you ask me, things couldn't have gone better. I've done nothing but ride nonstop for the last day. Mr. Knight said I had time to make up for, but I'm pretty sure he was just wanting to kick my ass for quitting on him days ago.

I went to my house and passed out. I woke when Blake called me informing about the party. I told him I was gonna skip this one, and I went back to sleep. Then I woke up wide-awake at a little past ten and decided what the hell? I got up, showered, threw some clean clothes on, and jumped in my car. I know the guy who is throwing the party. He was one of Jake's best friends in high school. He was always cool with Blake and me tagging along. For some stupid reason, we looked up to them and wanted to be just like them. With their cigarettes and cheap-ass beer. Thankfully, we didn't keep up with the smoking charade. Every time Blake and I would try one, we sounded like we were choking to death. Jake and Bobby made it look cool and easy.

I pull up to the million-dollar mansion and park my Bentley next to a Porsche. I guess you could say we were all spoiled little rich kids. Now we're all adults and still rich idiots. We just spend our money on bigger and badder toys.

I walk up to the front door and the sound of the music carries through the walls to the outside night. It's now almost midnight. I try the handle on the door, and it turns, allowing me to enter. I stand in the foyer as I look around at the house. The marble floor of the entryway shines, ahead of me stands one large staircase that, once you get to the top, you can choose to go left or right. I start to move forward, and go around the staircase to find the kitchen.

"Dash!" a girl that we all went to school with hollers at me from behind the kitchen counter.

I nod my head and give her a smile. I fucked her once and you never wanna acknowledge that when you are at a party. Unless you wanna climb on top of it again. And last thing I had heard, she has four kids. Too fertile for me.

"Hey, man," I turn around to see Blake standing by the open the fridge as he speaks to me. "I didn't think you were gonna come." He reaches in and grabs two beers.

I shrug as I walk over to him. "I changed my mind."

He hands me a beer and claps me on the shoulder. "Drink up. You're gonna need it."

"Why's that?" I ask tilting the bottle back.

"Well…" He pauses. "Tabatha is here," he says before he tilts his back and takes a swig of his own. "And she's drunk."

I grip my beer bottle tighter to the point my knuckles turn white. God, I miss her so much. I need to see her. "Who's she here with?" I look down at my bottle and start to pick at the label, trying to act as if I don't really care.

"She came with us," he says simply, and I nod my head to him. Makes sense. She wanted to party with her friend, Jackie. Who is dating my best friend. Well, and of course, the fact that her father is my boss…I take a bigger swig of my beer. I hate that she made me love her with no intention of loving me back. I hate that I acted like a little bitch and fell for her so fast. I hate that Rodger hurt her. What I don't hate, though, is the fact that I kicked his ass. Which Mr. Knight has been true to his word. I have not heard one peep from any lawyers or Rodger himself about pressing charges. So far.

"Where is she?" I start to look around. I just need a glimpse of her. I just wanna see that smile on her face. I know I won't be the reason for it, but it would make me happy.

He spins around, surveying the kitchen. "She was here just a minute ago." He frowns. "She must be with Jackie in the bathroom or something."

I turn around and walk away before I can change my mind. I need to see her. I need to explain something to her. I need to apologize for the way I acted at the police station. Maybe once I apologize, I will be able to move on.

I take off down the hallway, saying hello and shaking the hands of guys I remember from high school. For the ones who haven't moved away, we have stayed pretty close over the last four years. Shockingly, most of them have settled down, gotten married, and even have a kid or two. That's quite a bit for four years.

I come to the end of the hallway, and I come to a closed door. I knock, afraid some random person may be having sex in there. You never know at parties what you may walk into. Once I get no response, I reach down and turn the knob and it opens up for me. As soon as I step into the bedroom, I instantly feel like I just stepped off a plane in Africa. Cheetah print everywhere. A big area rug covers the wooden floor with cheetah print on it. A big four-poster bed sits elevated in the middle of the room with a dark brown comfortable and cheetah print pillows. The walls are also painted a dark brown with a cheetah type of border.

I just turn to leave the room when I hear a woman laugh from behind a door that's at the other end of the room. I know that laugh. It's hers. Tabatha's.

I tiptoe my way over to the door and press my ear up against it. I don't hear anything so I very carefully and quietly twist the doorknob and push it open just a little.

My heart pounds in my chest and my throat tightens. I see her sitting on the bathroom counter. Her long dark hair is down and over one shoulder, messy and looks to be tangled. Her high heels lay on the tile floor as her bare feet swing back and forth, hitting the cabinets softly. She wears a shirt—a man's shirt. I know this because the man standing in front of her is shirtless. A man who was supposed to be my friend, Jake. He leans over as he looks her eye to eye, both hands on either side of her on the countertop.

He says something that I can't quite understand due to the ringing in my ears. I watch as she throws her head back and laughs as if it was the funniest thing on earth. She loses her balance and her arms come up from the counter and she grabs on to him as if she thought she was gonna fall off of the counter. He starts to laugh as he wraps his arms around her and holds on to her tightly.

She goes to giggle, but he covers her mouth with his.

I've seen enough. Anger, anger like any other I have ever felt runs through me. I should go in there. I should yank him off her and demand to know what the fuck they are doing... but she doesn't love me. She didn't choose me as I did her. I need to be a fucking man and live with that no matter how much it hurts.

I shut the door and make my way back through the bedroom. I shut that door as well and down the rest of my beer as I head for the front door. I don't acknowledge a single soul as I walk right out the front door. I throw my beer bottle out to the side of me as I walk to my car, and I hear it break as it hits the concrete. Hope Jake drives his Range Rover over it and flattens his tires. I get in my car and fire it up as I get the fuck out of there.

# CHAPTER THIRTY-TWO

## *Tabatha*

My skin tingles and my heart races. His hands on my back and his lips on mine…I close my eyes and I allow him control over my lips. My body pushes into his, and my hands find their way to his bare chest.

His lips pull away from mine, and they travel down to my neck. "Jake…" I breathe, my head foggy.

His breath lands on my neck. "I love the way you breathe my name," he whispers, sending shivers down my neck. "Say it again."

"Dash…" My eyes spring open, and I shove him away. "Oh, my God." I gasp.

"Tabatha…" Jake holds his hands up in the air.

"What were you doing?" I demand. What the hell was I doing?

"It's okay that you accidentally called me Dash. I know you guys are over…"

"You know nothing," I scream at him as I jump off the bathroom countertop. My ankle gives out, and I find myself sprawled out on the bathroom floor cussing myself. Why did I call him Dash? He kisses nothing like Dash. Why did I even allow him to kiss me in the first place? Tears start to well up in my eyes. I blink a few times.

He reaches down to help me up, and I shove his hand away. "Don't touch me," I snap as I find my way to stand.

"Tabatha. Calm down. It was just a kiss."

"A kiss?" I squeal. I wanna bang my head up against the wall. That's all it was, yes. But what made him think he could kiss me? Was I flirting? Was I acting like some cheap whore? "Just how far would that kiss have gone?" I demand as I bend over and pick up my heels. I knew this was a bad idea. I should have never come out here tonight. We've been here for a few hours, I've had plenty of drinks, and somehow I find myself in the bathroom with Jake. I've become an alcoholic whore. Oh, just give Tabatha some drinks, and she'll let you fuck her. "Jesus," I chide myself.

"Are you asking at what point I would have stopped you?" His voice shows no anger like mine. Just pure curiosity.

"Yes." I hop on one foot as I put my other in my heel still trying to hold back the tears.

"I wouldn't have," he says simply.

I stop jumping around and stare at him wide-eyed. "You would have slept with me?" Before he can even answer, I continue. "How could you? You're friends with Dash." I run my hands through my messy hair. It's in tangles; some drunk bitch placed her sucker in my hair. Don't ask me how it happened because no one knows the answer.

He sighs heavily. "Dash is not good for you."

"And you are?" I demand. I can't believe he is saying this. I can't believe I am listening to it.

"I would treat you better," he says matter-of-fact. "If you were mine, I sure as hell wouldn't be chasing after other girls."

Other girls? Is Dash seeing someone else now? So soon? I shake my head as I look down at my feet. Of course, he is. He's a man who laid his heart out to me, and I stomped on it. "Don't pretend like you know what happened to us," I decide to say. He doesn't know anything about our relationship. I'm the one who walked out on him. I take a step up to Jake, and I hate that a tear runs down my cheek. It's not one of those tears of sadness, but anger. I am so angry at myself, at Jake, and at Dash. I hate the fact that I feel guilty that Jake kissed me when I just found out that Dash is seeing other people.

"You're beautiful, Tabatha." His words are spoken softly, and his hand comes up to wipe the tear from my cheek. "But you're not the girl who is going to change Dash's ways."

"Just shut up," I order as I rip his shirt off and pick mine up off the floor. It's still soaked in alcohol from another drunk idiot. Fuck, this was just not my night.

I storm out of the bathroom with my soaked shirt on, and as soon as I enter the kitchen, I start yelling for Jackie. She spins around to look at me, and I take a deep breath. "I'm ready to go."

Blake frowns. "Go?"

"Yes!" I yell causing everyone to stare at me awkwardly. "I'm ready to fucking go." And then I spin around and start for the front door.

As I'm running down the stairs to the house, I hear the front door swing open. "What happened?" Jackie asks.

"Jackie, I can take her…"

"No!" I shout as I spin around to face Jake. "I don't want to be around you. I just want Jackie to take me home. Now!" I demand.

He sighs heavily as he digs into his pocket of his pants and pulls out the keys to his Range Rover. He tosses them to Jackie, and she automatically unlocks it for me. You would think that I would eventually learn to start driving myself.

"Are you okay?" she asks as she climbs behind the driver's seat.

"I'll explain in a minute," I say as I dig through my purse looking for my cell phone. I go to Dash's number saved in my phone and press send. Hey, you've reached Dash. Leave a message. I hang up and try again. Same.

"Fuck!" I say as I throw my phone down into the floorboard. I start rocking back and forth.

Jackie looks over to me quickly and I rub my face with my hands. "Are you having some sort of breakdown?"

"Jake kissed me," I blurt out.

"What?" she demands. "Like on the mouth?"

"What are we in grade school? Yes, on the mouth. With tongue. And I kissed him back."

"Oh." She mouths as she watches the road.

"And now Dash won't answer his phone." I wrap my arms around myself.

"Why are you calling Dash? Don't tell him what you did." She speaks frantically.

"I just need to talk to him." I know why I couldn't tell him how I felt, but now I realize that I need to. He may tell me to go to hell. He may turn me down the way I did, but at least then I know that I tried. I told him how I truly felt and he can make the decision. I don't want anyone else. I want him.

## CHAPTER THIRTY-THREE

*Dash*

I bring the bike to a quick stop and jump up off it. I tear off my helmet and unzip my leather suit. I only unzip it far enough for me to remove my arms out of the sleeves. I'm sweating and fucking hot as hell.

"You need to take it easy," a man wearing a Knight Racing shirt says as he kneels down next to the bike. "You're gonna burn up the motor."

"Well, fix it to where I won't," I snap back.

"It can only take so much. You're pushing it too hard."

"I'm doing what it's made to do," I growl. "If this motor can't handle it, then fucking fix it."

"Dash…" Mr. Knight says as he walks onto the racetrack. We've been at it all day, every day, for a week now. A fucking week and I still can't get it right. "Let's take a break." He softly taps my shoulder. And I stretch my neck to each side, giving it a little crack. My back is sore, and my entire body is tight. I need to relax. I need to get laid.

I place my arms in my sleeves and start to pull my leathers up when Mr. Knight grabs it. "Take the rest of the day off."

"Are you serious?" I ask wide-eyed. "We have a race in a week."

"I am. You need a break, Erik. I need your head in the game, and we both know it's not there."

I throw my hands out to my side. "What do you want me to do?" I question. "I'm here. I'm racing. And I'm doing a damn good job, if I might add," I say defensively. We've spent every day this week out at the track. Today they were having an open track day, and I paid the fee it required and jumped on the bike. I've whooped all of their asses. Hell, I'm a damn good rider, but I am going to be up against pros soon. And if I don't qualify, then I won't even get to race.

"So far, you're driving reckless. It's amazing you haven't gone down yet while practicing this week. And you can't race if you injure yourself."

I hang my head and run my hand through my sweat-drenched hair. I know he's right. I've been riding the bike too hard. I've been pushing it to the point it smoked. I've been going through tires like I go through beer on any given weekend. And even though I know he's right, I continue to argue. "I'm doing what you hired me to do. And I'm getting a faster time every single time I get out on that track," I say pointing to it.

"I'm not gonna tell you again," he growls, getting tired of arguing with me. "Go home and blow off some steam." He nods down to the mechanic who is kneeling by my bike. "Load it up," he tells him and then looks back at me. "You gotta know when to quit, son."

I spin around and tighten my left hand into a fist. If this helmet wasn't my favorite, I would throw it to the fucking ground. Instead, I hold on to it. I quickly make my way back over to where I parked my car and pop the trunk. I place my helmet in it and peel my leathers off the rest of the way. I'm left in my boxers and Under Armor t-shirt that fits like a glove. You have to wear them or the leathers will rub your skin raw. I grab a new t-shirt out of the back of the trunk along with a pair of shorts and pull them on.

"Not gonna finish?" I hear Blake ask from behind me.

"Nope. I've been sent home for the day," I inform him as if he didn't just hear the conversation.

It's been a week since I saw Tabatha at the party, and I haven't told a soul what I saw. Not even Blake. He has to know that she's seeing his brother. What hurts is that he hasn't mentioned it to me, either. I've been avoiding all of them, especially her. It's for the best. I have to get over her and we both need to move on. She obviously already has. And that brings me to Valerie. She would be very useful right now, if we were talking. But she has not called me since the night of my party when she confessed to cutting my brakes. So that is a no-go. The sad thing is that I would totally fuck her if given the chance. Women give us too much credit. We really are pieces of shit.

"Dash?" Mr. Knight hollers as he stands over by the bike. I turn to face him. "Change of plans. Meet me at my house. We need to go over a few things." Then he dismisses me by turning back to the mechanic.

I slam my trunk closed and climb into my Bentley, not even bothering to say good-bye to Blake.

I walk into their house and make my way to the kitchen. I need a water. My mouth is dry, and all I've done today is sweat my ass off. I open up the fridge and grab a bottle. I twist the lid off and turn around to leave when I pause the bottle at my lips. There sitting at the kitchen table is Tabatha. She's staring at me with wide eyes and open mouth. God, it's hard to look at her after what I saw. But I can't look away, either.

"Dash," she breathes, and my cock starts to harden remembering what her breath felt like on my neck when we were in bed. Then I remember the fact that my best friend's brother is also experiencing that side of her. Bitch!

"What are you doing here?" She licks her lips as if they're dry.

I clear my throat. "I have a meeting with your father."

She nods, and I watch her swallow nervously. "I've been trying to call you."

"I know." I've been ignoring them.

She hangs her head for a second, and I take the chance to drink some of my water. "I wanted to tell you thank you," she says softly.

I swallow and pull the bottle of water slowly away from my lips. "For what?"

She licks her lips and it reminds me of the taste of them on mine. How soft they were wrapped around my cock…Stop, Dash! "For what you did to Rodger," she whispers.

"He deserved it!" And I deserve you. Not really, that's me just being selfish.

She nods her head slowly, and I allow my eyes to search her face. Her bruises look better, almost gone. She almost looks like the beautiful girl I saw walk into my parents' kitchen, but I know it's not the same girl. The one who had confidence and knew the world was at her fingertips. I would give anything to be her world. My chest tightens as she opens her mouth to speak.

"So…uh…" She stumbles over her words. "How have you been?"

"Not as good as you." The words leave my lips before I have the chance to stop them.

Her back straightens. "What does that mean?" she demands, finding the words pretty easily now.

Why lie? Why not tell her that I know? Just get it out in the open? "I know you're fucking Jake." I hate how jealous I sounded. Pathetic.

She gasps. "You're the one out sleeping around with other women."

I hate how much I love the sound of jealousy coming from her lips. It's crazy how good it feels when the tables are turned. But it's not true. I chuckle. "So you fuck my best friend's brother and then accuse me of sleeping around? Classic," I say, my words dripping with sarcasm.

"Dash...I swear it's not..."

I hold my hand up. "You don't have to pretend. I saw you with him in the bathroom at the party." I laugh at myself. She must think I'm crazy, but that's what she has made me. Crazy.

"You were there?" She starts to shake her head quickly. "I swear that's not what it was."

"Quit lying."

"Lying?" she sneers as she pushes her chair back from the table. "You're the one who lies. Or do you not remember the conversation we had at the police station?"

"I remember," I snap. "I remember you acting like you had no idea why Rodger came over to your house after I had just been there."

She points her finger at me. "You wanna know the truth? Fine." I have moment of panic. Do I really wanna hear that she is still in love with Rodger? That I'll never live up to the woman-beating fuckface that he is. "My doorbell rang, and I answered it thinking it was you coming back. He came inside and told me that he had messed with your brakes. He said that if I didn't give him what he wanted, that he would go after you again. To teach me a lesson." Her voice rises. "He asked me what I was willing to give up in order to save you. And I told him me. I would give him me to make sure you were safe." Her chest rises and falls rapidly, and I see the tears start to well up in her eyes. "But I couldn't do it." Her voice breaks. "I couldn't go back to that life. To being controlled.

215

To being numb to everything." She lifts her hands and angrily wipes the tears from her face. "I'm sorry that I failed you. That I didn't go with him to ensure your safety," she says with bite.

"Tabatha," I say softly. "I would never want you to…"

"I had to fight. Fight for myself. I was gonna die trying." She takes a deep breath. "And as for Jake. Some drunk ass spilled her mixed drink all over my shirt. And he helped me to the bathroom. He gave me his shirt to wear. Yes, he kissed me. And I freaked. I yelled at him. I made a fool of myself in front of everyone there. But I haven't spoken to him since. It was a mistake. A mistake that I regret more than anything."

"More than me?" The words slip from my lips before I can stop them

"I don't regret you." She wipes her hands on her jeans and takes another step toward me. "I have tried to call you to explain myself. I understand why you came to my house after what happened with you and Valerie. I was so mad that I had been right. The night before, when I left you that note, I was letting you off the hook. Because I knew that you were going to do stuff with her, and I didn't want you to be a cheater. Our relationship had already been so fucked-up to the point that I didn't wanna add more to it." She swallows. I go to speak, but she lifts her hand to stop me. "I…" She takes a deep breath. "I was with Rodger for a year. And in the beginning the relationship, what we had was what I thought I wanted. But over time, I slowly lost myself. I became dependent on him. And that first night I met you, I just wanted to be me. Find the old me who I loved. And when I saw what you were willing to do with Valerie to get that information…"

"I told you I would give up racing for your dad for you," I remind her.

"I didn't want you to do that," she cries. "Because I don't wanna change you."

"People change," I say taking a step toward her. "Dreams change. You start to want things that you never knew were possible," I say as I lift my hand and cup her face.

She sniffs. "I love you, Dash. I wanted to tell you how I felt the moment you walked into my house that night, but I was too mad at you for what you had done. I was pissed that I had been right."

"Right about what?"

"That you would put her and your dream before us." I can't argue with her because I did. I was mad at her as well for writing that stupid note. But none of that matters now. "You love me?"

She nods her head. "I thought us being apart would be best for me. That it would give me a chance to find myself. But I realize that I'm at my best when I'm with you. I feel strong when you hold my hand. I feel loved when you cuddle with me. I love the way you make me feel about myself. Not what you try to make me be."

I lean down and kiss her hair before I wrap my arms around her and pull her in for a tight hug. She quickly looks up at me and her eyes shine from the tears. "I didn't sleep with Jake. I swear it. I kissed him and it was a mistake. Please forgive me."

No more secrets. No more lies. They've all been laid out on the table, yet we're both still standing here waiting for the other one to walk away. But the thing is that I do believe her. I understand more than anyone does how something can look one way but the truth be exactly the opposite.

"Dash…?"

I breathe a sigh of relief. "Shh. I believe you." I pull her head back against my chest. She has to feel my heart pounding and my pulse racing.

Just as I go to speak again, she pulls away and wipes the tears off her face. "My father raised me to always say what I feel. He would say, 'Sweet pea, people can't read your mind. In order for them to understand what you want, you have to tell them.'" She chuckles to herself. "Rodger took that part of me away. To him, women weren't allowed to have opinions or wants." She looks up at me. "I was afraid to tell you how I felt, but you weren't. You were much stronger than I was. But if you just give me the chance, I will show that I can be just as strong as you."

Her words are like a knife to my heart. I didn't realize how much she was hurting. When I was with her, she seemed so happy. How was I supposed to know what she felt when she was alone?

I reach up and place my hands on her soft face. My fingers run across her cheeks, wiping away the tears. "I don't want you to be afraid of what you feel," I tell her. "I want you to feel safe." My eyes scan her forehead. You can barely see the scar where her stitches were. "I would never want you to lose yourself in order to love me." I love a strong-willed woman who has a mind of her own. That's what made me fall in love with her in the first place. She was so free.

She reaches up and grabs a hold of my shirt. Her hands tightly grip it, and she buries her face into my chest once again. "I've missed you so much," she cries.

I lean down and kiss her hair. "Not as much as I've missed you," I admit.

We stand there in her parents' kitchen for a good ten minutes as we hold each other. Her cries start to subside, and her grip on me loosens. She eventually pulls back and looks up at me. "I do love you." She licks her lips. "I've wanted to tell you that ever since you told me that night."

I smile down at her. "I love you. But you already know that." She chuckles to herself and nods her head.

"So you say."

"I'll prove it," I say, and her smile widens.

She pushes her chest into mine and whispers, "Kiss me."

I grab her face and lower my lips to hers. I kiss her desperately. As if she's air and I've been drowning. Because that is what she does for me. She helps me survive. Her body presses into mine and her lips work with mine as if they know what I'm gonna do next.

She sighs as she pulls away. "I have to leave," she says, and I grip her tighter.

"Please. Stay," I beg her as I look around and realize that I am still at her parents' house and her father is probably going to walk in any minute.

She actually gives me a small smile. "I have to get home. But I wouldn't mind a little company when you're done here," she suggests. "That is if you don't already have plans." She nibbles on her lower lip nervously.

"Even if I did, I would cancel them," I say in all honesty.

She giggles, and God, does it sounds amazing. It's crazy how only minutes ago, I hated her for turning me away. How low I felt that she broke my heart. And now...now, I feel high and drunk at the same time. All because I now know that she loves me. She reaches up and gives me a soft kiss. "I'll see you soon." And then she pushes away from me and leaves me standing in the kitchen alone.

# CHAPTER THIRTY-FOUR

## Tabatha

I can't explain what kind of high Dash's kiss has put me on. I was not expecting him to show up there. I knew he was up at the track with my father. My mother and I had lunch and then she had to leave when we returned to their place. I was just about to leave when he walked into the kitchen. I thought I was gonna have a heart attack. I hadn't seen or heard from him in so long. But that didn't matter. The time apart wasn't helping the slow ache that I had in my chest for him. Just smelling him had my knees weak. His arms wrapped around me had me coming undone. It was all too much yet not enough at the same time. And that kiss…God, it tilted my world upside down in a good way. Took my breath away. That man has a lot of power over me, and I don't think that either one of us understands what that means, but I'm tired of questioning it. My father raised me to say what I feel when I feel it. Rodger made me keep those feelings inside. But I finally realize that it's okay to love. To be vulnerable. So I'm gonna cut myself open and lay it all out on the table for Dash to see. He said he loves me and I love him. Now I'm gonna show it.

I get home and run up to my room. I had stayed the first few days at my parents' after the Rodger incident. I was afraid to come home. The smell of blood. The memory of what had happened. Little did I know that my mother had hired a team to come in and rip up the carpet and the floors. She had most of the entryway and stairs redone for me. And oddly enough, it helped.

I just get out of my shower when I hear my doorbell ring. "Coming," I yell, running down the stairs and wrapping the towel tighter around me. As soon as I open the door, two arms wrap tightly around me. "You took a shower without me." Dash frowns, dropping an overnight bag at our feet.

I wrinkle my nose as I sniff just joking around with him. I know he's been sweating at the track with my dad all day, but to me, he smells amazing. "I can take another one."

"That's what I wanted to hear," he says as he buries his face in my neck. And then I feel his hands on my thighs and he lifts me up in the air, causing me to lose my towel. His lips land on mine, and he kisses me the entire way up the stairs and to my bathroom. He sets me down on my feet long enough to reach over to turn the water on and then I'm pulling him into me again. He lifts me and places me on the counter as I yank his shirt up over his head. Then I get to work on his jeans and he shakes them off along with his boxers. His hardness presses up against my thigh, and I start panting. It's been too long.

His hands grab my face and force me to look up at him as he stands between my legs. "I just want you to know that I don't expect this…"

"I do!" I say interrupting him, and I go to reach down to grab his hard dick. But he reaches down and grabs my wrists before I can get to it.

"I'm being serious."

"Me, too," I say looking into his eyes. "You're all I've thought about. You're all I've dreamed about. I need you, Dash. I need you to fuck me. Please." I'm to that point of begging. I want him! I need him! I'm tired of pretending like I don't.

He releases my wrist and his hands find their way into my hair. I close my eyes when he tightens them, making my skin break out in goosebumps. "Do you have any idea how fucking sexy you sound when you say that?" he asks against my lips. "Tell me again. Tell me how much you need me."

"I need you," I say immediately. "Quit making me wait and fuck me."

He lets go of my hair and grabs my right arm. He yanks me off the counter and my legs threaten to give out on me, but he grabs a hold and spins me around.

He holds my back to his front and his hand comes up and wraps around my throat. He forces me to look straight ahead at us in my bathroom mirror. I can see the steam spilling over the top of the shower since the water is still on. "So beautiful," he says, getting my attention as his eyes slowly run up and down my naked body in the mirror. His free hand comes around and cups my pussy. I suck in a deep breath as I move up onto my tiptoes.

My pussy throbs and I spread my legs, needing more. He smiles at me in the mirror. "Always in a hurry." He takes his fingers and spreads my lips allowing him to push a finger into me. "Do I make you this wet?" he asks with a raised brow.

I nod.

"Tell me," he demands.

"Yes." I hiss in a breath as he tightens his hand around my throat. I love when he's like this. It was so different with Rodger than it is with Dash. He makes me feel wanted. Not used.

"Well, then I think I need to do something about it."

His hand leaves my throat and places it on my back. He pushes me forward and I put my hands on the countertop. His one hand stays between my legs and he adds another finger. I moan as I drop my head forward and take in a deep breath.

"Oh, no," he says. "You're going to watch." His removes his fingers, and he lifts my head. I stare at him standing behind me in the mirror. "I want you to see how beautiful you are when you come."

I stand in my kitchen as I try to cook Dash breakfast. I've lived here for three years, and I can probably count on one hand how many times I have used the kitchen to cook something. It's not because I'm lazy or prefer to eat out, it's just that I don't know how to cook. My mother never taught me; I'm not sure she even knows how. Growing up, we had chefs.

I woke up this morning and saw Dash sleeping next to me, his long shaggy hair covering his forehead. I reached over, kissed his warm face, and then got out of bed, wanting to do something special for him. And what else says I love you better than breakfast in bed?

Too bad it's not going as planned because I've already burned two pancakes. I managed to pull the third one off before it burned, but it's not done.

I raise my hands in the air trying to fan the smoke out of my face and then I hear the smoke detector in the kitchen going off. "Shit!" I grab a towel off the counter and yank a chair from the kitchen table. I place it under the smoke detector and start fanning. By the time it shuts off, my arms are tired from being lifted above my head.

"What is happening in here?" Dash calls out as he walks into the kitchen. He waves his hand in front of his face as he looks around.

I jump up off the chair and sit down in it. Defeated. "I was trying to cook you breakfast, but I failed."

He laughs, and I narrow my eyes on him. He coughs to try to stop it. "You don't have to cook me breakfast."

"I know. I was just trying to be nice."

"Aww…" He reaches down and pulls me to stand, wrapping his arms around me. "That's so sweet."

I pucker my lips, and he gives me a soft kiss. "But it looks like we're going out for breakfast or I'm gonna starve to death."

I pull back and playfully slap him on his bare chest, which makes him laugh even harder.

I walk away from him and over to the counter to answer my now ringing phone. "Hey, girl," I say with a silly smile on my face as I watch Dash shake his head at my attempt of cooking.

"Oh, my God, Tabatha," Jackie screeches. "Have you seen the news?" she all but screams in my ear.

"No," I respond frowning. I try not to watch the news. It's so depressing. And last I heard, my and Rodger's incident was still a very heavy topic.

"Turn on the TV," she says in a rush. "It's on almost every channel."

"What is?" I ask not even bothering to move. Dash stands across from me, leaning back against the other countertop as he watches me carefully. My mouth waters as my eyes roam over his body. The only thing he has on is a pair of black boxers.

"Dash. You and Dash. Pictures have been released of you guys kissing up at the track. People are saying it's why Rodger did what he did. Because you were cheating on him with Dash."

"Pictures?" The only pictures I can remember ever being taken are the ones that the guy tried to blackmail us with. "How could they have been released?" I ask out loud.

"The hell if I know. No one cares who took them or how they got released. Just the story behind you two."

My eyes scan Dash's face, but there isn't one wrinkle. Not one frown. Not one sign of concern of the situation on his face. "I'll call you back." She starts to ramble, but I hang up on her. "I know you could hear her. Why don't you look surprised? Or mad?"

"How do you want me to look?"

I narrow my eyes on him. "That didn't answer my question."

He goes to open his mouth when my phone rings again. I go to press ignore thinking it's Jackie, but my father's name lights up my phone. "Hello?"

"Is he with you?" he demands, and I know he means Dash.

"Yes."

"Put his ass on the phone." I place the phone out in front of me and Dash takes it.

"Hello, Mr. Knight," he says politely. I tilt my head to the side as I analyze him, and he still looks calm as can be. Shouldn't he care that someone has violated us by releasing pictures?

"I've been calling your phone, boy," I hear my father growl.

"It's not on me at the moment, sir," he responds.

"Well, find it and get your ass over to my house. And bring my daughter with you."

"Yes, sir," he says before he hangs up.

"Dash…"

"We'll grab breakfast on the way to your parents' house. Get dressed," he insists then leans over and kisses me on the forehead.

I quickly throw all the dishes into the sink and then run upstairs to change into something more appropriate than a pair of cotton shorts and one of Dash's t-shirts. Dash is already walking out the door while I rush to slip my tennis shoes on. So I grab a ponytail holder and run after him.

The car drive over to my parents' house is extremely quiet. After about five minutes into it, I realize he isn't going to talk so I reach over and turn on the radio while I put my hair up into a ponytail. But the closer to their house we get, the more nervous I get. My father sounded pissed, and well, I can't decide how I feel about it. Just weeks ago, I was saying that we should release them ourselves. The boy would have no leverage if the pictures were released. Now they are. What does that do for us?

We walk in and head straight to my father's office. I allow Dash to sit down first, and then I sit down beside him. He places his left arm over the back of the couch and pulls me closer into this side.

"Why is this such a big deal?" I'm the first one to speak. "It's good that they are out, right? Now that kid can't use them as leverage."

My father's black eyes travel from Dash to me. "Have you not turned on the TV?"

I shake my head. Why do people keep asking me that? Jackie asked the same thing. "Why?" They can't be nudes, can they? "Are they not of us kissing at the track?" I ask as I start to panic. "Are they more...intimate pictures?"

He bangs his fist on the desk. "Have you taken intimate pictures?" he demands.

"No, sir," Dash says immediately, and I shake my head quickly.

My father lets out a long breath of relief. "The point is what they are saying about you." He looks at me.

"What could they possibly be saying? Dash and I are together. Who cares if the world knows?"

"What I care about is your image. They are saying that you have been seeing Dash for a while now and that is why Rodger 'attacked' you."

It takes me a few seconds to understand what he is saying, but once it sinks in, I let out a laugh that has Dash and my father both looking at me like I'm crazy. "Who cares what the public thinks. They are going to think whatever they want." I shrug carelessly.

My father rummages through some papers on his desk. "Well, I care, and I'm going to find out who is responsible for this. I will take care of it."

"I did it."

My head snaps to look over at Dash so fast that I get a pain in my neck. "You what?" I ask as I rub it.

"What?" my father snaps.

Dash looks across the room to him. "I released them," he says with no remorse.

"Why would you do that?" he demands.

Dash turns to look at me. He gives me a big smile as he reaches out and takes my hand. "Because I promised your daughter that I was gonna prove to her that I loved her. And I thought the best way to do that was to shout it to the world."

Oh, my God. My heart just melted. He did tell me he would prove it, and by proving it, he allowed the world to see it.

"How…What…You mean to tell me that you released these pics on a dare?"

"No. It wasn't a dare." He takes a deep breath. "We both have secrets. We both have a past. I wanted to show the woman that I love off to the world." I smile. "And I agree with her. Who cares what the people think. She and I know the truth, and that's all that matters to me."

*Dash*

My father pushes his chair back and comes to stand in front of his desk. "So, you're saying you love her?"

Dash stands from the couch and bows his chest out but places his hands in his front pockets of his jeans. I take a quick look at how hot his ass looks in them. "Yes, but you already know that. And if you're mad at me over the pictures, I understand why. I did it behind your back. But if you're about to tell me that I need to pick a side — racing or her. I pick her. Because, yes, I love her."

Hearing him say those words to my father has me smiling like a huge idiot. I jump up from the couch and loop my arm into his. My father looks over at me with hard eyes; I try to hide my smile, but it's just not possible.

"Is this how you feel about him?" Before I can answer he adds, "I didn't know it was this serious." He places his arms over his chest and leans back against his desk.

"Yes," I say simply, "it is that serious."

He looks away from me to look over at Dash for a few seconds. He finally uncrosses his arms and reaches out his hand to Dash. "Okay. Then. I expect this won't affect your racing?"

"No, sir." Dash responds as he places his hand in my father's to shake.

My father takes his hand from Dash and walks back to sit at his desk. "I'm going to make a call. Maybe we can spin this in our direction." He starts to go through papers on his desk, and I give a sideways glance at Dash. He's staring at me with a smile on his face. "You two will do an interview…"

"No," I say in a panicked voice. "I can't give an interview." I'm horrible with interviews. I mean, I never even gave one for Rodger. His father always wanted us to do one, but I always said no. That was one thing Rodger never pushed, and I'm pretty sure it was because he knew

228

I would just make the world think that he was dating an idiot.

"You'll be okay," Dash says running his hand down my back.

I shake my head quickly. "You don't understand; I can't even give oral reports in school. I get terrified."

"You've never had a problem with giving me oral," he whispers, and I shove him. He laughs. "There's nothing to be afraid of."

"Why do we need to do an interview?" I whine.

"Because we need to clear the air. Your pics are public, yes. But now we need a headline to go with those pics. Plus, it will get Dash's name out there."

"What does that have to do with anything?" Dash asks.

"The more you're in the public, the more people will watch you race. Motorcycle racing isn't as popular as like say...football. The more people who see you will mean more who will cheer for you. Plus, everyone loves a love story."

"So, you wanna use Dash?" I ask in a rush. "Daddy...How could you?"

He holds his hand up. "The interview will only be about your relationship. You guys wanna go public with it? This is how it needs to happen."

I take a deep breath and look over at Dash. The smile on his face helps reassure me that I can do anything.

## CHAPTER THIRTY-FIVE

Dash

It's been three days since I leaked the photos to the public. It was the best decision I have ever made. After our yelling match in her parents' kitchen, which ended in us making up and being stronger than ever, I realized just what she wanted. She told me to prove it and that was exactly what I had to do. We were past the point of no return. We had tried to survive without one another, and it just wasn't working. So, why not dive right into what we both want? Each other.

After she left her parents' house, I went into his office and found that guy's contact information. I called him up and paid him a very pretty penny in order to leak them. Yep, it was that easy. To be honest, I didn't think he had the resources to release them that fast to the right people. But it worked. Now I'm just waiting for him to release a statement saying that I paid him to release them. I'm hoping he won't but only time will tell.

We just finished the interview, and I must say that for as nervous as Tabatha was, she did amazing. They asked us question about how long we had been together. They asked us what it was like for her to be seeing someone who works for her father. They also asked her a few questions about Rodger, but she refused to answer any of those. All in all, it went well.

What didn't go well was the phone call I got right after we walked out of Mr. Knight's office. My cell rang, and it was my mother. She said she had seen my face on the local news and wanted to meet this girl who I had my hands all over. To say I have been avoiding her is an understatement. But I can't hold out anymore. I have three days before my race, and we fly out in the morning for it. So here Tabatha and I are, pulling up to my parents' mansion. The same house where I first met Tabatha. The same house where Tabatha and I had sex. A shiver runs up my back, causing my body to jerk.

"What's wrong?" she asks, placing a soft hand on my shoulder.

I look over at her and stare into her beautiful brown, golden eyes. Her long hair is down and a little windblown from having the windows cracked, but I like it the best when it's a little messy. She has a black, sleeveless, button-down shirt on with a pair of white jean shorts and a pair of black high heels. She looks classy yet comfortable. But it won't matter what she wears, my parents will still hate her.

"Nothing," I say, picking her hand up and kissing her knuckles. "Ready?"

She nods and gives me a big smile. I wish I could warn her how awful this dinner is going to be; I would, but I don't wanna worry her. So instead, I let go of her hand and get out of my car. Walking around to the passenger door, I open it up and help her out.

"Well, aren't you a gentleman?" she says playfully hitting me on the shoulder. "If I remember correctly, last time I saw you here, you were nothing close to a gentleman."

I laugh. "I can't be bad all the time."

"Guess not," she says as I walk her up the stairs. I twist the doorknob and push one of the stained glass doors open. I walk right in, pulling her behind me. As I enter the kitchen, I can't help the smile that spreads across my face as I remember meeting her in here the first time. She was so feisty. Bitchy. And the most beautiful thing I had ever seen, and now she's all mine.

"Hello, Erik," my mother says as she wipes off her hands and starts to walk toward me. I allow Tabatha to pull away in order to hug her. For us to act like we are actually a loving family.

"Mother…" I say but come up with nothing else.

She pulls away, and her gray eyes, I got my eyes from her, look from me to Tabatha. She smiles, but it's a half smile. That's all she knows how to give. "Who is your girl, Erik?" she asks already pushing me out of the way and stepping up to her.

"Tabatha," she says happily and holds out her right hand. "Tabatha Knight."

My mother stops midstride and turns to look at me. "Are you dating your boss's daughter?" she asks accusingly. But she knows the truth. She saw the headlines and the pics. She just likes to put on shows.

"I am," I say carelessly, and her eyes narrow on me. Here we go.

Tabatha goes to speak, but my father decides to join us. "Hello, son," he says giving me a pat on the back. That's as close to hugging we get.

"How was your trip?" I ask as I go to the fridge, grabbing Tabatha a water and myself a beer. She already told me earlier that she didn't wanna drink any alcohol tonight.

"It was great. Such beautiful real estate in Venus," he says, and I nod as if I would know.

"How's racing coming along?" my mother asks as if she cares. The three of us know she doesn't. Not really. She's just trying to look good in front of Tabatha.

"Great."

Tabatha places her arm in the crook of mine, and she smiles brightly. "His first race is in a few days. You guys should come."

She sounds so proud of me. So happy to see me succeed. The amount of faith she has in me almost hurts. I've been the one to push myself. Some call me cocky; I call it determination. No one else has ever wanted me to succeed or ask what I wanted to do with my life. Not until Mr. Knight. And he didn't even ask. He just offered me my dream. But I would give up that dream for my world. Thankfully, she chooses to stand beside me.

"I believe we will be out of town," my mother says as she gestures for all of us to sit at the table.

"Didn't you just return?" Tabatha asks, and I can see my mother's eyes narrow on her.

"They travel quite a bit," I inform her as I pull out her seat.

"Oh," she says softly. "That would be fun," she adds with a smile. "I've always wanted to travel the world. Do you have to travel for business?" she questions as she places a napkin on her lap.

"For pleasure," my mother responds. Tabatha looks over at me with a look of confusion on her face as if to ask why can't they cancel their next trip to see you race? I give her a soft smile and then reach for my beer.

I just take a drink when my mother speaks. "How is Valerie, Erik?"

I start to choke on it, and I slam my fist into my chest thinking it will help, but it doesn't. "Busy," I say through a cough.

My mother frowns as she sits across from me. "We had dinner with her parents yesterday. They said she's been going through a rough time." I bet she is. She's probably hiding out thinking she is gonna get her ass kicked next. "You should call her." She looks over at Tabatha. "Maybe offer her to go out to dinner with you guys. I'm sure she'd love to meet Tabatha."

"We've met," Tabatha answers flatly as I try to regain my voice.

My mother gives her a big smile. "Isn't she adorable? She is the best." She goes on and on as I burn holes in her with my eyes. They always thought I would marry her. That's only because they found it convenient. They are best friends with Valerie's parents; therefore, we were destined together.

"She's…something," Tabatha says with a fake smile of her own. And I grab for my beer again. This is exactly why I have been ignoring my mother.

We walk into Tabatha's house after dinner, and I follow her up to her bedroom. I was hoping to avoid any question regarding my parents, but I know it's not gonna happen.

"Do you wanna talk about it?"

I sigh. "Not really," I say pulling my shirt up over my head.

She undoes her shorts, and I watch carefully as she shakes her hips side to side as she pushes them down her tan legs.

"Come on," she continues as she walks over to her side of the bed. "You looked uncomfortable the entire time we were there. Maybe talking about it will help you."

I undo my pants quickly, ready to release my achingly hard cock. "Just nervous about the race."

"You're lying," she says matter-of-fact, and I laugh. She knows me too well. Or maybe I'm just that easy to read.

"What do you wanna know?" I ask her as I climb in beside her. Maybe if she asks the questions then I won't have to give certain details.

She cuddles up next to me and places her warm palm on my chest. She softly runs her fingertips soothingly in little circle as she takes a deep breath. "You guys aren't close."

If she meant it as a question, then that is not how it came out. It was clear that she saw the distance that I have put between my parents and myself.

"No," I say simply.

"Why not?"

I sigh. We've decided to go all in. I've lied enough so I'm going to be honest with her. That's what this relationship is all about, after all. "My parents never wanted a child. They married young, but they had big goals. They wanted to travel the world — spend a few years at a time in other countries. My parents had only been married for six months when they realized my mom was pregnant with me." I swallow and catch my breath. "I guess my grandmother, my dad's mother, had found out that they were expecting and was beyond the moon excited to be getting a grandchild. They felt obligated to keep me."

She sits up quickly and looks down at me. Her long brown hair falls down the left side of her face and softly touches my bare chest. "Oh, my God, Dash. They were going to…"

"Give me up for adoption," I finish before her mind wanders too much. Her bug eyes start to fill with tears, and I hate that she pities the life that I might have had. And I hate the odds that I might not have found her if my parents would have had their way.

"Is that why you are the way you are?" I frown, confused by her question. Her eyes drop down to my chest, and she whispers as if she's ashamed to say what she is thinking out loud. "Do your own thing. Never abide by authority?"

I actually give her a soft smile. "A child knows when they are not wanted," I say truthfully. As a young child, I remember all the fights my parents had over me. "My grandfather and grandma—my father's parents—pretty much raised me until I was ten. They are in all of my childhood memories."

"What happened?" she asks, and I reach up to tuck her hair behind her ear.

"It was a week before my tenth birthday...I remember sitting at my grandparents' house eating breakfast before school. And the phone rang. I sat there and watched my grandma's face turn white, and I knew it was bad. She started crying and then hung up the phone. She never said one word. She didn't have to. I knew what the phone call had been about." I close my eyes and take a deep breath. "My grandfather was big into oil. He owned a ton of offshore rigs around the world. I mean, the guy was a billionaire. He loved what he did, but it also cost him his life."

"I'm so sorry," Her voice breaks, and that's when I notice the tears running down her flawless face. "You and your poor grandmother." She hangs her head. "I can't even imagine what that must have felt like."

"She was never the same after that day."

"Do you still see her?"

"She died shortly after he passed away." She sniffs and more tears runs down her face. "It was like she just gave up. Like she wasn't strong enough to go on without him."

She lies down on my chest and wraps her arms around my neck. "I'm so sorry," she cries into my neck.

"It's okay." I push her hair out of the way and rub her back.

She sits up quickly and wipes her eyes. "Then what happened?"

"My grandfather left my grandma everything. But then she passed and she had split what he had left her between my parents and myself."

Her eyes widen. "I bet that pissed them off."

I shrug as well as I can lying down. "They already had money. My parents are in real estate and have always made more than enough."

"So, what did you do?"

"What was there for me to do?" I ask. "I was twelve when my grandmother passed. By then my parents thought that I was old enough to be left home alone. So, they continued to go where ever they wanted, whenever they wanted."

"Why didn't you go with them?"

"I was in school. And like I said, a child knows when they are not wanted. So I stayed behind. I learned to do things for myself. And when they were home, it was a constant fight. They tried to tell me what to do, and I just didn't give a fuck. I'm not saying it was right; I'm just saying that I didn't need them. I got my money from my grandparents on my eighteenth birthday. I bought my house that day and moved out. It was the best thing I've ever done."

"I'm so sorry, Dash."

"Don't be. It's not your fault."

"I know. But still…"

"Stop." I reach up and pull her back down into me, wanting to feel her warm body. "It wasn't all that bad. I had Blake, and his parents were cool about letting me stay over there sometimes." I know there are kids out there who had it much worse. I was never beaten. I was just ignored.

"It sounds awful. Your parents should have been there for you. They should have cared about you more," she says into my chest. And I hate that she is right. I loved my grandparents more than I loved my own parents. The moment I watched my grandmother answer the phone and I saw the look of terror, the look of heartbreak on her face, I wished that it had been my mother or my father who had died, not my grandfather. What kind of person does that? A sick bastard is who. I would have gladly given up all that money in order to have them back. I went into a deep depression. My parents lived as if it was no loss to them. But they never really saw them anyway. Me, on the other hand, I lived with them. Then I had to go back to my parents' house. A place that I should have called home, but it felt foreign. It was cold and quiet. No one was there to wake me for school. Or to help me with getting ready. I was in a dark place for quite a while. My father only showed up to pick me up from the police station or to tell me to get the fuck over their death.

I guess you could say, as I have gotten older, our relationship, what relationship there is, has gotten a little better. But I can still go months without talking to them. Weeks without even thinking of them. And as true as it is, I know it's sad. But that's just how we are and nothing will ever change that.

I lean my head up to look down at Tabatha cuddled up next to me and I smile when I see her eyes are closed. I place my lips on her forehead, giving her a good night kiss. I lie back down and close my eyes thinking of her. She reminds me what it's like to be wanted. To be important. To be loved.

# CHAPTER THIRTY-SIX

## *Tabatha*

I sit in the back of Dash's racing trailer. He's about to race, and I am scared shitless. I'm so nervous that I'm shaking. I expected to be nervous but not terrified. This is our second day here in Florida. He already raced once this morning for qualifying, and of course, he made it. I thought it would ease my fear, but it didn't.

I turn around and look at the trailer. Of course, my father has the best trailer there is. It's a fifty-three foot double decker and has everything that they could possibly need. Up against the right wall is a toolbox nailed to the wall. It's taller than I am. In the center of the trailer is a place where Dash rides his bike up and locks his bike in place to keep it from falling when traveling. I haven't even went up to see what is on the second level yet.

The trailer and crew have been here for two days. We just flew in last night. My father kept telling Dash that he needed to be here earlier than that, but Dash assured him that the night before would be plenty of time.

I jump when two arms wrap around me. Dash chuckles in my ear. "You're so jumpy."

I spin around in his arms and smile up at him. "I'm nervous," I admit.

He lowers his lips to mine and softly speaks against them. "Don't be. I know what I'm doing."

"You're so cocky," I whisper.

He softly brushes his lips against mine. "Speaking of cock…" He pushes his hips into mine, and I can feel the hardness behind his jeans.

_Dash_

"Dash…" I moan as his hands start to tangle in my hair.

He lowers his face to the crook of my neck and kisses my neck. I let my head fall back to give him better access. I grip the back of his shirt as he kisses up my neck to the base of my ear. "You are mine as soon as I finish." Then he pulls away, leaving me breathless and wanting. "I want you in this trailer waiting for me when I'm done; do you understand?"

I nod, and he grabs my head and gives me a soft kiss on the lips. Then he pulls away and walks over to the front of the trailer to grab his leathers. I walk over to him knowing that he needs help to get into them. After a couple of minutes, he is fully dressed in leathers, riding boots, and holding his helmet. And I'm back to shaking.

He grabs my hands and realizes how sweaty they are. "Hey," he says as he leans down and rubs his nose on the tip of mine. "I'm kinda sad at what little faith you have in me."

I let out a little laugh. "I'm just nervous. I know you're good, but anything could happen out there. Another biker could cause you to wreck."

"Dash, it's time to go," I hear Greg, a crew member, yell from the back of the trailer.

He nods. "I'll be right there." Then he looks back down at me. "If it scares you that much, stay in here. Okay?" And before I can respond, he kisses me on my forehead and walks past me. I spin around in time to see him walking down the ramp of the trailer and out of a sight.

"I love you," I call out, hoping he heard me, but I doubt he did.

I walk to the end of the trailer and sit down on the ramp. I look out at all the other trailers positioned inside the middle of the track. They all have the same concept—

the back wall of the trailer pulls down to make the ramp, easy access to get their bike in and out. They have tools and equipment inside to help them work on their bikes, if need be. Some trailers have more than one bike in them.

A man's voice comes over the speakers positioned throughout the raceway, and my heart starts to beat harder in my chest and my hands instantly start to get sweaty.

"He's gonna be okay," I chant over and over to myself.

Then I hear all the bikes start up, revving their engines. I drop my head in my hands and pray. I pray that win or lose, God keeps them all safe out there.

The second I hear them take off, I start rocking back and forth. As I take deep breath after deep breath, I try to think of anything other than him racing. Watching him go down last time was scary as hell. Seeing him get up and then fall, my heart fell with him. I don't want to see that happen again. And that was just a practice; this is a race. He is out there to win. He is out there to prove that he deserves to be here.

I stand up quickly and dust my ass off with my shaky hands. He does deserve to be here, and I should be supporting him. I mean, he's doing all the hard work. All I have to do is stand on the sidelines. I love that man, and he deserves for me to cheer him on.

I straighten my homemade DASH tank top and brush off my white denim shorts one more time before I start to walk on shaky legs.

"How's he doing?" I ask as I come up next to my father.

"Great! He's made his way up to third."

It's hard to watch motorcycles races because their course is much different from say Nascar. They don't have an oval track. They have more like a road course track. It has small hills and sharp turns, which makes no sense to me. They're on motorcycles, they should have a raceway that doesn't have any turns, but I guess that would defeat the purpose.

I look up at the big billboard-like screen that shows all the racers, and I spot him immediately. It's hard to miss him. His bike is normally black, but you can't tell that now. It has stickers all over that say Knight Racing. And he has a number eighty-eight on the front.

I hold my breath as he comes up on a corner. He leans over to the right, and it looks like he is about to fall off the side of the bike when his knees appear to scrape across the track. I start to jump up and down as I bite my nails.

"He is badass!" Jackie squeals beside me. I was sad when Dash told me his parents weren't going to come to his race. But I'm thankful that Jackie and Blake were able to make it.

I can't seem to look away as he zooms down the track. "How, how…How fast is he going?" I ask with a stutter. My nerves are still getting the best of me.

My father doesn't even realize it as he watches the track. "Depends on the turn. Maybe one thirty right now. He can hit one seventy-five in the straightaways."

"Holy fuck!" I hiss.

He chuckles at my choice of words, and then begins to clap as he calls out Dash's name. I turn my attention back on the screen above us, and I see he is now in second place and closing in on first. "Oh, my God," I squeal.

He comes into another corner and cuts it sharp as he leans over to the far right this time, once again his knee dragging the ground. As soon as he makes it through the corner, he pulls the bike to an upright position and passes the first place bike.

My father starts to call out his name, and I start jumping up and down. Jackie wraps her arms around me, and we jump together like two little kids at a birthday party.

"Come on, Dash. You got this!" Blake screams out as he slaps my father on his back.

We all jump up and down, and I grit my teeth so hard that my jaw starts to hurt as we watch him keep first place. We all stop what we're doing and hold our breath as he speeds to the finish line. Once he crosses over it, all hell breaks loose.

Blake picks Jackie up, and twirls her around in the air. My father starts hugging all the guys who are in his crew. And myself...well, I take off running. I don't know where I'm going or what I plan on doing, but I run. With a racing heart and a smile so huge on my face that it hurts, I run toward the track as fast as I can.

I watch as he brings his bike to a stop and yanks off his helmet. He turns around and the first thing he sees is me running toward him. He places his helmet down and runs right to meet me.

I squeal loudly as he bends down and picks me up off the ground. I wrap my legs around him and squeeze him with all that I have. "Oh, my God, you..." He cuts my rambling off with his lips on mine.

I open my mouth wide allowing him to kiss me deeply as he holds on to me tightly. I can taste his victory. I can feel his heart pounding, even through his leathers. And I can smell the sweat that is dripping off him.

He pulls away and he laughs. "You did it," I whisper against his lips.

"We did it." He smiles. "We fucking did it."

He loosens his grip, and I place my feet on the ground. By now, people are coming up to us and pulling him away from me. My father being one of them. Jackie

*Dash*

pulls me in for a hug, and we start jumping up and down again.

I can't even imagine how excited Dash feels because I am on cloud nine and I wasn't even the one who did it. "We need to do an interview," my father says, slapping him on his back. Dash nods his head as he takes a drink of the water that Blake hands him.

I go to pull my phone out of my back pocket for some photos but realize it's back in the trailer. "I'll be right back," I say as I take off in a mad dash across the track to the trailer.

I run up the ramp breathing heavy and holding my side. "Shit," I hiss. "I am out of shape," I say to myself as I look for my phone. I see it over on the floor by his backup bike when I hear the door close shut. I spin around and see Dash coming toward me. "Geez, babe, that scared me," I say still trying to catch my breath.

He gives me a sly smile as he pushes his damp hair out of his face. "Why did you shut that?" I ask pointing to the ramp. He's closed us in here.

"Because I need some you time."

My mouth drops open. "Babe," I take in a deep breath. "You have to go out there and do an interview." I know there's no way he has already done it.

His smirk grows. "They can wait on me." He starts to walk toward me.

I smile. "Becoming a diva already?" I tease.

He chuckles. "No. I just wanna be with you at this moment."

Before I can say anything, he is standing in front of me. His hands are on my face and his lips are on mine. His tongue slips between my lips and dances with mine as I throw my arms around his neck. He deepens the kiss as he steals my breath. His hands leave my face and grab my ass as he lifts me up off the ground. His kiss more desperate

244

as he spins me around and slams my back against the wall. I pull away and cry out as a few things fall off the wall and hit the floor with a thud.

He lifts his hand and places it over my mouth. "Shh, baby." He hushes me. "Others can hear us, these walls are thin."

I nod my head. He takes his hand from my mouth, and I suck in a breath. "We shouldn't..."

"Oh, but we are." He pulls away from the wall. "Stand up," he says as he releases my legs. As soon as my legs hit the ground, he's yanking my shirt off my body. I undo my bra as he undoes the zipper on my white denim shorts. They pool at my ankles, and I go to kick off my heels, but he stops me. "Leave them on," he demands so I step out with one leg and then kick my shorts across the room with the other.

He grabs my arm and pulls me over to the side where a toolbox is nailed to the wall. He lifts me up and sets me on it. "Lay back." I hiss in a breath as I lay down on the cold steel. As soon as I do what he says, I can hear him pushing his leathers down to free his cock. He grabs my ankles and holds them up in the air. "Keep your legs up," he orders.

"Okay," I say breathlessly. The anticipation is killing me. Knowing that someone could come in at any moment and catch us. He's supposed to be doing an interview. Of course, my father will be looking for him.

My right hand grabs the side of the toolbox while I place my left hand above my head when I feel him positon himself in front of me. The toolbox puts me at the perfect height for him to do whatever he wants to with me.

I bite my bottom lip and arch my back as he enters me in one hard thrust, remembering that I need to be quiet. He spreads my legs, and I bend them so they fall over his shoulders and he begins to fuck me wildly. Hard and fast. His fingers dig into my hips as he tries to hold me in place.

I close my eyes and my mouth falls open as my legs tighten and that familiar feel of orgasm starts to build. My head thrashes back and forth and my pussy tightens around his cock, causing him to cuss harshly. I arch my back, and I can't help but cry out as I come. Through the haze of my orgasm, I hear him grunt and his cock jerks inside of me as he comes.

He pulls out and I whimper at the loss of him. He takes a few steps back and quickly pulls his leathers up.

I go to get up. "Here, let me help you," he says reaching out to me. He pulls me to sit and then he walks away to go fetch my shorts. He comes back and slips them over my heels.

"Wait. My underwear?"

"You don't need them," he says and gives me a wink. I give a little laugh as my body continues to shake.

He helps me with my bra and top, and then pulls me from the toolbox. I stumble but right myself.

He walks over to the back where the ramp is and opens it up. "Smells like sex in here." He laughs to himself.

"You're gonna be in so much trouble," I say, and he comes back over to me.

He gently kisses me on the lips. "You're worth it." Then he reaches down and grabs my hands. "Come on."

He pulls me back across the parking lot over to where the big crowd still stands. I let go of him as we get close and I stay back as he walks over to my father. I smile when my dad slaps him on the back and they start to talk to a reporter.

Jackie comes bouncing over to me and hugs me tightly. "Whoa," she says pulling away. "Why are you still so nervous? He won."

"Nervous?" I question.

"Yeah. You're shaking."

I laugh to myself. Yes, I am. But not due to being nervous.

# CHAPTER THIRTY-SEVEN

*Dash*

I sit back in my chair as my left arm hangs over Tabatha's shoulder. My other hand rests on the table. Her dad sits across from me telling a story about a time back when he was racing cars. Blake sits to the right of me and then Jackie sits next to him. The rest of the crew members fill up the other seats.

Earlier this afternoon, after I won my race and we got back to the hotel, Mr. Knight told me that he wanted to take us all to dinner. I couldn't say no. He chose a quiet but upscale restaurant. They seated us outside at a round table right on the water. I can literally here the waves and feel the ocean breeze on my skin. It's amazing.

I smile brightly and pull Tabatha closer to me as she lays her head on my shoulder. We've already finished dinner, and the sun has started to set. We've been sitting here for hours on the deck. The sound of the ocean is behind me, and I have my girl under my arm. I can't tell you how good I feel at the moment. I won my race today. It's just one, but that one made all the difference. I wanted more than anything to prove to Mr. Knight that I could do what he hired me to do, and it's an amazing feeling to know that I succeeded.

"Are you ready to go back to the hotel?" Tabatha whispers through a yawn.

"I am," I say bending down and kissing her on her forehead.

"Wait," Jackie says as she stands quickly. "We have to get a group picture of all of us with the ocean behind us," she explains as she pulls her cell out of her purse.

Blake sighs heavily. "I'm so full; I'm not even sure I can stand."

She starts to walk off to grab a server to take the pic when she throws over her shoulder, "Quit being a baby."

She comes back within seconds, dragging a young waiter behind her. She orders us all to stand up and then positions us on the deck before she starts to explain how to work her phone. Once she's satisfied, he gets in position. "Okay," he says. "On three." He counts down to three, and we all smile.

He snaps a few shots because that's what Jackie instructs him to do. I just release Tabatha from under my arm when I turn to my left to speak to Blake. I go to speak but stop when he gives me a sly smile. The kind of smile he used to give me right before he suggested we do something stupid. "What are you thinking?" Just as the words leave my mouth, he places his hands on my chest and he shoves me backward.

I swing my arms and kick my legs but nothing can stop the fact that I am falling. Just as I hold my breath, I feel my back slam into the water. I come up out of the water pushing my hair back and laughing. "Jackass," I call out.

He's bending over with his hands on his knees laughing his ass off. Tabatha comes running over to the edge. "Dash! Are you okay?" She reaches out to help me as she looks over at Blake with a scowl on her face. "Why do you have to be such a...?"

I yank on her hand and pull her in with me. She comes up out of the water with a gasp, and she slaps me in the chest. "Why...? What...?" she rambles, and I wrap my arms around her pulling her to me.

"I've always liked you better wet," I say with a smirk.

"Jesus," I hear her father hiss, and I laugh at the fact I forgot he was around. It's so hard to know when to be good or bad with her.

"This is awesome," Jackie says as she takes a few pictures of us as I tread water, keeping us from drowning.

"I'm glad you feel that way," Blake adds before he pushes her in as well. This time it's Tabatha who laughs as Jackie comes out of the water gasping and cussing Blake.

"You're lucky this phone is waterproof," she snaps as she lifts it up out of the water.

Blake just laughs it off before he jumps off into the water doing a cannonball.

"You guys are crazy," Mr. Knight calls out. Then he turns around quickly talking to the crew. "If any of you guys push me in, you're fired." His tone is serious and it makes all of us laugh. The guys shakes their heads quickly and throw their hands up in surrender.

I wrap my arms around Tabatha and hold her tightly to me. I'm ready to be back at our hotel alone. After the day I've had, I just want to be alone with her. People have surrounded us all day except for the little time I had with her in the trailer after I won. Now, I'm ready for her and only her in a bed under the sheets. "I love you," I whisper against her lips.

"I love you, too," she says seductively, and I know she is thinking the same thing that I am.

"Say cheese," Jackie says as she lifts her phone up in the air to take a selfie of us all in the water. But instead of smiling or saying cheese, I place my lips on Tabatha's.

We've been back from Florida for a week now, and we haven't left each other's side. We have spent most of our days lying in bed and most of our nights hanging with Jackie and Blake. It's been wonderful yet it still seems surreal. Things have been crazy since I won the race. I've had a couple of practice runs since we got back, and they feel different. Like something's off. I don't know if it's that my mind and body know that it is just a practice and not a real race. Or the fact that my mind is consumed with Tabatha. When I'm on the track, I find myself looking over at her. When I'm in the same room with her, I can't help but just stare at her.

Things couldn't be going better. I keep having these dreams…dreams of our future. I know I was once engaged to Valerie, but I never really saw a future for us. I didn't see us having a wedding, or growing old on a swing out on the porch while our grandkids played in the front yard. With Tabatha, I see all of that. I want all of that. Winning that race last week made me realize that was only half of my dream. The other half was having her there with me.

My mind continues to wander as I stand on the balcony of my house overlooking my backyard In my mind, I've already picked out the tree that I wanna put a tire swing on for our kids. I can picture what tree I can build a treehouse in.

"Dash…?"

I turn around to see Jake, Blake's brother, standing in the opening of the glass door to my balcony from my master bedroom. I haven't spoken to him since the night I saw him kissing Tabatha, and I still haven't mentioned it to anyone. Tabatha wanted to invite Jackie and Blake over for some drinks tonight and they showed up with Jake. I had an instant urge to punch him in the face the moment I saw him, but I didn't want to explain to everyone why I did it.

"Yes?" I ask as I turn back around and look over my backyard again.

"May I talk to you for a minute?"

"Sure," I say not bothering to turn around.

He walks up next to me and places his forearms on the railing as he leans over and looks at the backyard as well. "Tabatha…She told me…" He pauses and takes a deep breath. "I know that you know what I did. But I want you to know it wasn't what it looked like."

"Looked like you were kissing the woman you knew I was in love with," I say flatly.

He sighs. "I don't know why I did it." He pauses. "Well, that's a lie."

I finally turn to the side to face him. "Are you going to start making sense anytime soon?"

He turns to face me, too. "I just want you to know, I kissed her. And she freaked out. Started talking about you. I told her that you couldn't change for her." My anger toward him grows. "That you couldn't love her like I could." He rubs his hand over his forehead. "I didn't get it. How much you loved her. But I see it now. I see how much you love her. Just like I…" He swallows, and I know what he is about to say. "Just like I loved Amelia." He hangs his head. "Tabatha just reminds me so much of her, and I got caught up in the moment. I thought that she could fix an ache that won't seem to go away. I'm sorry, man. I truly am. I hope you can understand that."

As I look up at him, I see the sadness in his eyes. I see the pain that he still feels. Amelia was Jake's high school sweetheart. Their senior year, while he and Blake were on vacation with their family, he got a call from a friend that her and her parents died in a house fire. I don't remember much about Amelia, but I do remember how much they were in love. And what it did to him. How it made him who he is today. I couldn't even imagine what I would do if I lost Tabatha forever.

"It's okay," I say, and I mean it. He might have kissed Tabatha, but who wouldn't want her? She's mine now; my own stupidity allowed them the moment to share that kiss. I guarantee you that it won't happen again.

"It was my fault…"

I place my hand on his shoulder. "Jake. I said it's okay."

He nods his head as he rubs his hand against his thighs. "Thanks for understanding. You know I would never want to do that to you."

"You're a good guy, Jake," I say honestly. He may drink Blake and me under the table, but there's a reason behind that. And Amelia is that reason. It must be hard to shake the memories and feelings.

"I just needed to explain myself," he finishes. "Thank you." He turns around and walks back through my sliding glass door before I can respond.

I sigh heavily and run a hand through my hair as I look back over my backyard. I stand there silently as I hear the door open once again. Then two small arms wrap around my waist, and I smile. "Why are you up here?" Tabatha asks, laying her head on my back.

"Just wanted some fresh air," I answer truthfully. I spin around in her arms and wrap my arms around her as well. I look down into her beautiful eyes, and I place both hands on either side of her face. "Move in with me."

Her eyes widen and her lips part slightly. "Dash…"

"I know it feels like we've been moving fast, but I'm not ready to slow it down. I know I love you, and I know that you love me. I'm ready for us to take that next step." I

Dash

push my body up against hers. "Please. Say you'll move in with me," I ask once again, and I hold my breath. This is what you do when you're in love. When you know you have found the one. And I know that I have.

I watch as her parted lips start to turn into a smile, and her wide eyes soften. "I do love you." She speaks softly. "And yes, I would love to move in with you."

A smile spreads across my face, and I pull her in for a hug. I couldn't be more grateful that she said yes, but I also can't help but think about Jake. What he must have felt being around her? He had mentioned her healing his pain. She does that. Just looking at her makes you feel invincible. Seeing her smile is like watching the sun rise. I couldn't imagine losing her like Jake lost Amelia. Life is short, and I wanna make the best of it with her.

## CHAPTER THIRTY-EIGHT

# Tabatha

It's been two weeks since Dash asked me to move in with him and three weeks since he won his race. The first week back from Florida we spent ninety percent of our time together. Now, we're lucky if we get fifty. I'm back in school now; my father got word that Rodger had transferred schools, to New York nonetheless. Guess he decided he needed to get away, or his father made him transfer. Either way, I'm not sad about it. He's out of our lives for good, and that's all that matters.

I've moved all of my stuff that I thought I needed to keep into Dash's house and put mine up for sale with a lot of help from my mother. I swear, it doesn't matter how old you are, you will always need your mother. Dash has been busy spending all of his time with my father. They are building him another race bike, and they are looking for another guy to join their team. I don't understand why they need another member, but Dash tells me that it's a common thing. I just nod my head and say yes, honey I understand what you're saying even though I truly don't.

I was in the middle of rearranging our furniture when he called to tell me to meet him at my parents' house. I swear I don't know why we just didn't move in with them. There's plenty of room, and I feel like we spend all of our time there.

I open the front door and can already hear them talking in my father's office. I make my way down the long hall and walk right in. Dash sits looking relaxed on the far couch with both arms fanned out across the back of the couch as he speaks to my father. When he sees me walk in, he winks at me and pats the spot next to him.

I snuggle up next to him and let them finish their conversation before I speak. "What's going on?"

"I told Dash to call you here to celebrate," my father says excitedly.

"Celebrate what?" I question.

"Two things actually." He smiles. "One, the fact that Rodger didn't press charges on Erik for beating the shit out of him." Dash chuckles. "And two, the fact that I just got off the phone with a company who wanted to sponsor Erik."

"Oh, my gosh, that's great!" I say excitedly.

"It is," my father agrees as he nods.

Then a thought hits me. "Did he need a sponsor? Is there a problem with funds?" I ask nervously.

My father laughs as if that was an absurd question. "No. Of course, not. If that were the case, I never would have asked him. I was planning to back him a hundred percent of the way, even though that's not how this normally works. Usually the rider, or racer, has sponsors. But it was not a requirement. Although we didn't need it, we are going to accept it. People saw that he won and they want him to represent them. That is fantastic news!" he finishes as he smiles brightly.

"What about Valerie?" I ask, hating to rain on his parade, but no one has mentioned her.

"Uh, what about her?" My father asks slowly.

I look from him over at Dash. "Didn't you press charges on her as well?"

Dash shifts unconfutable beside me. "No."

I pull away from him. "Why not?" I demand.

"She was not a problem," my father answers for him.

I spin around to face him. "Not a problem? She was the one who actually cut your brakes," I remind them.

Dash runs a hand over the back of his neck, and my father sighs heavily. "I told Dash not to press charges against her," he says simply. I go to speak but he holds up his hand. "It would have looked bad against Dash filing charges against a woman. Especially one who he was once engaged to." I grind my teeth. "It would have just brought her into the spotlight, and we didn't want her anywhere near it."

"But…" I turn to Dash.

"I swear to you," he states, looking me in the eyes. "I have had no contact with her whatsoever since the night of my party."

I cross my arms over my chest and fall back onto the couch. I hate how this works. How your celebrity status has to come first before your personal life. I hate how people who don't know you can judge you over things that they don't understand. I take in a deep breath, dropping the subject. It's two against one; I've already lost. "So, what do we do now?" I ask.

"We party," my father answers simply.

"Party?" I laugh. "Dad, you don't party," I remind him.

He nods. "I will tomorrow." He looks over at Dash. "We have five weeks until your next race. Tomorrow night, I will throw a party here at the house for you." He points down at his phone. "I already have my wife planning it. And it will be huge. There will be reporters, along with photographers. She has already ordered you a tux." Then he looks at me. "And she has already gotten you a dress. It will be…"

Dash raises his hand to stop him. "That sounds like an awful lot. You don't have to do all that for me," he says softly as if he's embarrassed.

"Son…" He places his forearms on his desk and leans forward. "I do. This is how this works. You're all over the news. Calls have been pouring in about you doing covers for racing magazines. More interviews. You're the kid with a dream who came out of nowhere. And after tomorrow night, you will be a household name."

Dash shifts uncomfortably on the couch once again. "No offense, sir. I am very thankful for everything that you have done for me. Given me my chance at my dream, but my dream was to race. Not become a star."

"It comes with the territory." My father leans back in his seat and crosses his arms over his chest. "Tell me, Erik. Why did you want to race in the first place?"

Dash looks at him with an intense stare and no emotion on his face whatsoever. A few silent yet awkward seconds pass before he speaks. "I used to hate being at home," he admits softly, and I know he means when his parents would leave him there on his own. "I was always looking for things to keep me busy. One day, Blake and I found this abandoned dirt bike on the side of the road. I talked his mother into stopping, and we threw it in the back of her truck. It took us months to get it to run." He licks his lips before taking a deep breath. "Once we got it to run, we spent all of our time on it." He chuckles softly. "We even fought over it. It was never about the racing. Although, I liked to go fast. I liked to see what it could do and then push it a little more. So much to the point it broke on us all the time." He speaks softly as he stares over at my father, but I don't think he's really seeing him. I feel like he's back in that time of his life. "Blake's dad ended up finding us an old beat-up motorcycle and put us on that. We were unstoppable. It was faster and more durable. It became an escape." He blinks a few times as if he just returns to us. "It was never about the race. It was about the power that the bike allowed me to have. It was about the freedom I felt when I was on her. When I'm on a bike, I'm free. And who doesn't want to be free?"

I sit next to him on the couch trying not to let the tears fall from my eyes. There's so much about Dash that I think he keeps hidden. Mainly because he was never asked how he felt. Or what he wanted. His parents never cared.

My father smiles softly at him, and I know he understands exactly what he is saying.

I hang up my phone as I walk into our bedroom. "Well, my mother has officially covered everything," I say, tossing my phone onto our bed. "And I do mean everything. She even has a tux picked out for Blake and a dress for Jackie," I say in awe of her. I swear that woman can accomplish anything in a matter of seconds.

Dash pulls his shirt off and sits down on the end of the bed as he stares down at the floor.

I crawl on the bed behind him and softly run my hands up his smooth back. "What's wrong?" I ask.

He reaches up behind him and grabs my right hand. He pulls it over his shoulder and kisses it before he wraps it around his neck. "Nothing."

"Hey," I say as I pull him to where he has to lay down on the bed, with his feet still planted on the floor. I look down at him. "Why are you lying?" I ask softly as I run my hands through his hair.

He sighs. "Because this isn't what I asked for."

"I know, but you won your first race. Why shouldn't you celebrate it?"

He stands up and turns around to face me. "I did. I celebrated it with you. Why do you think I followed you back to the trailer after I won instead of doing the interview?"

"Uh…" I don't have an answer.

"Because I didn't want to do some stupid interview."

"You did that interview with me after the pics leaked," I remind him.

"I did that interview because it was how I felt about you, not because of my racing."

I sit up on my knees and stare at him confused. "I don't understand what you're trying to say," I say truthfully. "I don't understand why you don't want the world to see how great you are. You won your first race…"

"God, I wish people would quit saying that," he all but shouts, causing me to scoot back on the bed. "It was just a stupid race," he adds with a growl.

"Whoa. A stupid race?" I question shocked. "How can you even say that?"

He runs a hand through his hair and his muscles flex at the motion. "You wanna know why I don't want a party with reporters and photographers?" He doesn't allow me to answer. "It's because I don't want to rub it in people's faces. I don't want to plaster that I won all over the papers or the TV. Yes, I won; we celebrated at a nice quiet dinner afterwards with my friends and the crew. Let's leave it at that."

This isn't like the Dash I know. The cocky one who thinks he's the best. The one who gives that sexy smirk and gets everything he wants. Why would he not want to the world to see…? Unless… "You're afraid." He narrows those beautiful gray eyes at me. "Afraid that you won't win the next one." Of course. Like my father said, he came out of nowhere and won. Winning will bring haters. And those haters will laugh in his face if he were to lose the next one.

"Babe, it's okay to be afraid. But you're gonna win the next one," I tell him.

He gives a right laugh. "Because you can see the future?" he asks sarcastically.

"No because I know how hard you have worked. And how hard you're going to continue to work." I crawl over on my hands and knees to the end of the bed and place my hands on his face. "There's nothing wrong with being confident, Dash. There's nothing wrong with celebrating your victory. You don't have to mention anything about the next race or the fact that you're going to blow everyone out of the water." He rolls his eyes, but his lips tug at the corners. "Let the world see what you have accomplished. Let the world see the support system that you have. There are other people out there who believe in their dreams; let them know that they can be achieved."

He places his hands on my face and leans forward placing his forehead against mine. "I love you." His voice is soft.

"I love you, too." I reach out and undo the button of his pants. I look up to his beautiful gray eyes as I slowly undo his zipper.

"What are you doing?" he asks softly.

"I wanna show you how much I love you."

He gives me a soft smile. "I like the sound of that." His pants fall to the floor and he steps out of them and then removes his boxers. I reach up, bring his face down to mine, and kiss him as I pull him onto the bed. Ready to give him everything that I have.

He rolls us over to where he's straddling me and I smile up at him.

## CHAPTER THIRTY-NINE

*Dash*

"Nothing is more amazing than this," I say truthfully, as I run my hand down her stomach.

"Really?" She cocks an eyebrow. "You're comparing winning a race to sex?" she questions with a laugh.

"No." I shake my head. "I'm comparing it to you." I place my hands on both sides of her face. "Nothing in this world compares to touching you. Winning that race was all I ever wanted. Until you." She smiles. "I want to spend the rest of my life with you. I want to wake up every morning knowing that you're mine."

"I am," she says without a doubt.

"Nothing in this world could compare to that feeling." It's true. You could win every award there is in the world but having the feeling of knowing that someone loves you — well, nothing could beat that. Because all those awards are just gonna sit on a shelf and collect dust. People will forget what you worked so hard to accomplish — that dream. But she will wake up every morning loving me. And every night knowing that I love her just as much.

"Why am I so emotional?" She lets out a little laugh.

I smile down at her. "I don't know. But I'll spend the rest of my life drying your tears."

I wake up to the sound of the shower running. I push the covers off me and make my way into the bathroom. I open the door quietly and I allow my eyes to roam over her back and ass. My already hard cock aches as my eyes continue down past her thighs and down her legs. She pushes her head under the water as she runs her hands down her hair; bubbles pool at her feet from her shampoo.

I step in and close the door behind me. "Can I join you?" I question, and I can almost hear her smile as she keeps her back to me.

"Only if you wash me," she says as she turns around to face me.

"I'd love to," I say with a smile.

Her eyes drop down to my hard cock, and I realize I'm stroking it. Her smile widens, and she tilts her head to the side. "I'll make a deal with you." She steps into me, throwing her arms around my neck.

"I'm listening."

"You wash me and then I'll wash you."

"Deal," I say before my lips attack hers.

Once we finish in the shower, I throw on an old pair of worn-out jeans, a black t-shirt, and grab my helmet.

"Where are you going?" she asks as she comes out of the bathroom with her hair now dry.

I stand and give her kiss on the cheek. "I have some errands to run."

"What? On your bike?" She questions.

"It's a beautiful day." I smile. "It won't take long," Last night when we fell asleep in each other's arms, I realized what we have isn't enough. I want more! "You have a busy day with your mother and Jackie. I'll be back in plenty of time to get ready for tonight," I say with a smile, and she nods. I'm still not a big fan of the idea of this party, but I have an idea of how to turn it into a celebration. I thought that it would be the perfect time to tell her just how much she means to me. To prove it to her. I'm a big man of actions to back up the words.

I run out to the garage and jump on my bike. I was telling her the truth when I said it was a beautiful day. I take my time riding into town. I stop at the first flower shop I come to. Parking my bike, I go in and order her a beautiful bouquet of flowers to be delivered an hour before the party is to start tonight. I would have them delivered tomorrow, but I don't know what our plans are for tomorrow and I would hate for them to not be delivered. We both already have so much going on that I'm not sure she will be home.

Once I finish with that, I jump back on the bike and go a few blocks to my main stop. This one takes me a little longer. I spend two hours in the store trying to make a decision. The right decision. I want her to love it.

"Thank you," I say to the man behind the counter, and he smiles.

"Good luck," he replies. "She's gonna love it."

I place the box in the inside pocket of my leather jacket as I walk out the front door. I come to a stop next to my bike to place my helmet on when I hear my name being called.

"Dash?"

I turn around to see a little boy who looks to be the age of seven. "I knew that was you." He turns to his mom who stands beside him. "I told you, Mom," he says excitedly.

She smiles down at him. "You did. Let's not bother him." She tries to walk off with him, but the little boy runs to me.

"I watched you race." He jumps up and down. "You were awesome!" He gives a fist pump.

I chuckle. "Thank you!"

"I wanna be just like you when I grow up." He points to the helmet as it sits on my bike. "I want one of those helmets. And a trophy. Oh, my gosh!" He squeals between rambling on. "I'm your biggest fan. That would be a dream come true—to be just like you."

His mother laughs as she grabs his hand. "I'm so sorry," she says and starts to pull him away.

"Oh, no reason to be sorry," I say with a smile. And I finally start to understand what Tabatha was talking about last night. I've never seen myself as an idol. Being thrown in jail doesn't quite scream role model.

"Mom," he says digging his heels into the concrete. "I didn't get an autograph," he whines.

She huffs as she lets go of his hand and looks up at me. "Do you mind?" she asks as if it would put me out to sign my name.

"Not at all," I say. I pat my jacket and all I feel is the box holding the ring. "I don't have a pen…" I pat my jeans.

"Oh, I have a Sharpie." She starts to dig in her purse. She produces a silver Sharpie but frowns. "I don't have my notepad with me. I wrote my grocery list this morning and forgot to put it back in my purse."

"Mom," the kid whines, "you have to…"

I smile as I get an idea. "Here." I turn around and grab my helmet off my bike. Tabatha had said that my story could help others believe their dreams could come true. Maybe this helmet can help this little guy believe in himself. And that's the least I can do for my biggest fan, right?

"Oh, no…" The mother shakes her head as I start to sign my name on it. "I'll go get some paper. Please, don't do that!" she begs.

I finish signing my name and hand it to the little boy who is jumping up and down in front of me as he squeals. "You keep it," I say as I put my hand on his head and mess up his hair.

"Are you sure?" the mother asks wide-eyed.

"Absolutely!" I reassure her.

The mother hugs me, and I pose for a picture with the little boy. Once they thank me and I hug the kid one more time, I pull out my phone and send Tabatha a quick text. Then with a huge smile on my face, I pat the ring in my jacket pocket one more time before I get onto my bike and pull out into traffic.

I once told Tabatha that your dreams change as you grow older. And my dream is to be her husband. To be the father of her kids. My dream is to belong to her and only her for the rest of my life. I hope she understands that only she can make my dream come true when I ask her tonight in front of the world.

# CHAPTER FOURTY

## *Tabatha*

I stand in front of the bathroom mirror as I put my pearl earrings on. My mother had bought them for me on my sixteenth birthday, and I wear them every chance I get.

I walk out of the bathroom and into our closet to look at myself in the full-length mirror. I run my hands down my white silk dress. My mother has impeccable taste when it comes to…well, anything. But I have to give her mad props for this dress. It's strapless and has a thick black silk band that goes around the waist and ties in a bow at the back. It's going to look amazing when I stand next to Dash in his black tux.

Speaking of Dash, he still has not returned home. I walk out of the closet and go to look at my phone that is charging on my nightstand. He's been gone all day, but I haven't bothered him. I know he has a lot on his mind right now regarding the party tonight, and I don't want to make it worse on him.

I smile when I see he had sent me a text a few hours ago.

*Hey baby, I can't stop thinking about how much I love you. I want you to be mine…forever! Love you!*

Forever? Hmm. I hope that means what I think it does. I place my phone back down when I hear the doorbell ring. I make my way down to the front door. I smile when I open it to a man standing on our doorstep with a huge bouquet of white flowers in his hands.

"Miss Knight?" he questions.

"That's me," I say excitedly.

He hands me the flowers and I shut the door as he leaves. I all but run into the kitchen and place them on the kitchen table. I take the card out and read it.

*Here's to a night you'll never forget.*

I place the card on the table and go to run up to the stairs to grab my phone and call him when the doorbell rings again. "What now?" I ask running to it.

"Hey girl," I smile brightly when I open the door to see Jackie standing there. Her cream dress looks elegant yet sexy as it hangs off her shoulders and has a little dip to show off her cleavage. I look up at her face, and the smile drops off my face when I see her makeup is smeared from tears. "What's wrong?" I demand as I watch tears run down her cheeks.

"It's Dash…"

"What about him?" I demand as my heart begins to pound in my chest.

"He's in the hospital. Your dad told me to come get you…"

I shove past her, slamming our front door as I run to her car.

I run into the hospital, sweating and breathing heavily. Signs of my body telling me I need more than just yoga classes. The once pretty dress clings to my sweat-drenched body. "Where is he?" I demand, coming up to my father in the waiting room.

Jackie had informed me in the car that a car had hit him while on his bike and he had to be brought to the hospital by ambulance. I guess someone recognized him and went through his phone and contacted my father.

He spins around and looks down at me. And his black eyes soften as he opens his mouth to speak. He closes it quickly and then sighs heavily.

"No." My voice cracks. "Where is he?" I shout. "Where is Dash?"

"He's in surgery," he finally answers.

"What happened?" I demand.

"A car crossed the center median and hit him head-on. He's been in surgery for a couple of hours." He places his hands on my shoulders and speaks softly. "They think he may have brain damage..."

"No." I shake my head. "His helmet," I say in a rush. "He always wears a helmet," I inform him.

He shakes his head. "I'm not clear on the situation, but there was no helmet at the scene."

"No," I cry out as I feel like I was just stabbed. "When he left, he had it in his hand. He always wears a helmet," I repeat brokenly.

My father wraps his arms around me and gives me a hug. "I believe you."

I pull away, fall down into the seat beside me, and place my head in my hands. Surgery. It's better than nothing. That's what these surgeons do. They save lives.

This is gonna be no different than his last wreck. He's gonna wake up and demand that my dad come back there and pull some strings to get him out of this place. And then he'll come back to our home where I will take care of him. That's what we do; that's why we found each other, to take care of each other.

269

I lift my head and take a deep breath when I see Blake enter the waiting room, and Jake following behind him. Blake looks at me and my breath gets stuck in my throat when I see his bloodshot eyes. And I realize he must know more than I do.

I go to stand, but my father approaches him first and pulls him to the side. He places his arm over his shoulders and starts to walk him away from me as he speaks down to him. I hate that I can't hear what he is saying. But what could he possibly know? He's in surgery. I'm not sure that they could give him much information due to him not being relation. Oh, who am I kidding? The man can pull any information out of anyone.

I watch as Blake hangs his head and wipes his eyes, and I start to panic once again as a lump starts to form in my throat. What does he know? What did he tell him?

I stand and wipe the tears from my face. I take a deep breath and make my way over to them. "Dad?" I question, and they both look down at me. "Please?" I beg. "Please tell me what's going on?"

"It's bad." Blake's voice cracks and I place my hand over my mouth.

"What do you know?" I question just as brokenly.

"We don't know anything yet," my father says more to Blake than me.

I turn to face him with angry eyes. "What aren't you telling me?" I all but shout in the waiting room.

"She deserves to know," Blake says to my father, but he stares down at me.

"Tell me." My body shakes.

My father reaches into his suit pocket and pulls out a little black box. I stare at it with wide eyes. "What is this?"

"It's what Dash was out doing," my father says as he hands it to me. "The paramedics found it in the pocket of his riding jacket, and they gave it to me."

I close my eyes tightly and tears run down my face. This can't be what I think it is. The text- the flowers- the card that said to a night you'll never forget. This is not how this is supposed to happen. "I can't..." I choke on the words. "How bad is it?" I whisper still keeping my eyes shut as I grip the box in my hand. "I need to know." I open my eyes, and Blake immediately pulls me in for a hug.

"It's bad," he repeats. "But we both know that Dash is a fighter." I wrap my hands around his neck and nod my head quickly. He is. And he obviously has big plans for our future. He will fight for that.

# CHAPTER FOURTY-ONE

# *Tabatha*

*"Do you take this man to be your lawfully wedded husband? As long as you both shall live?"*

*"I do," I say with a smile on my face and a happy tear runs down my cheek.*

*Dash stands in front of me in an all-white tux and a proud smile on his face. His shaggy hair is slicked back and his gray eyes are shining into mine.*

*Never in a million years would I have guessed that I married a man who I once had a one-night stand with. But, somewhere, our story fell together as if a puzzle. It was made to be. We just fit.*

*"Do you take this woman to be your lawfully wedded wife? As long as you both shall live?" the preacher asks Dash.*

*"I do," his deep voice says, and my smile grows bigger as another tear falls down my face.*

*He reaches up and runs the back of his thumb over my cheek wiping it away. "I will forever wipe your tears away," he whispers, and it just makes another fall.*

*"You may now kiss your bride."*

I'm pulled out of my dream as my head falls forward and a small snore comes out of my mouth. I reach up to wipe the drool off my chin and push my unbrushed hair off my face. It's a dream that I continue to have every time I close my eyes. But it's become a nightmare. Hanging me.

I haven't left the hospital since I got here, five days ago. My mom showed up while Dash was still in surgery. She brought all of us a change of clothes and brought me some bathroom products. Even she knew Dash was going to be in here for a while and that I wasn't going to leave his side. My father pulled out all the stops and got the largest room possible, and I refuse to leave, afraid as soon as I do that he'll wake up. And I wanna be the first person to see those beautiful gray eyes. I wanna be the first one to hold his hand and tell him it's all gonna be okay.

His room smells like flowers—so much to the point where it makes me nauseous. The wreck has been all over the news and the gifts, flowers, and balloons have been pouring in from all of his fans to wish him well.

I remove the blanket from my legs and walk over to his bed. I grab his hand; I swear it gets colder every day. I softly run my hand through his long shaggy hair as I look at the tube that is down his throat—the ventilator that is keeping him alive. But I know he'll fight it. He's a fighter. "Good morning, sweetie," I say softly. "Wake up for me, baby," I whisper giving him a kiss on his forehead. I then sit down next to him. "I have a confession. I know what errand you were out doing." I smile. "I still haven't opened it, though. I don't wanna ruin your surprise." I give a little laugh. "I still expect you to get down on one knee, ya know? I expect a big display of love." I sigh. "I'm sure you had planned on doing it at your party." I know him very well, and I would bet everything I have that he was going to make that party about us and not his racing. He's sneaky like that. "You do you know that Dad is just going to throw you another one when you get out of here? You can do it then," I tell him. I lean down where my face is close to his. "But I have a little secret for you, too. I'm going to say yes." I softly kiss the side of his face before I pull back and look at him. He's almost unrecognizable. His face is swollen and bruised. The left side of his head is shaved where they had to open it up to relieve the pressure off his brain so the swelling could go down. His collarbone is broken, along with his right knee. His right ankle is shattered along with his left wrist. The car that hit him head-on wasn't paying attention. They were speeding and somehow went across the center median. A car that was behind Dash, who witnessed it, said he never even saw it coming. I hope that he didn't feel any pain. I pray that he wasn't awake for any of it. A part of me, the selfish part, wants him to wake up and see that I'm here. The other part of me wants him to stay asleep, to just sleep through all the pain and wake up once he heals.

I stand up, lean down to give him a soft kiss on his bruised face, and then pull away. I go back over to the couch and grab my bag before walking into the bathroom that is connected to his room. I wash my ashen face with some cold water and start to brush my teeth. I change out of one pair of yoga pants for a clean pair and a fresh t-shirt. I step back out of the room and see his parents along with my dad now standing in his room. His parents, who have only been here twice. I hate them more every time I see them.

"Good morning," I say trying to give them all a soft smile. I've really been holding it together pretty well. I have my moments where I break down but, for the most part, I try to stay happy for him. I know he can hear me, and he needs to know that when he wakes up, I'm gonna be here for him.

"Tabatha…" My father's voice cracks, and he clears his throat.

"What is it?" I ask, taking a step toward him. "Did they get the results back?" I ask in a panic. They keep testing him. I'm not sure what for, but I heard one nurse say something about brain activity.

His mother goes to speak, but a nurse walks into the room and closes the door. We all stand quietly and I can feel the pressure in the room start to build. I can literally hear a humming in my head.

I jump back like someone shocks me when the nurse pulls the blinds shut, closing out the rest of the hospital.

"How long will it take?" his mom, asks as tears run down her face.

"How long will what take?" I demand. "What are you doing?"

"Tabatha...they've made a decision," my father says as he turns to face me.

My heart stops and my knees wobble. "Please don't do this," I cry walking over to his mother. My father wraps his arms around me. "Please don't do this," I beg.

"Come on, Tabatha." My father gently pulls me toward the door, and I realize he wants me to leave. I start to fight him, but he tightens his arms around me.

"I'm his wife," I yell as I hold up my left hand but realize I haven't opened the box. "I won't allow this," I shout furious. How can they do this? I have rights. I'm going to be his wife; I have rights.

The nurse has an instant look of panic on her face and looks at Dash's father. He leans over to whisper in her ear, and she looks at me with pity in her soft blue eyes. "I'm truly sorry for your loss, but..."

"No," I try to say but I don't have enough breath to even say the two letter word.

His mom looks at me with anger in her eyes. As if I'm making a scene when she is the one who is about to kill her own son. "He's gone," she declares as she straightens her back. Like she has to have some kind of fucking pride.

"No," I shout making his mother jump. "He just needs more time," I say as my eyes look back over at him lying in the hospital bed. He looks so helpless. Just lying there as if he's begging me to fight for him. "Please," I beg, looking at his mother. "He can fight this," I cry. "Miracles happen every day." I try to push my father off me once again, but he holds me tightly. "I beg you. Please don't do this to him." They've been talking about this since he came out of surgery. The odds of him ever waking up. And the

275

odds of him breathing without the ventilator. Without it, he will die. He needs to wake up before they try to remove it. He's not awake yet, though.

"I'm sorry…" his mother cries.

"You're gonna kill him!" I shout angrily. My father starts to move as he drags me out of the room, and I try to fight him. Try to grab on to anything that will keep me closer to Dash. But I find nothing. He slams the door shut with his foot, and I cry out.

A man comes running up to us as I scratch at the window that separates me from Dash. Those stupid curtains block my view of him. "I can sedate her."

"No," my father growls and the man runs off.

I turn to face my dad. I grab a hold of his shirt and force him to look down at me. "Please don't let them do this, Daddy," I sob. "I love him."

"I know," he says as he runs a hand over my hair. "I'm so sorry, sweet pea. But it's their choice."

"What about my choice?" I cry. "What about Dash's choice?" I lift my left hand and point to my ring finger. "He wanted me. He loves me." He wraps his arms around me and pulls me into his chest. "They can't take him from me." I feel my lungs tighten, and my body gets heavy; it's as if I'm dying with him. I'd be better off dead. I have no life without him. I have no reason to keep going. Dash came into my life like a whirlwind and now he's leaving me with nothing but a massive hole. "I…Need…" I swallow. "Water." I find myself breathing heavy and unable to talk due to my throat closing.

My father leaves me right away to get me some water, and I look up to see Jake standing at the end of the hall, just staring at me blankly. I wipe my face quickly and waste no time in turning around and going back to his door. I slowly and quietly twist the knob and open it up to where I can look inside.

His father stands with his back against the wall while he holds his wife. She sobs into his shirt as his face nuzzles into her neck. The nurse stands back by the foot of Dash's bed; she's eying me nervously, waiting for me to make a scene. But I have no fight left in me. Instead, I take what little strength I have left and make the ten steps over to his bed. It's as if I'm walking in quicksand. The ground pulling my body under. My chest tightening to the point of suffocation.

I crawl on his bed and cuddle up next to him, softly placing my hand over his chest. I hold my breath as I feel his chest slowly move as he breathes with the ventilator no longer there. I close my eyes and remember what his laugh sounded like. I remember what his touch felt like. "Don't make me live without you," I whisper as tears run down my face.

I cry uncontrollably as my body shakes. "Miracles happen every day," I repeat in a broken mess. I close my eyes tightly and pray to God that he continues to breathe on his own. Seconds tick by. Minutes pass by. And I start to relax. I feel my body start to calm as I talk to him. About our future. About how much I love him. And then, just when I thought I got my miracle, it was taken from me.

His chest stops moving. And I feel it down in my soul. I feel him leave me. I feel the room grow colder and my heart be ripped out of my chest. I cry out and two arms wrap around me. I look up to Jake now standing beside Dash's bed. He rips me from him, and I start kicking and screaming. I feel a prick in my arm and then those strong arms soften, yet hold me up as my legs grow weak and my eyes grow heavy. But it doesn't help the massive hole in my heart. The part that Dash left me behind with.

I numbly get out of Jake's car and walk up the stairs to the house that Dash and I shared. My mom walks in front of me, and my father silently walks next to her. He opens the door for us, and I find myself walking to the kitchen. I fall down into a chair at the kitchen table. I look up to see the flowers that sit in the crystal case in front me. They're dead. Just like Dash. Just like me.

He's gone. Dash lived for twenty minutes off the ventilator. Then, as the clock in his room read 9:32 AM, he left us for good. He died in my arms. I held him as he took his last breath. That does something to a person. When Jake ripped me from him, it ripped my soul out. I'm nothing now. I woke after the sedation they had given me wore off in Jake's arms, and I prayed that God would take me with him. I prayed that God would strike me dead. He didn't. He left me behind to live out my life, which could be fifty more years without Dash. Why is life so cruel? Why did God give me something so special just to take it away? I can't answer any of those questions, but I try.

I ignore Jake as he walks past me and stands to the side. He constantly watches me, waiting for me to do something, but I have nothing to do. Nothing to live for. My mother silently places all the flowers from the hospital on my kitchen table as my father stands over in the corner talking quietly to Blake. Jackie hangs on to him as if she were to let go, she may lose him like I did Dash.

I reach out and touch the card that sits in front of me. Tears roll down my face in waves so strong that I can't even read what the card says, but I don't have to. I remember what it says. Here's to a night you'll never forget. How right he was! I throw a hand over my mouth as a sob comes out.

I use what strength I have and stand up. I want to tell everyone to leave, but I don't even have the strength to speak. I make my way up to our bedroom and slam the door shut. I then fall onto our bed and sob into the pillow.

My body shakes and my throat tightens. I feel a hand on my back and I jump as if it stung me. "Please...just leave me alone," I cry out as I look up to Jake.

"I don't wanna leave you alone," he whispers.

I close my eyes tightly as I grab my chest. "It hurts so bad," I admit.

"It gets easier."

My eyes spring open, and I stare at him as if he's lost his mind. My body jolts as I hiccup. I've cried so hard that I have given myself the hiccups.

I shake my head. "It will never be easy living without him."

"I feel your pain."

"No, you don't," I shout, feeling the anger that I feel toward Dash. Angry that he gave up so easily.

"I do. I once lost someone I loved." He drops his head and looks down at the comforter. "The woman I wanted to spend the rest of my life with died," he admits.

I want to feel sorry for him. I want to tell him that I'm sorry. But I can't. No one can know how much I love Dash, and I'm not about to compare my love for him to the love that Jake felt for someone else.

He reaches out and places a hand on my leg. "The pain, it won't go away, but it will get easier. You'll forget..."

"I'll never forget him," I shout as I shove his hand away.

"That's not what I meant." He speaks softly.

"Just please stop talking." I wipe the tears from my face. "Please," I beg with all I have. "Please stop. I'm begging you." My vision has turned blurry once again, and I hiccup once more.

He's quiet for a few seconds before he finally speaks. "I'll be downstairs."

I fall back down onto our bed when I hear the bedroom door shut softly and I continue to sob.

# CHAPTER FORTY-TWO

## *Tabatha*

I sit in our bedroom on the floor with my back against my wall as I look at the bed that we shared. All the memories we made in such short little time. It's crazy how you have only been with someone for a short time, and it feels like you've known them all your life.

I sleep on his side of the bed because his smell still lingers. I find myself walking into the bathroom and spraying his cologne, and I swear I can feel him wrap his arms around me. I can hear his voice telling me that I'm gonna be okay. But it's not and I won't.

As I sit here on the floor with my knees pulled up to my chest, I think about the day I have ahead of me. And I refuse to face it. I refuse to go through the motions when all I feel is an ache as if someone has stabbed me in the heart and I'm slowly bleeding out.

I look over to the far wall and see that the TV is on. I have to place my hand over my mouth to quiet my sob when I see Dash on the screen. He's sitting next to me on a brown leather couch as he smiles at the cameras. It's our interview my dad made us give. They've had it on every local channel since the news of his death broke.

"How did you two meet?" the pretty blonde asks as she sits across from us.

"At a party," Dash says with a little laugh. He turns to look at me and reaches down to grab my hand. I smile brightly at him as he soothes my nerves. "Who knew I would have so much to celebrate."

"I assume you're referring to your racing contract?" she questions.

"No." He frowns looking back at her. "Falling in love."

I hang my head as a sob wracks my body. He left me! What about me? I fall over to my side, and I open my eyes. There in front of me in a blurry haze is the little black box. With shake hands, I reach out and grab it. I still haven't opened it. I keep hoping that I will wake up and Dash will be on bended knee. I keep hoping I will see his big smile again with the open box in his hand. But it's never gonna come.

With shaky hands and tear-filled eyes, I open the box and sob as I see the beautiful oval diamond. I close my eyes as I sit up. I cry out into the room as I think of him buying this. How much thought he must have put into it. How excited he must have been.

I open my eyes and look down at it. I slide it on my finger and whisper, "I do." Tears run down my face like a river and my chest aches. I stare down at the ring and cry uncontrollably.

The doorbell rings, but I ignore it. I don't want visitors. Everyone finally left on the second day, but they just won't stay away.

"Tabatha!" I hear Blake's voice yell.

I close my eyes, and my head falls back down to my knees. "Please go away," I say softly.

It rings again. "Tabatha! If you don't open this door, then I will break it down." His voice is so loud; I can hear it as if he was standing in front of me and not downstairs.

Then I hear Jake's voice growl. "Don't give her a choice."

I shake my head as if he can see me. No one cares about what I want. No one cared I wanted to give Dash a chance to pull through. That I wanted to spend the rest of my life with him.

I hear some commotion and then I hear the breaking of wood. The pounding of the door coming off the hinges. "Blake…" I hear Jackie cry out to him, and I hold in the sob of what's about to come. For what he is about to make me face. My biggest fear.

My bedroom door swings open also hitting the wall, and I tighten my arms around my knees as I keep my head buried into my knees. "Get up," Blake commands.

I look up at him; the tears falls so fast that it makes him nothing but a blurry blob. But I can see two figures standing over by my door. Jake and Jackie, for sure. "You can't make me."

He grabs my hand and jerks me to a stand. "You will not do this," he yells.

"Blake…" Jake growls as he walks toward us.

"Shut up, Jake," Blake snaps. Something has happened to him since Dash left us. His death has changed all of us. And we're all falling apart in our own way.

"I can't go." I wrap my arms around myself. "Please," I beg of him. "Don't make me." I continue to beg everyone for something, but none of them listen. No one but Jake.

His eyes narrow on me. "You think this is easy on me? On any of us?" he questions. He places his hands on my shoulders, and his eyes soften. "I know you loved him. But you knew him for months. I've known him my entire life. I lost a brother and a best friend." His anger breaks and his voice cracks. "I love him just as much as you do." He sniffs. "And the time has come for you to show your respect."

I hang my head, and he pulls me in for a hug. "Good-bye is never easy," he whispers, and I sob into his shirt knowing that he is right. "But Dash deserves a proper good-bye." I hate how right he is. Dash deserves to have the woman that he loved at his funeral. It's time for me to say my final good-bye.

We all four sit in silence as the limo drives us to the cemetery. My black hat is so big that it covers most of my makeup-less face. Tears silently roll down my face, and I keep my head down. Jake sits next to me, and Blake lays with his head in Jackie's slap. I try not to stare, but it's so hard. He looks like I feel. Lost. Betrayed. How could Dash leave us? How could he not fight for us? He loved us, yet he gave up so easily. I don't know why, but I have this feeling that this isn't how it was supposed to end. I know people die. But not Dash. He was so young and had such a promising future. He had dreams that he still needed to fulfill. I had dreams for him that involved us. A family. I look down at the ring on my finger and that stabbing sensation in my chest returns. It takes my breath away. I place my hand on my chest and try to breathe, but there's nothing there. I start to pull on my black dress.
"I...can't..." I try to speak, but my throat burns. My chest tightens, and I close my eyes tightly.

"Tabatha?" Jake's voice demands as he shakes me.

Nothing. I try to say something, but nothing comes out. I try to push his hands off me, but he doesn't let go.

"Help her," Jackie cries out.

I reach up and grab my throat, trying to get air, but there's nothing there. Just this pain. The suffocating pain that Dash is gone. That in less than an hour, he will be in the ground. Gone forever. This can't be how our love story ends. The one that we fought so hard to keep.

"Tabatha?" Jake yells as he shoves a bottle of water in my face. I try to push it away, but he grabs my arms with one hand and pushes the water to my lips with the other. He tilts it and water runs down the back of my throat. It chokes me, and I cough it up. I suck in air as I continue to cough, water spilling down my chin and onto my black dress. I bend over, and he roughly rubs my back. Tears sting my eyes and my throat burns. Dash would be so ashamed if he could see me now. How pathetic I am. How much I truly relied on him.

"It's okay." He wraps his arms around me and pulls me into his side. "You're gonna be okay. I promise," Jake whispers as I continue to take deep breaths. I should push him away. I shouldn't allow myself to lean on a man considering he's not the love of my life, but at the moment, I need this support.

"He left me," I cry. "How could he leave me?" I understand how the world works. You're born. You live your entire life chasing dreams that most don't achieve. Except love. People find love every day and they waste it. They tarnish it by cheating or lying. Or just because they're scared. I do believe that Dash was my soul mate — the one person in this world for me. Now I have to face this world alone with a broken heart.

"I'm here for you," he whispers.

By the time we pull up to the cemetery, I have my breathing under control. My hands shake and my knees wobble, but with the help of Jake, I get out of the limo and make my way to where all the chairs line up in rows. There are hundreds of people already here. Bikes line the entrances, some crotch rockets and some Harleys, decorating the cemetery of men and women to pay their respects for a man who loved to ride. Most, I'm sure, are people who Dash didn't even know, but many wear his name across the front of their shirts with his number eighty-eight written across the back. His death has been on the headlines for the last five days now, and I see no end in sight. Everyone here wants to come and pay their respects for the kid who was going places. The man who had big dreams as a little boy and who had almost accomplished them. It wasn't any secret the type of man he was. Reckless. He liked everyone, and everyone liked him. He was good hearted and truly a carefree spirit.

I come to a stop while I look around. The cemetery is as beautiful as one can be. Beautiful green grass and rolling hills. It has to cover fifteen acres. At least. His parents are laying him to rest next to his father's parents. I'm glad that he is once again close to the people who raised him, but it also hurts me. Even when I pass, which can't be soon enough, I won't ever be near him. Ever again!

"What's wrong?" Jake leans down and whispers in my ear as he holds onto my arm.

Looking at the people who stare at me with pity in their eyes is a feeling of sadness on its own. It's been part of the headlines. Erik Dashling passes before getting the chance to propose to girlfriend. They've had pictures of us at the race he won. The look of love in our eyes. The intimate kiss that they now plaster all over the world is earth shattering. I have come to fucking hate social media. Some bastard at the hospital spilled the beans about finding the ring on him. For what? A little cash.

I feel so lost. "I...I need to leave." I choke on the words as I try to avoid the black casket that sits ahead of me. I feel like I'm going to suffocate again like I did in the limo, knowing he's in there. I pull on my dress that is still damp in spots from the water I coughed up. Jake grabs my hands, pulling them away before I rip this dress off my body.

He positions his body in front of mine and looks down at me. "Take a deep breath," he orders, and I do as he says as I look deeply into his soft blue eyes. "Good.

Another one." I do it again, and I feel my shoulders relax a little.

Blake and Jackie walk past us and to the front row. I lower my head as we follow them. I keep my eyes on my hands as we sit in softly covered chairs. I'm thankful for the hat that keeps people from seeing my tear-streaked face.

A hand reaches over and grips mine. I look up quickly when I see it's my mother's hand. She doesn't even try to give me a smile as the tears run down her face. My father sits next to her, and I've never seen him cry, until now. He looked at Dash as a son, and in a way, that's exactly what he was going to be. His son-in-law.

I look next to my father and see Dash's parents sitting there. Tears run down their faces as well, and I want to scream at them to stop pretending like they care that their son died. They killed him. Don't they understand that? How can they cry for something that they did?

I look down at my hand when my mother runs her finger over my engagement ring that he had purchased for me, and it comes crashing into me like a wave on a shore. I've been blaming his mother and father when the real person to blame is myself. That was why he left the house. To buy me that ring. "It's my fault." The broken words fall from my lips as the sob wracks my body.

"Oh no, honey," my mother says softly as she wraps her arms around me. "It's not your fault. None of this is your fault." She places her head on mine, and she kisses me as we cry together.

## CHAPTER FOURTY-THREE

# Tabatha

I remember every word spoken during the ceremony. As much as I tried to avoid what was being said, I couldn't. I remember every sniffle, every sob, and every tear that fell from my eyes. The ceremony ended minutes ago and people have started to leave, but I stay seated as my eyes remain fixed on his casket. It's beautiful and hideous all at once.

It's black. All black. With chrome accents that cover the corners. I don't know why I'm still sitting here. I don't want to watch them put him in the ground. I don't want to say good-bye anymore. I want to say hello. I want to go back to the first time I saw him, and I never wanna let him go. I would do things so differently. I want to say that I choose him forever, but I don't get that option. Not anymore.

I look down at my purse sitting on my lap and start to dig through it. I had one thing that I wanted to do before I left here, and I'm going to do it.

I find what I'm looking for and pull it out. Jake takes my purse from me without me even asking and I stand. On shaky legs and a heavy heart, I walk over to the casket. It's open. It's been open for the past few minutes for people to say their good-byes. But I just couldn't find the will to do it until now.

He looks so different. So pale. So not Dash. His mother dressed him in a suit and I just want to rip it off him. He hated wearing suits. He preferred t-shirts and jeans. She knew nothing about her son.

I lift the small piece of paper to my lips and kiss it, leaving what little lip-gloss I had on the card that he had given me with the flowers. I then place it in his casket as I whisper, "I said yes." And then with a broken heart, I turn around and start to walk away, but a little boy stands in front of me. Tears run down his face as he looks up at me with bloodshot eyes.

"I'm sorry," he whispers brokenly.

I don't know what to say to him. Thankfully, Jake comes to stand beside me. "Thank you," he replies to the little boy and it sounds stupid.

"You're the one, the one that is in the photos with him that I see on TV?" he asks me and I nod as I wipe the tears from me face.

"I want you to have this." He turns around to the woman standing behind him and she hands him something when he turs back around to face me I almost fall over.

"His helmet," I take it from him with shaking hands and heart pounding. "How do you have it?" I ask trying not to fall over.

He looks guilty as he lowers his eyes to the ground. "He gave it to me. He signed it and gave it to me outside of a jewelry shop."

I look down and rub the tips of my fingers over the four letters where he signed DASH along with his number below it and my chest tightens. "Thank you," I say brokenly as I hug the helmet to my chest. This could have saved his life. This one thing could have made our dreams come true.

# CHAPTER FOURTY-FOUR

## Tabatha

I lay in my bed as I look up at the ceiling. Jackie sits on the edge of it. Dash has been gone for three weeks, and it still hurts as bad as it did the moment I found out he left us. I don't eat much, but I sleep often. He's always in my dreams. Always smiling. Telling me that he loves me. He holds me while we bask in the sun on a beach. Or sitting by a warm fire on a cold, winter night. But wherever he takes me in my dreams, it's always just the two of us. I cry, and he tells me it'll be okay. That he is with me every day. That he truly never left me. And when I wake up, all alone, I cry my eyes out. I've closed myself off from the world. Jackie comes over daily, but it's gotten to the point where we don't even talk. She grabs my mail out of my mailbox and brings it in for me. I might have moved in with Dash, but I wasn't on the deed and he didn't have a will. His parents put the house up for sale shortly after the funeral, and I bought it. There was never a doubt in my mind that I wanted to stay here. Where we had planned to build a life. It has a different feel to it now, but he's still here with me.

Jackie sits on the end of the bed and just stares off into space for about thirty minutes then she leaves. At first, she would tell me that it was going to be okay — at times she even brought Jake or Blake with her — but after a couple of weeks, she gave up on me. I don't blame her; I'm a lost cause. And I'm actually thankful that she doesn't try to cheer me up. She doesn't understand how I feel, and it's hard for me to put it into words.

I close my eyes as I feel the bile taste in my mouth. It's been happening often lately. But what do you expect your body to do when you starve it? I've never understood what someone goes through when they say they have depression. Until now. It breaks you down to the point you feel crippled. My body has turned against me, and I don't even fight it. I can't even get out of bed. I keep the shades pulled tight to block out the sunlight. I prefer the darkness.

The bile rises and I sit up quickly, throwing a hand over my mouth. Jackie spins around to look at me wide-eyed. "Tabatha?" She reaches out for me, but I throw the covers off and run to my bathroom. My body finds the strength I didn't even know it had to move.

I fall to my knees and what little I had to eat yesterday comes up. Her soft hand rubs my back as I cough and spit out what my body has rejected. And when I finish, I lay down on the cold tile floor, once again unable to move. My body gives up on me again. Just those few seconds of vomiting left me utterly useless. She places a cold washrag on my forehead and lays down next to me. I look over at her as my eyes sting from the tears.

"I'm sorry for being such a shitty friend," I softly say. She's done nothing but be here for me, and I have taken that for granted.

"Stop," she says as a tear runs down her face. "I love you."

"I love you, too."

We lay there side by side on my bathroom floor like two kids afraid of what is to come. Because Dash taught me that you're never guaranteed tomorrow. And yesterday is never enough.

# EPILOGUE

## Six Years Later

I pull my short dark hair out of face, trying to tuck it behind my ears. I cut it a few years back. One of those moments when you go into the salon, and she asks, "What are we doing today?" And you say, "Something different." And that something different ends up making your hair almost ten inches shorter. I must have liked it though because I still keep it at that length. The wind blows again and it gets caught in my pink lip-gloss, and it makes me laugh.

"What's so funny?"

I look up to see Jake coming toward me with a big smile on his face and a little girl on his shoulders. "Mommy," she says excitedly. "Can I open my presents now?" she begs in the most adorable voice I have ever heard.

"Not yet," I say smiling. "We gotta wait til everyone gets here," I remind her, and she pushes her bottom lip out. It's hard to say no to that face. The face that looks so much like her father. I see him every time I look at her. Dash would be so proud of her. It took Jackie and me three full days of us living on my bathroom floor — me too sick to get up and her refusing to leave my side — before we thought of the possibility that I could be pregnant. I never even thought that could be a possibility, but I was wrong.

My life changed once again after reading those two pink lines. I had to be strong; I had to survive because Dash wasn't dead after all. A part of him was going to live on and I was going to be a mom. A mom to his child. That seems like so long ago now. But those nine months went by agonizingly slow. I was afraid to leave the house. I was afraid to do anything that could jeopardize my pregnancy.

He had left me with a gift, and I was afraid to lose it. Her room is covered in pictures of Dash and me. Some are of him winning his race. Some are from pictures of us that Jackie took with her phone. And some are magazine clippings. She knows her daddy is in heaven. And she knows that he loves her very much.

Our little girl squeals, getting my attention as Jake pulls her off his shoulders and places her on her feet. I smile as I look at the little pink toenails her white sandals are showing off. Her bright pink dress falls almost down to her feet and her dark brown hair is pulled up in a messy ponytail. I had fixed it earlier this morning, but she and Jake have been rolling around in the grass all day.

"Mommy?" She pulls on my shirt.

"What is it, sweet pea?" I ask with a smile.

"I want my bubbles," she pouts, and I reach into my pocket pulling out the small thing of bubbles for her. "Here you go."

She gives me a big smile and then turns around to run off after her friends. I stand in my parents' backyard on Erika's fifth birthday party, and I can't help but smile. I wanted to name her after him, so I named her Erika. Erika Noel Dashling. My smile grows as I watch her play. It hurts every day that Dash isn't here to see her. To see how much she looks like him and how much she already acts like him at only five. I see him in her every single day. I guess God gave me my miracle after all.

"Where is my brother?" Jake mumbles as he looks down at his watch. Jake also plays a big part in my and Erika's life. We started dating about a year back. I wouldn't say he has replaced Dash and he knows that he never could. But I do love him. It was a slow process. Accepting Dash was gone was hard to do. Then finding out that you are having a child to a man who will never get to experience that is even harder. But Jake was always there for me. We both have a hole that can't be filled by

*Dash*

someone we've lost, but I think that it helps. He loves
Erika just as much as I do. And in return, I love him. We're
not married, and I'm not sure if we ever will. But we have
built a life together. A different life than what I wanted
with Dash. People judge me for being with him, but I
don't care what they have to say. My father once told me
that he knows Dash would want me to be happy. And it
has taken six years, but finally I am.

I still have my engagement ring from Dash. I even
still wear it. I see Jake look down at it every now and then.
I don't know what he's thinking when he stares at it. All I
know is that I'm still not ready to take it off. Nothing
about my and Dash's relationship was planned, but what
little time we had together was beautiful. And every night
when I lay down in bed, I see him. His beautiful smile
hypnotizes me. His gorgeous eyes I get lost in.

I still feel his love. I still feel his strong arms around
me. I still see his cocky smile every time I close my eyes,
and I still smell him on my skin. He is still here, with me,
with us.

"God, it's hot as hell."

I spin around when I hear Jackie whining behind me.
"Well, look at you, little momma," I say with a smile as I
reach out and rub her big belly.

"Only you would have an outside birthday party,"
she complains, and Blake wraps his arms around her from
behind. The sun reflecting off his wedding band is almost
blinding.

He smirks over her shoulder. "Ignore her. He kept
her up all night kicking." He smiles proudly, and I let out
a chuckle.

"I just wish he would get here." She shoves him off
and stomps her foot.

"You only have a couple more weeks," I remind her.

294

"That's not soon enough," she declares. She looks around the backyard and her eyes widen and she smiles, before she waddles off toward the tables that showcase all the food.

I laugh as I watch her start shoveling finger food into her mouth. Jake takes off after her as she goes for the cake, and I laugh harder when she gives him the stare down. Never come become a pregnant woman and her food.

Blake places an arm around my shoulders as he pulls me into his side. We silently stand with our hips touching as we watch my little girl run to her Aunt Jackie once she spots her. Jackie places her plate down when Erika wraps her little arms around one of her legs.

"I wish Dash was here to see her," Blake says softly.

I let out a long sigh as I drop my head over onto his shoulder. "Me, too."

"I think about him all the time," he admits.

"Me, too. I can still feel him," I say as my throat tightens.

"I wish I could tell him that I loved him like a brother." He sniffs as he continues to watch Erika.

"He knows," I say softly. Blake has been my saving grace. He was tough on me when I need tough love, and he was also the shoulder that I needed at times. He's like the best brother a guy could have, and I know Dash loved him as if he was his brother.

"He would be so proud of you." He tightens his arm around my shoulders. "But I know he would hate to see you do it alone." He still looks at me as if I'm single. He is very supportive of my relationship with his brother, Jake. He just has a hard time with Dash being gone. I watch the way he looks at Erika. There are times that I still catch him rubbing his red eyes.

I lift my head to look up at him. "I'm not alone," I say truthfully.

*Dash*

He looks down and smiles at me. "You're right. You're not."

"Uncle Blakeeee." We both look to see Erika running for him with Jake right on her tail. He lets go of me and reaches down to catch her when she leaps into his arms.

"Happy Birthday, princess!" he says excitedly.

She wraps her arms around his neck as she giggles. "Wanna come blow bubbles with me?" she asks in her cute girly voice.

"Of course!" he replies. He starts to walk off with her still in his arms as she tells him about her princess cake. I can't help but laugh when I watch Jackie put her finger into the icing of said cake to try it. She stops and smiles at Jake, as he silently watches her.

"I told her the cake was off-limits," he mumbles next to me.

I turn and look up at him. "You're so cruel," I tease, and he laughs as he wraps his arms around me. We stand silently as we watch Erika play and I close my eyes and tell Dash that I miss and love him. Missing him hasn't gotten easier. It's a constant, dull ache, but a reminder of just how much what we had was real. Jake takes me to visit his grave often. I take him flowers and show him pictures that Erika colors for him. And it breaks my heart every time she asks if she can go visit Daddy. But we do it. Because I don't ever want her to forget how much I know he loves her. And every night when I lay down, I thank him for the beautiful gift that he left me with. A life that is full of heartbreak and fulfillment every day.

*The End*

# ABOUT THE AUTHOR

Shantel is a Texas born girl who now lives in Tulsa, Oklahoma with her high school sweetheart, who is a wonderful, supportive husband and their two seven year old daughters. She loves to spend time cuddled up on the couch with a good book.

She considers herself extremely lucky to get to be a stay at home wife and mother. Going to concerts and the movies are just a few of her favorite things to do. She hates coffee, but loves wine. She and her husband are both huge football fans, college and NFL. And she has to feed her high heel addiction by shopping for shoes weekly.

Although she has a passion to write, her family is most important to her. She loves spending evenings at home with her husband and daughter, along with their cat and dog.

You can find out more about Shantel and sign up for her newsletter at www.shanteltessierauthor.com

Be sure to follow her on Facebook and Twitter.

# ACKNOWLEDGMENTS

First I want to thank my amazing assistant Kelly Tucker. This woman is fucking awesome! She keeps me on track and makes me laugh. She is the best friend a girl can ask for. Thank you for always being there for me in my day to day life. I love you so much!

I would like to thank Jenny Sims my wonderful editor. I love you to pieces, girl. Thank you for all the help. I truly appreciate it.

I want to thank, Sommer Stein at Perfect Pearl Creative for making me such beautiful covers. Love you princess!

Thank you to the very talented photographer, Jennifer Voss who did the shoot for Dash's cover. I am in love with it. Thank you.

Thank you Emma VonDielingen for working so hard to get my books formatted when I give her little notice.

I wanna thank my wonderful friend Casey Peeler. You've been with me since the very beginning and I love you. Just wished you lived closer.

I want to thank my awesome street team, Shantel's Pimpettes; Amy Rangel, Andrea Wilkovich, Jackie Ashmead, Makayla Sasse, Michelle McLellan, and Stephanie Anderson-Cochran. This lovely groups of ladies are awesome at pimping and making me laugh. They make me smile on bad days and make me laugh every day with booty dances, foul language and dirty minds. It's amazing how you can become so close with someone when they live halfway around the world. These girls are my sisters, and I love them very much.

I also want to thank all my family members who are no longer with us. Not a day goes by that we don't think of you. We love and miss you.

And last but not least, my readers. Thank you for taking a chance and wanting to read Dash. I can never thank you enough for wanting to read and share his and Tabatha's story. I hope that you all love it as much as I do. These characters have become my children. I have cried with them and fought with them on this journey, and I wouldn't have it any other way.

This book would not be possible without any of you. Thank you!

Printed in Great Britain
by Amazon